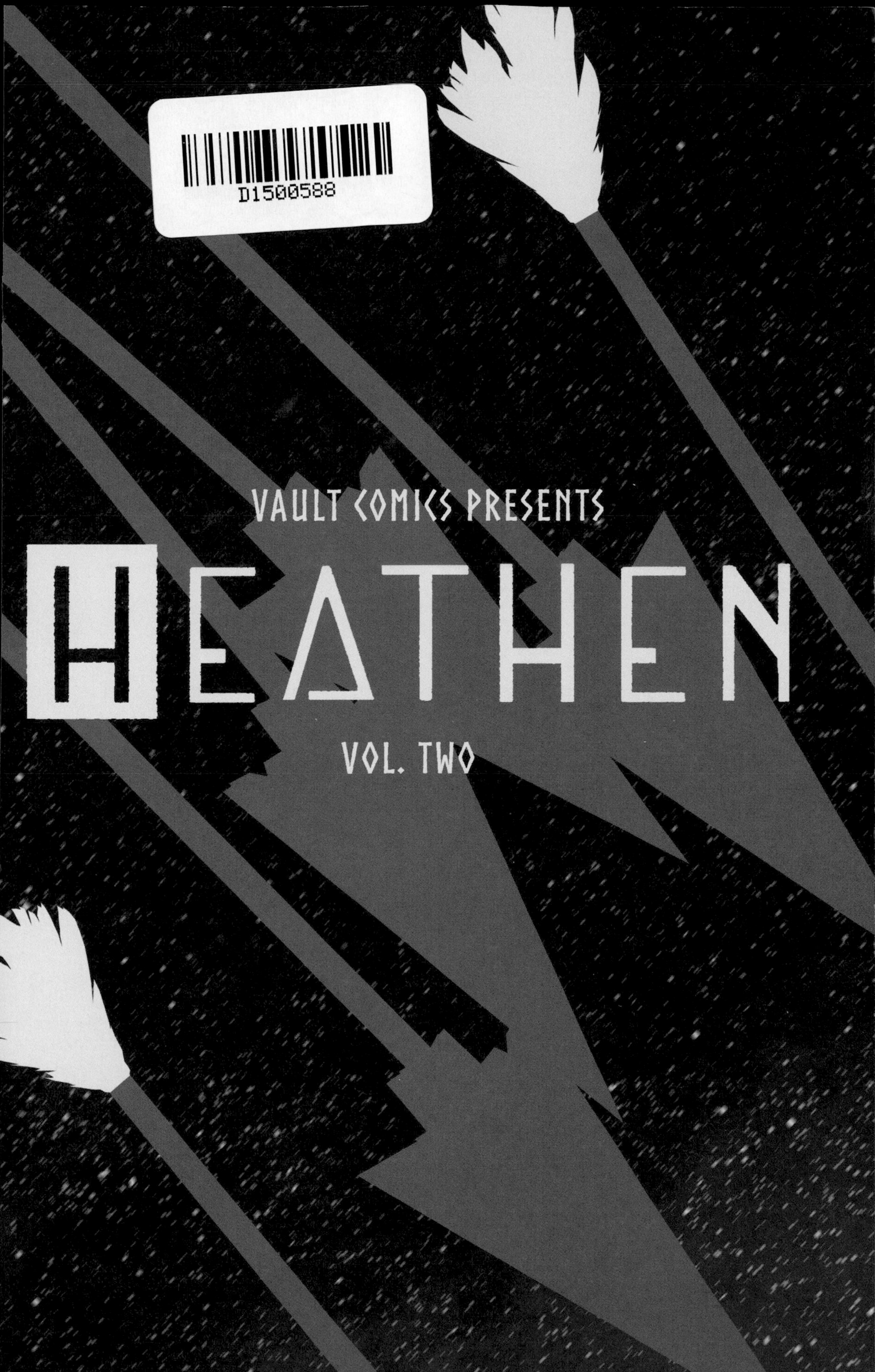
VAULT COMICS PRESENTS
HEATHEN
VOL. TWO

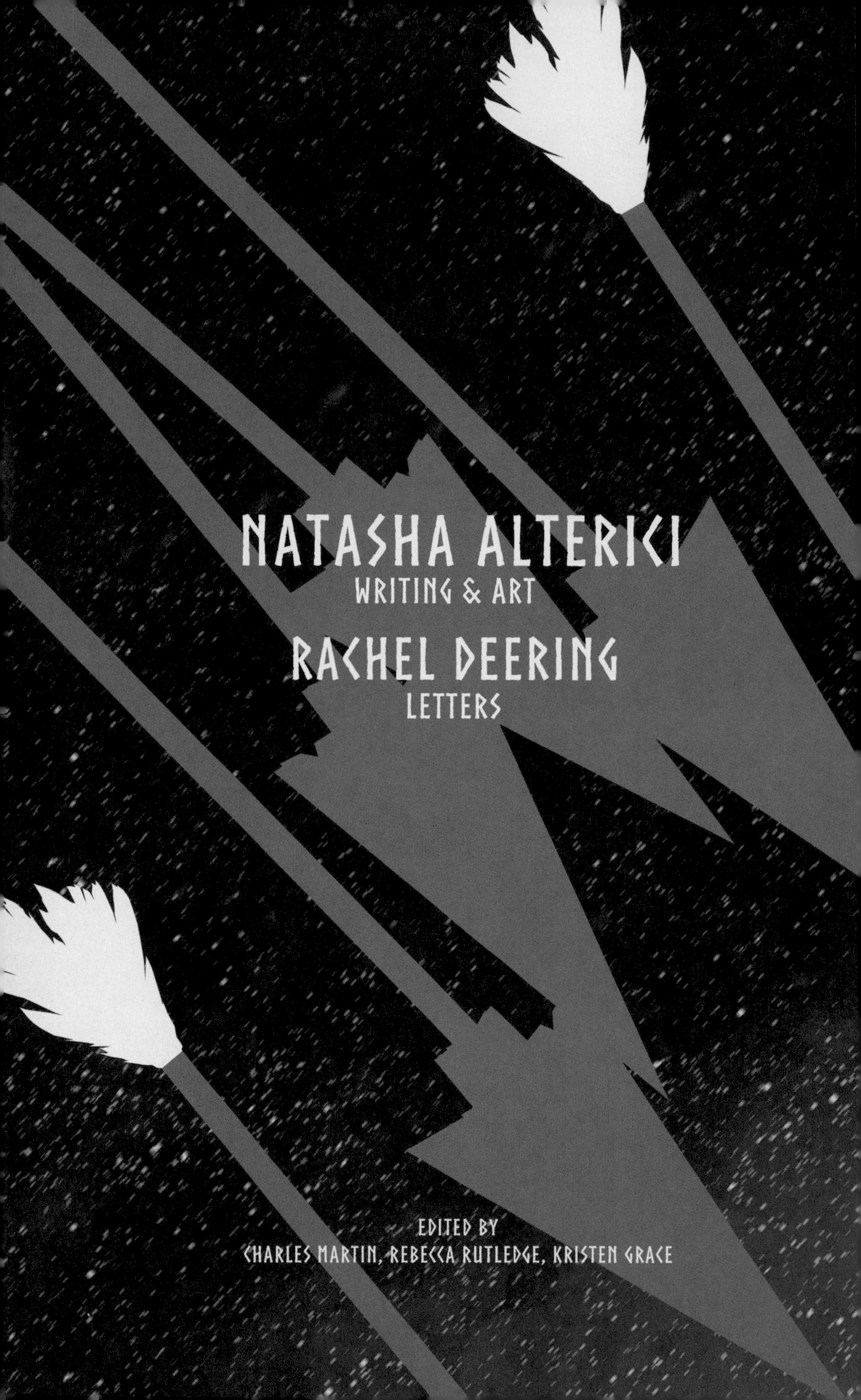

NATASHA ALTERICI

WRITING & ART

RACHEL DEERING

LETTERS

EDITED BY

CHARLES MARTIN, REBECCA RUTLEDGE, KRISTEN GRACE

FOR CHARLES, MY GREATEST CHAMPION;
AND FOR NICOLE, MY GREATEST LOVE.

DAMIAN A. WASSEL
PUBLISHER

ADRIAN F. WASSEL
EDITOR-IN-CHIEF

NATHAN C. GOODEN
ART DIRECTOR

TIMDANIEL
EVP DESIGN & BRANDING

DAVID DISSANYAKE
DIRECTOR OF PR & RETAILER RELATIONS

IAN BALDESSARI
OPERATIONS MANAGER

DAMIAN A. WASSEL, SR.
PRINCIPAL

CHAPTER 5

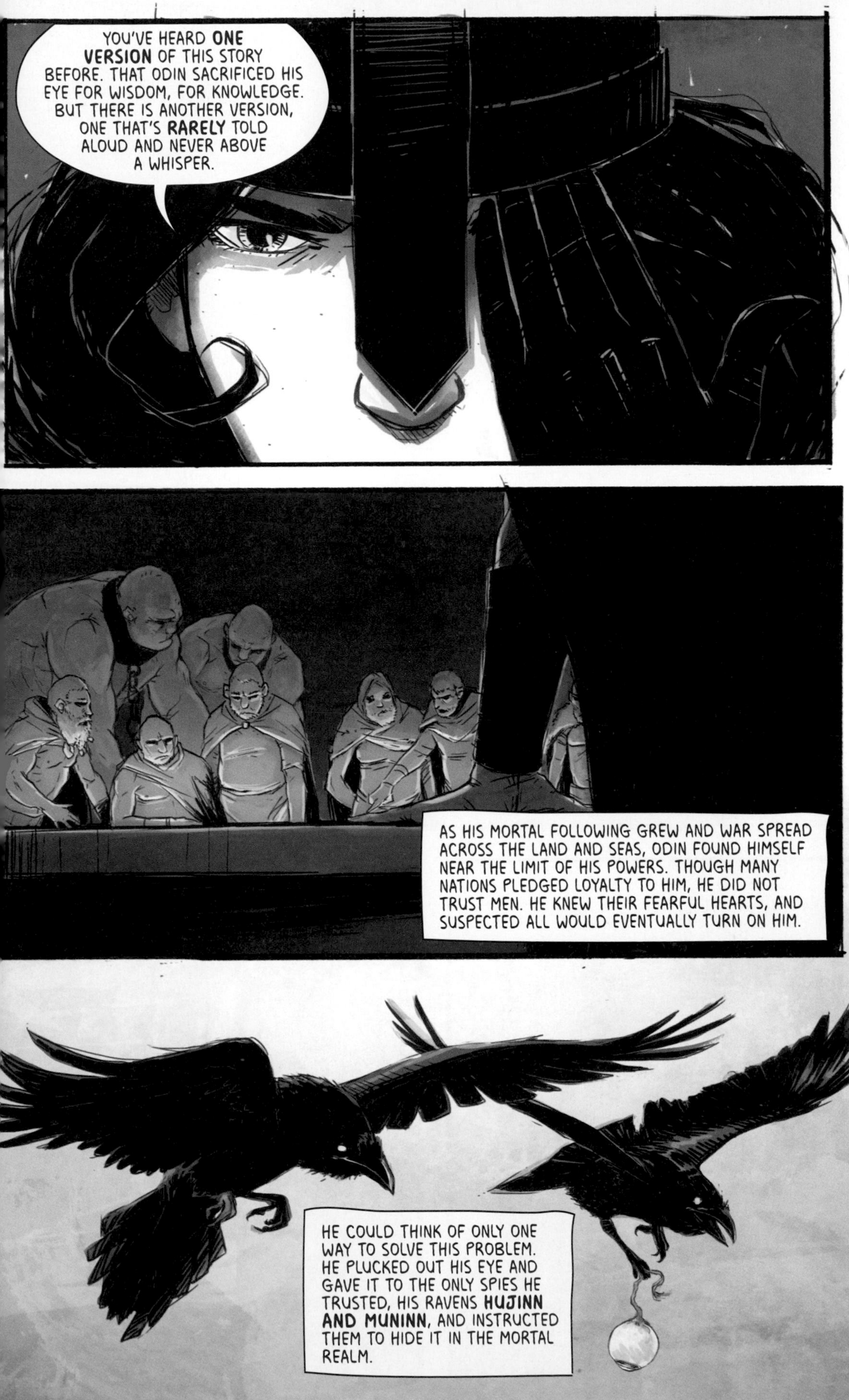
YOU'VE HEARD **ONE VERSION** OF THIS STORY BEFORE. THAT ODIN SACRIFICED HIS EYE FOR WISDOM, FOR KNOWLEDGE. BUT THERE IS ANOTHER VERSION, ONE THAT'S **RARELY** TOLD ALOUD AND NEVER ABOVE A WHISPER.
AS HIS MORTAL FOLLOWING GREW AND WAR SPREAD ACROSS THE LAND AND SEAS, ODIN FOUND HIMSELF NEAR THE LIMIT OF HIS POWERS. THOUGH MANY NATIONS PLEDGED LOYALTY TO HIM, HE DID NOT TRUST MEN. HE KNEW THEIR FEARFUL HEARTS, AND SUSPECTED ALL WOULD EVENTUALLY TURN ON HIM.
HE COULD THINK OF ONLY ONE WAY TO SOLVE THIS PROBLEM. HE PLUCKED OUT HIS EYE AND GAVE IT TO THE ONLY SPIES HE TRUSTED, HIS RAVENS **HUJINN AND MUNINN**, AND INSTRUCTED THEM TO HIDE IT IN THE MORTAL REALM.

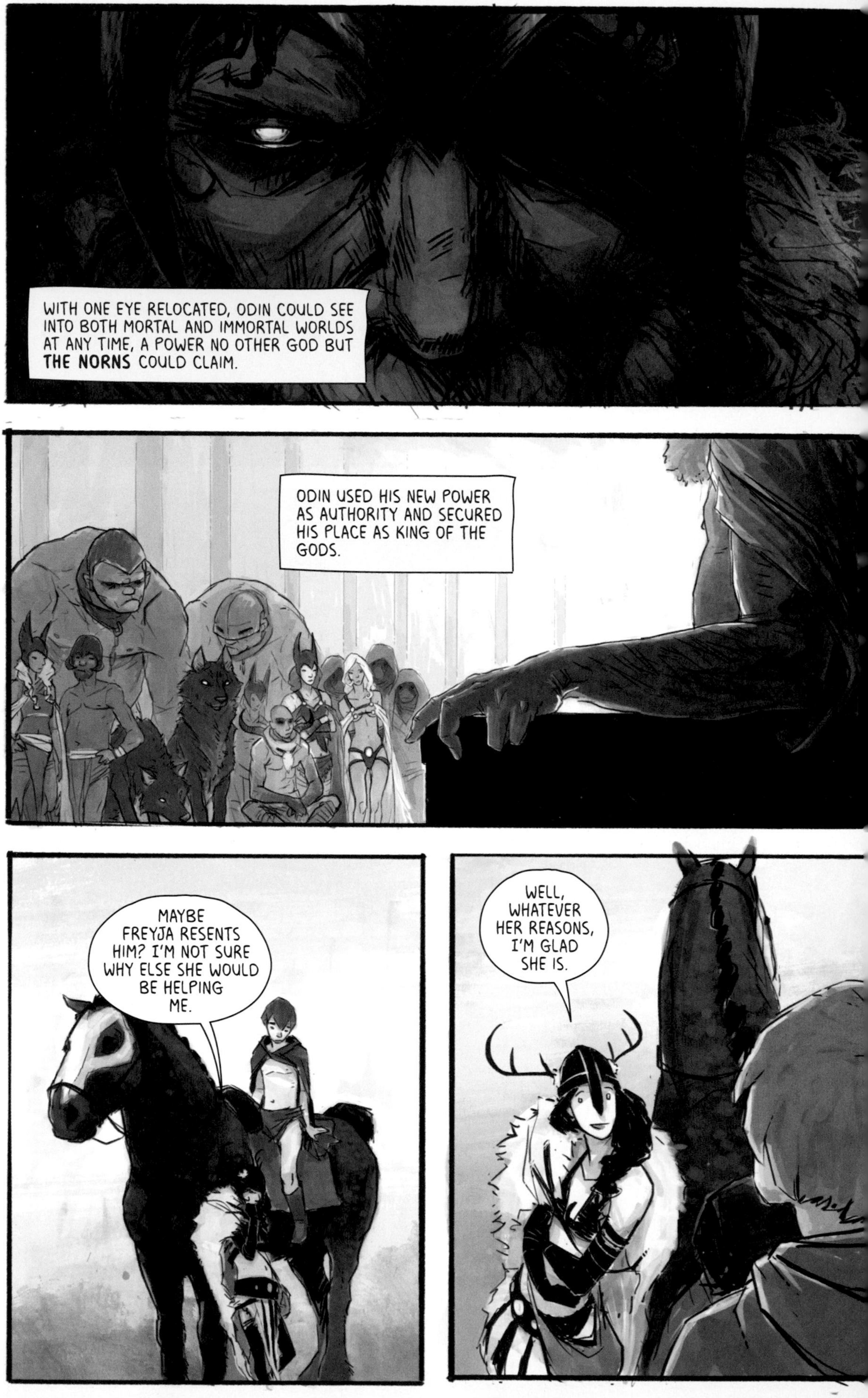
WITH ONE EYE RELOCATED, ODIN COULD SEE INTO BOTH MORTAL AND IMMORTAL WORLDS AT ANY TIME, A POWER NO OTHER GOD BUT **THE NORNS** COULD CLAIM.
ODIN USED HIS NEW POWER AS AUTHORITY AND SECURED HIS PLACE AS KING OF THE GODS.
MAYBE FREYJA RESENTS HIM? I'M NOT SURE WHY ELSE SHE WOULD BE HELPING ME.
WELL, WHATEVER HER REASONS, I'M GLAD SHE IS.

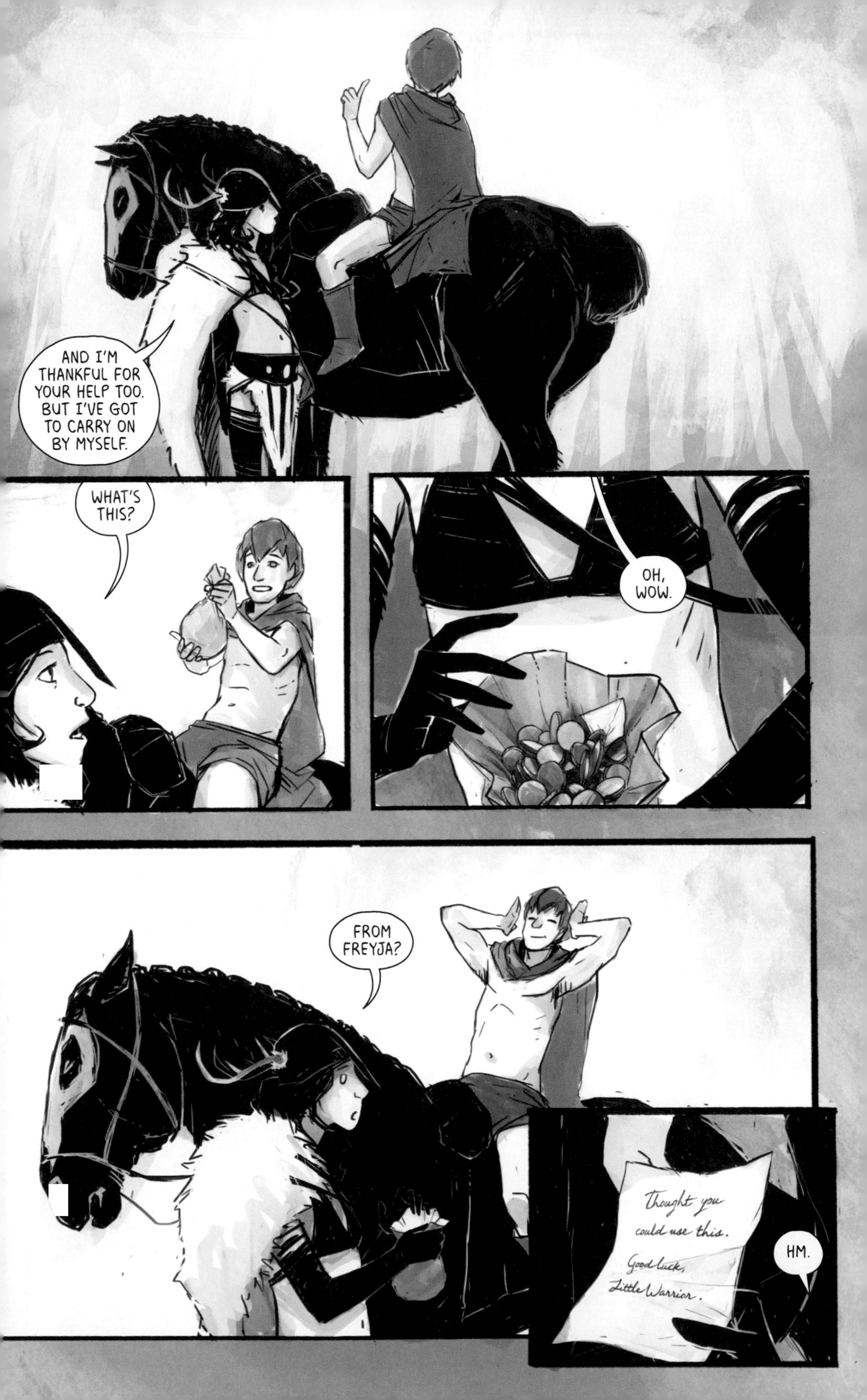
AND I'M THANKFUL FOR YOUR HELP TOO. BUT I'VE GOT TO CARRY ON BY MYSELF.
WHAT'S THIS?
OH, WOW.
FROM FREYJA?
Thought you could use this. Good luck, Little Warrior.
HM.

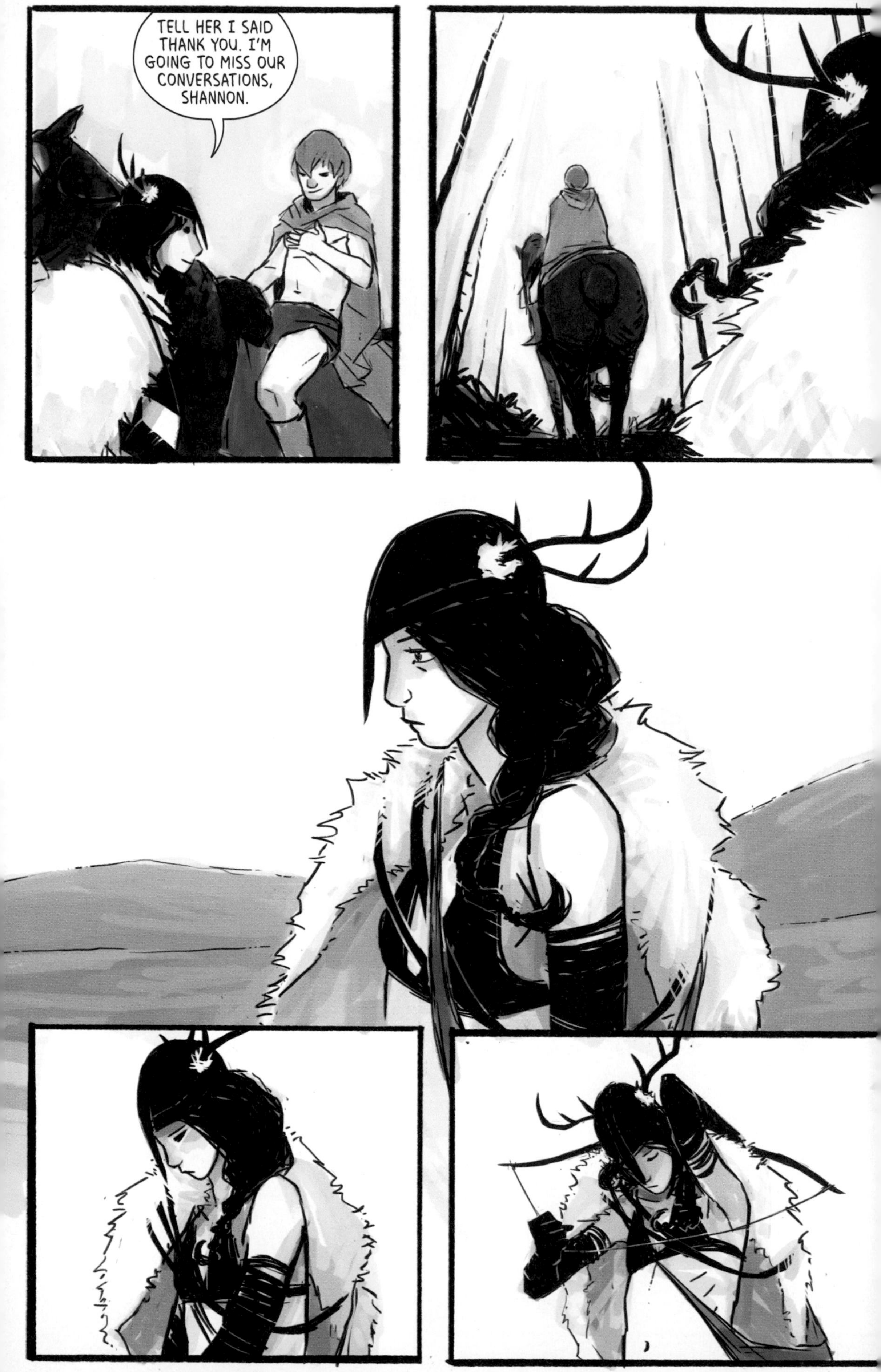
TELL HER I SAID THANK YOU. I'M GOING TO MISS OUR CONVERSATIONS, SHANNON.

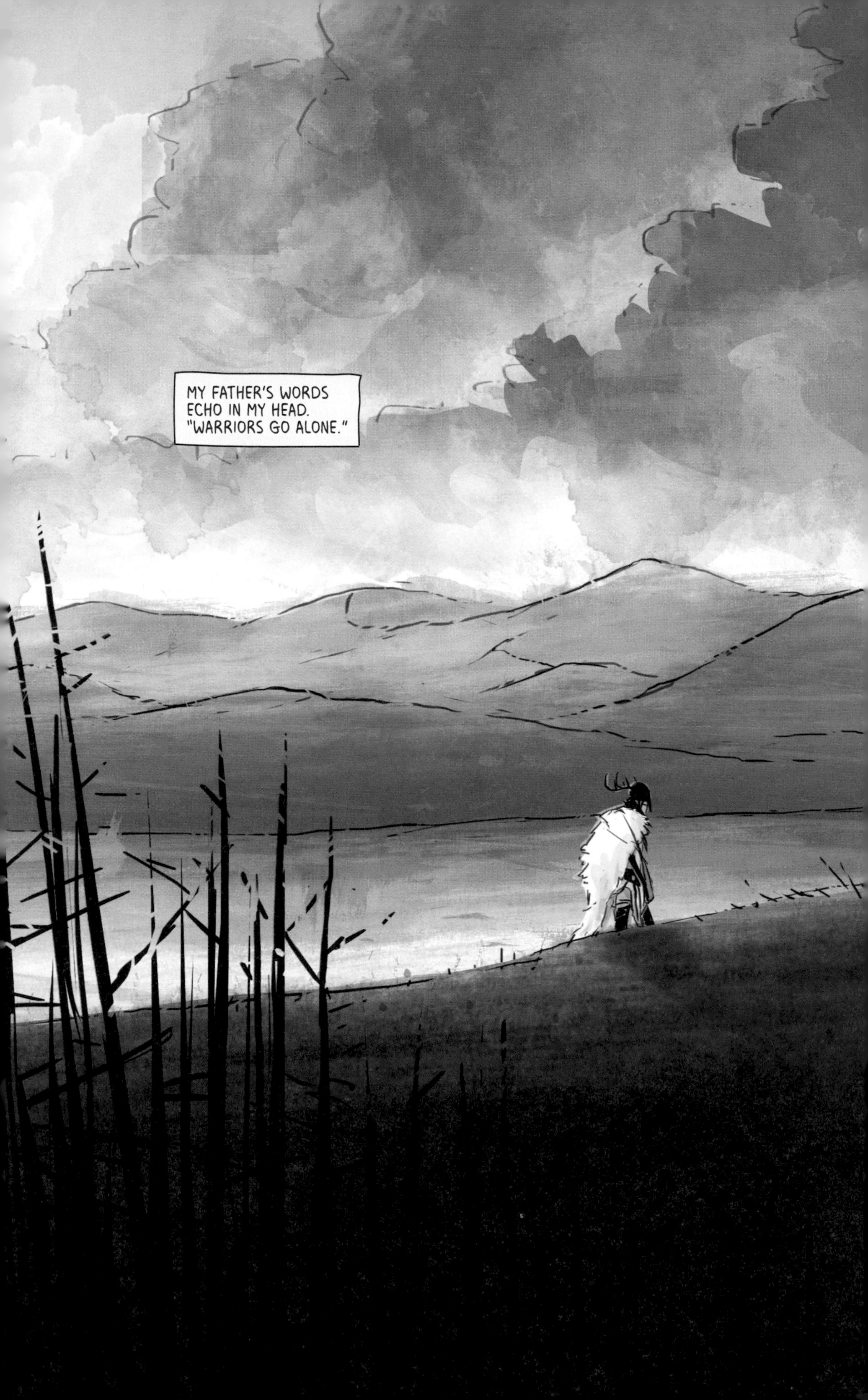
MY FATHER'S WORDS
ECHO IN MY HEAD.
"WARRIORS GO ALONE."

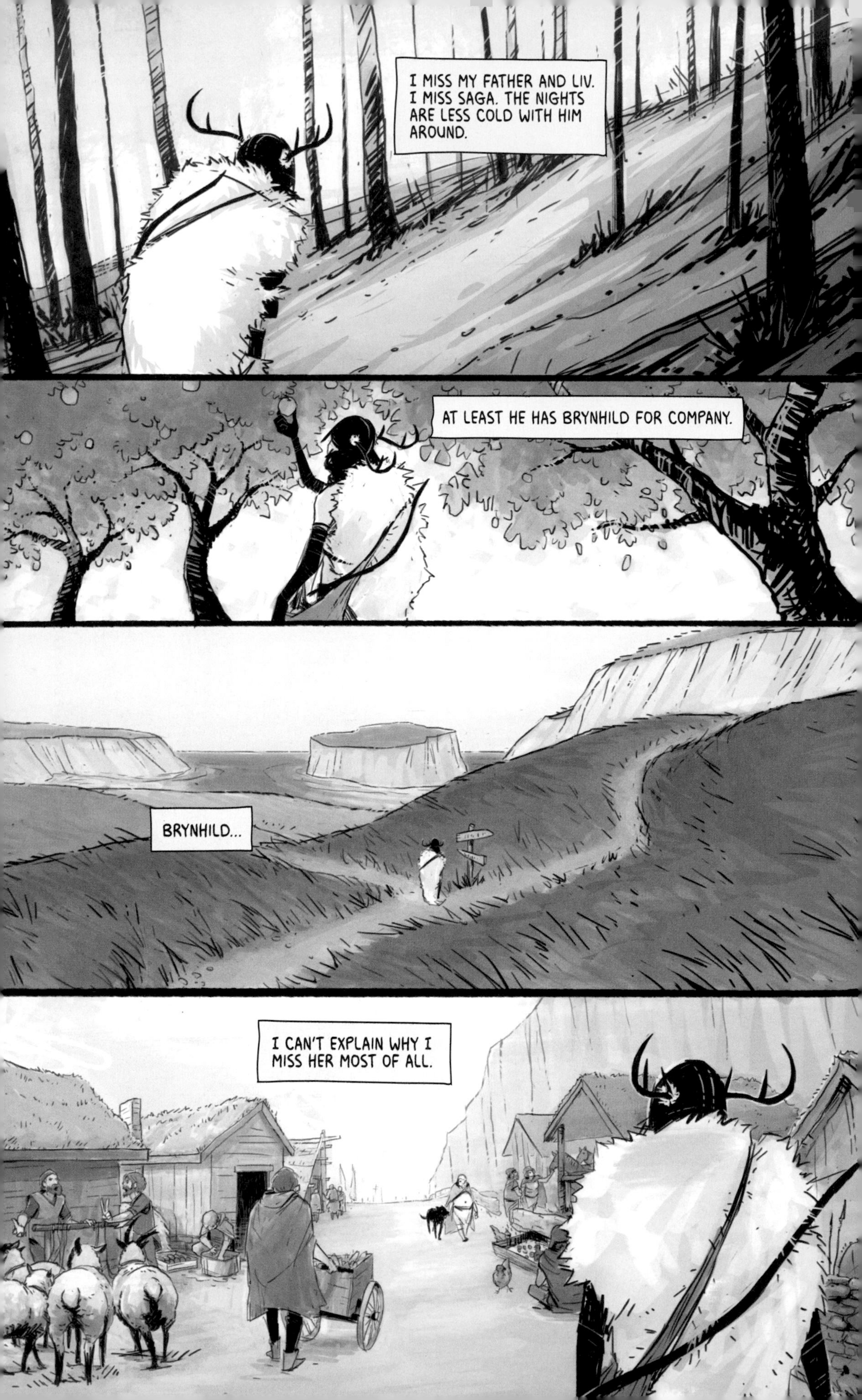
I MISS MY FATHER AND LIV. I MISS SAGA. THE NIGHTS ARE LESS COLD WITH HIM AROUND.
AT LEAST HE HAS BRYNHILD FOR COMPANY.
BRYNHILD...
I CAN'T EXPLAIN WHY I MISS HER MOST OF ALL.

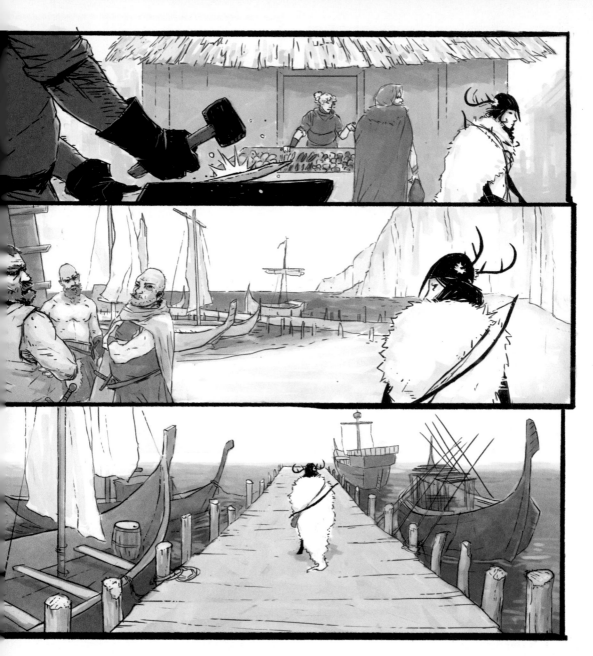

EXCUSE ME.

ARE YOU THE CAPTAIN OF THIS SHIP?

HUH. NO ONE EVER ASKS ME THAT. THIS IS MY SHIP, YES. I AM MAKEDA. AND YOU ARE?

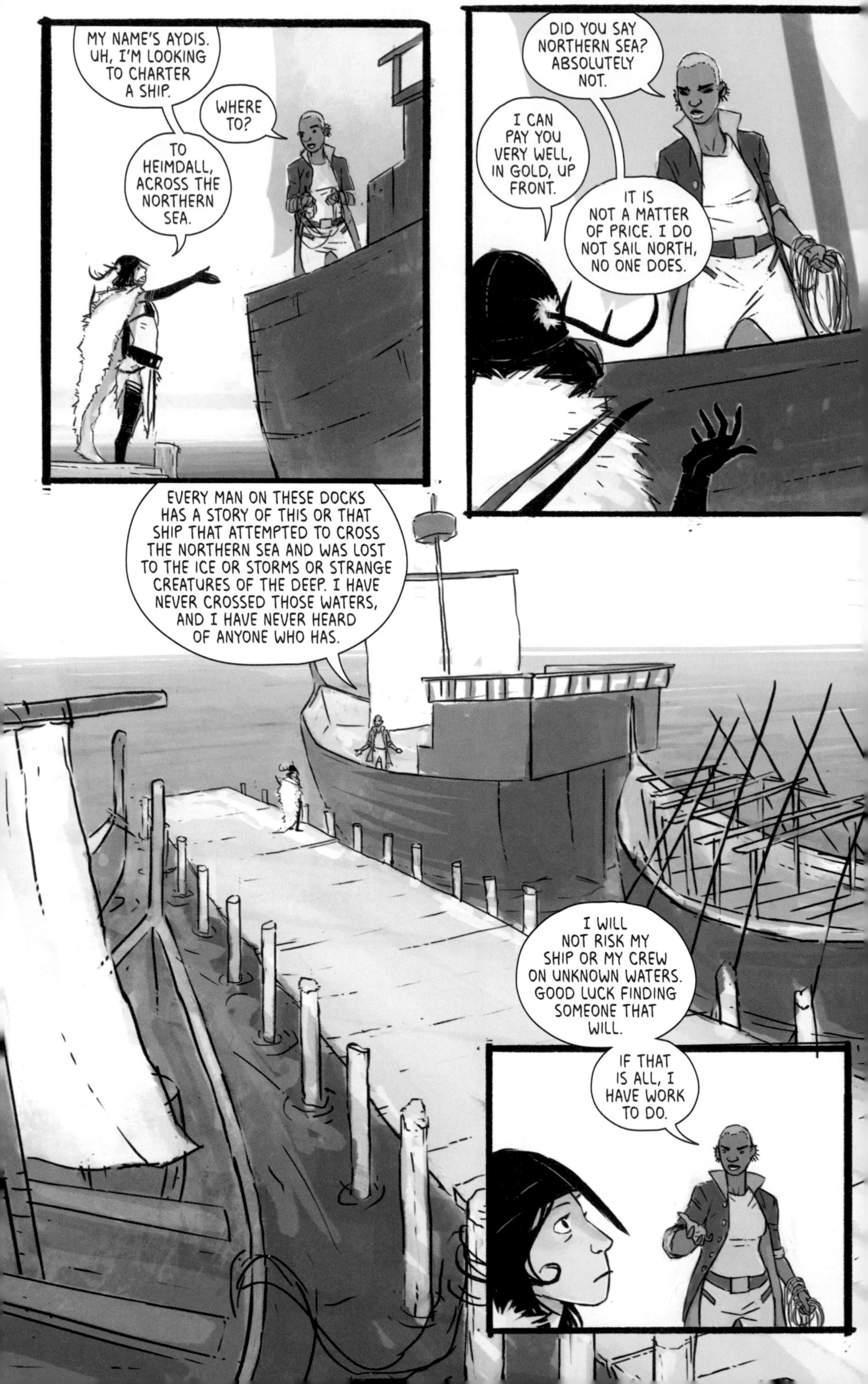
MY NAME'S AYDIS. UH, I'M LOOKING TO CHARTER A SHIP.
WHERE TO?
TO HEIMDALL, ACROSS THE NORTHERN SEA.
DID YOU SAY NORTHERN SEA? ABSOLUTELY NOT.
I CAN PAY YOU VERY WELL, IN GOLD, UP FRONT.
IT IS NOT A MATTER OF PRICE. I DO NOT SAIL NORTH, NO ONE DOES.
EVERY MAN ON THESE DOCKS HAS A STORY OF THIS OR THAT SHIP THAT ATTEMPTED TO CROSS THE NORTHERN SEA AND WAS LOST TO THE ICE OR STORMS OR STRANGE CREATURES OF THE DEEP. I HAVE NEVER CROSSED THOSE WATERS, AND I HAVE NEVER HEARD OF ANYONE WHO HAS.
I WILL NOT RISK MY SHIP OR MY CREW ON UNKNOWN WATERS. GOOD LUCK FINDING SOMEONE THAT WILL.
IF THAT IS ALL, I HAVE WORK TO DO.

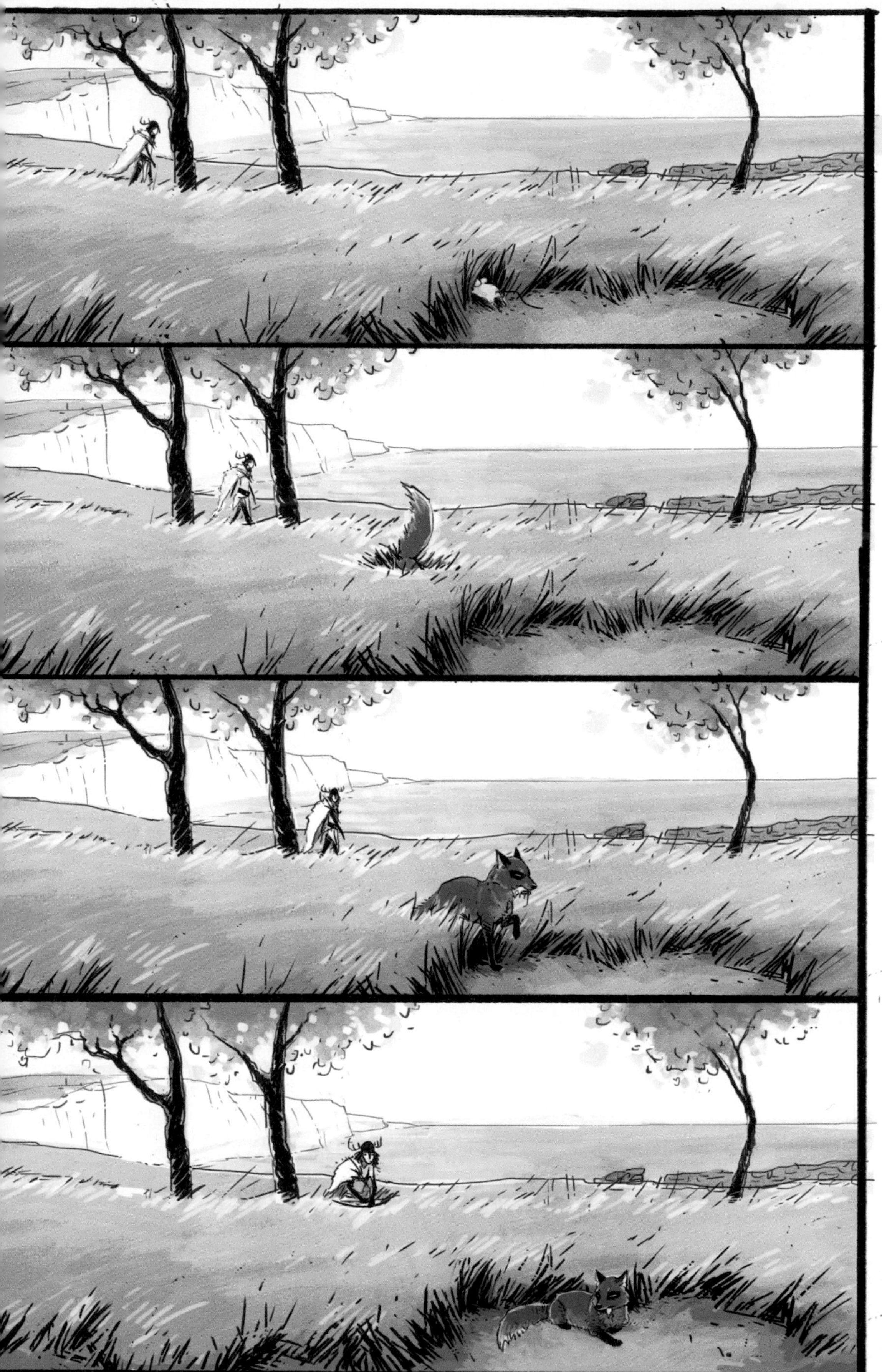

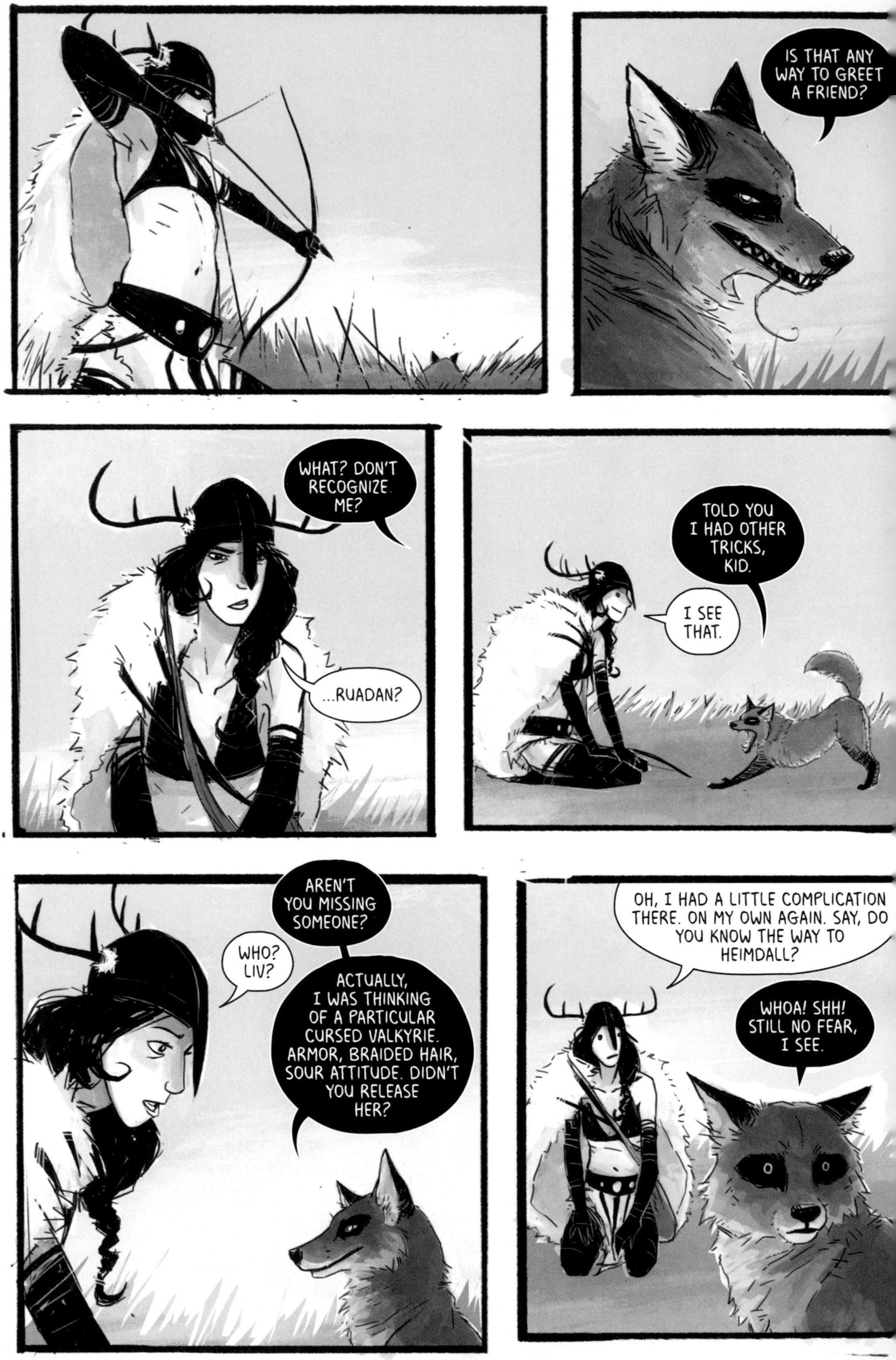
IS THAT ANY WAY TO GREET A FRIEND?
WHAT? DON'T RECOGNIZE ME?
...RUADAN?
TOLD YOU I HAD OTHER TRICKS, KID.
I SEE THAT.
AREN'T YOU MISSING SOMEONE?
WHO? LIV?
ACTUALLY, I WAS THINKING OF A PARTICULAR CURSED VALKYRIE. ARMOR, BRAIDED HAIR, SOUR ATTITUDE. DIDN'T YOU RELEASE HER?
OH, I HAD A LITTLE COMPLICATION THERE. ON MY OWN AGAIN. SAY, DO YOU KNOW THE WAY TO HEIMDALL?
WHOA! SHH! STILL NO FEAR, I SEE.

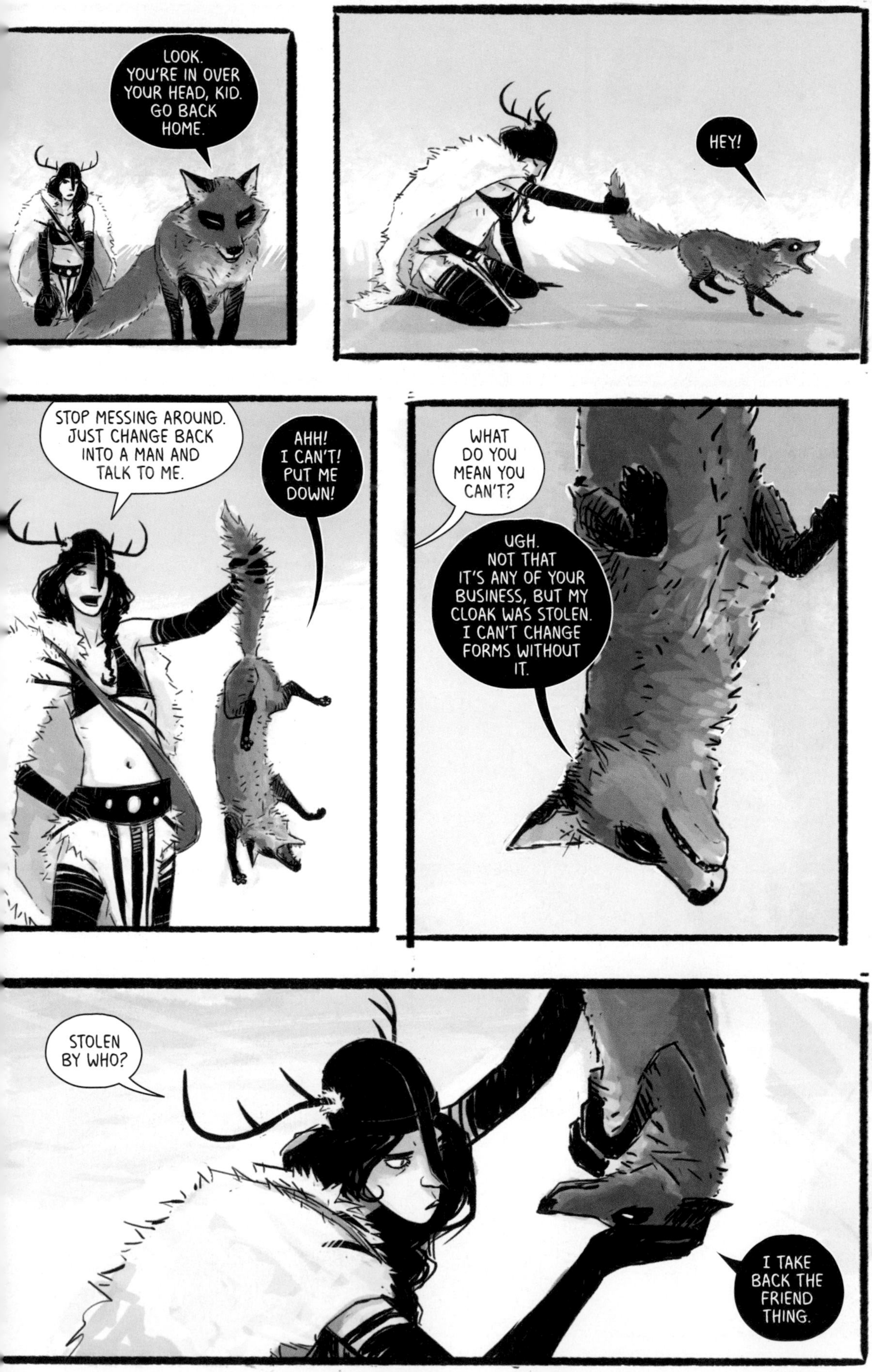

LOOK. YOU'RE IN OVER YOUR HEAD, KID. GO BACK HOME.
HEY!
STOP MESSING AROUND. JUST CHANGE BACK INTO A MAN AND TALK TO ME.
AHH! I CAN'T! PUT ME DOWN!
WHAT DO YOU MEAN YOU CAN'T?
UGH. NOT THAT IT'S ANY OF YOUR BUSINESS, BUT MY CLOAK WAS STOLEN. I CAN'T CHANGE FORMS WITHOUT IT.
STOLEN BY WHO?
I TAKE BACK THE FRIEND THING.

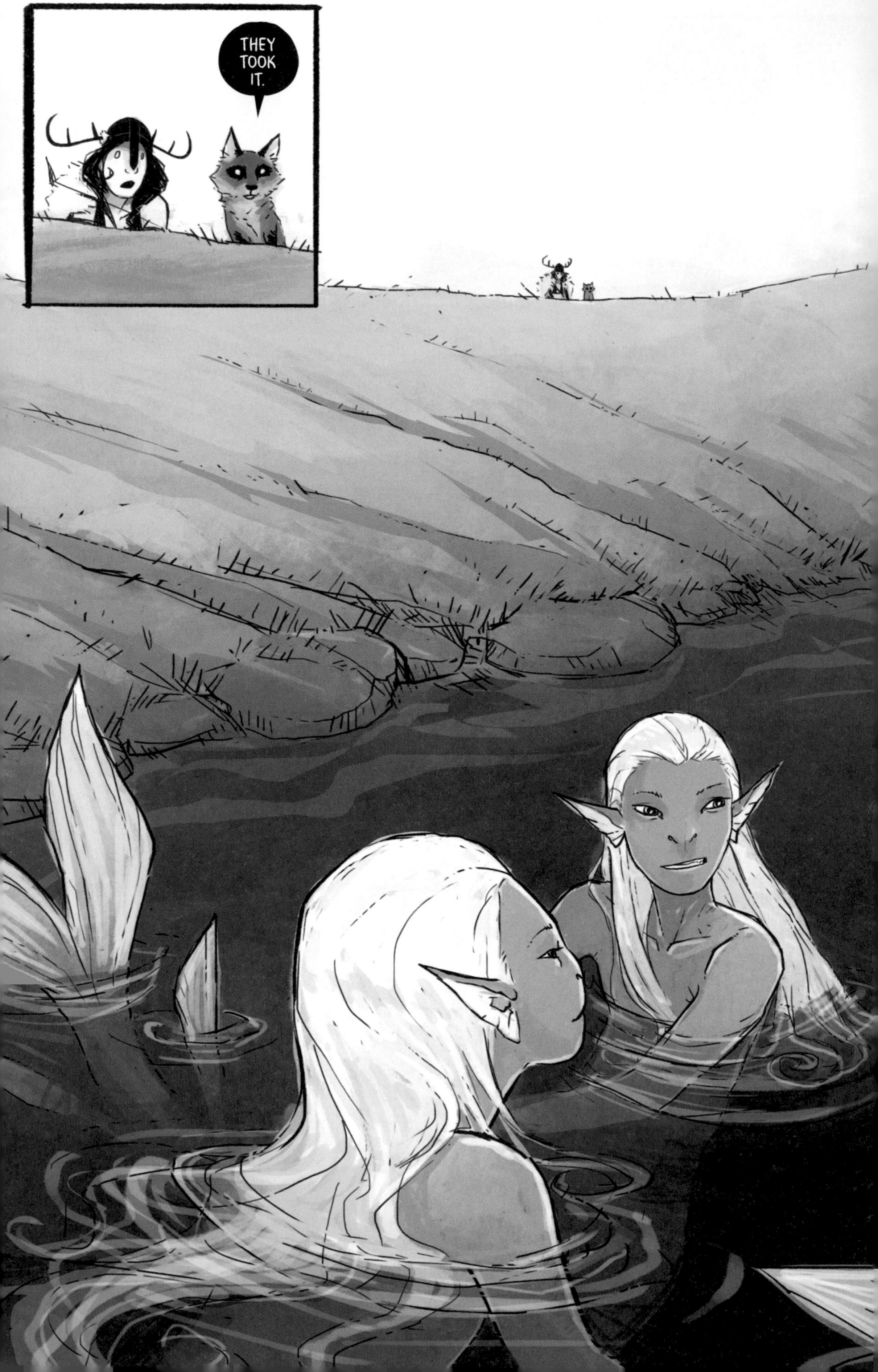
THEY TOOK IT.

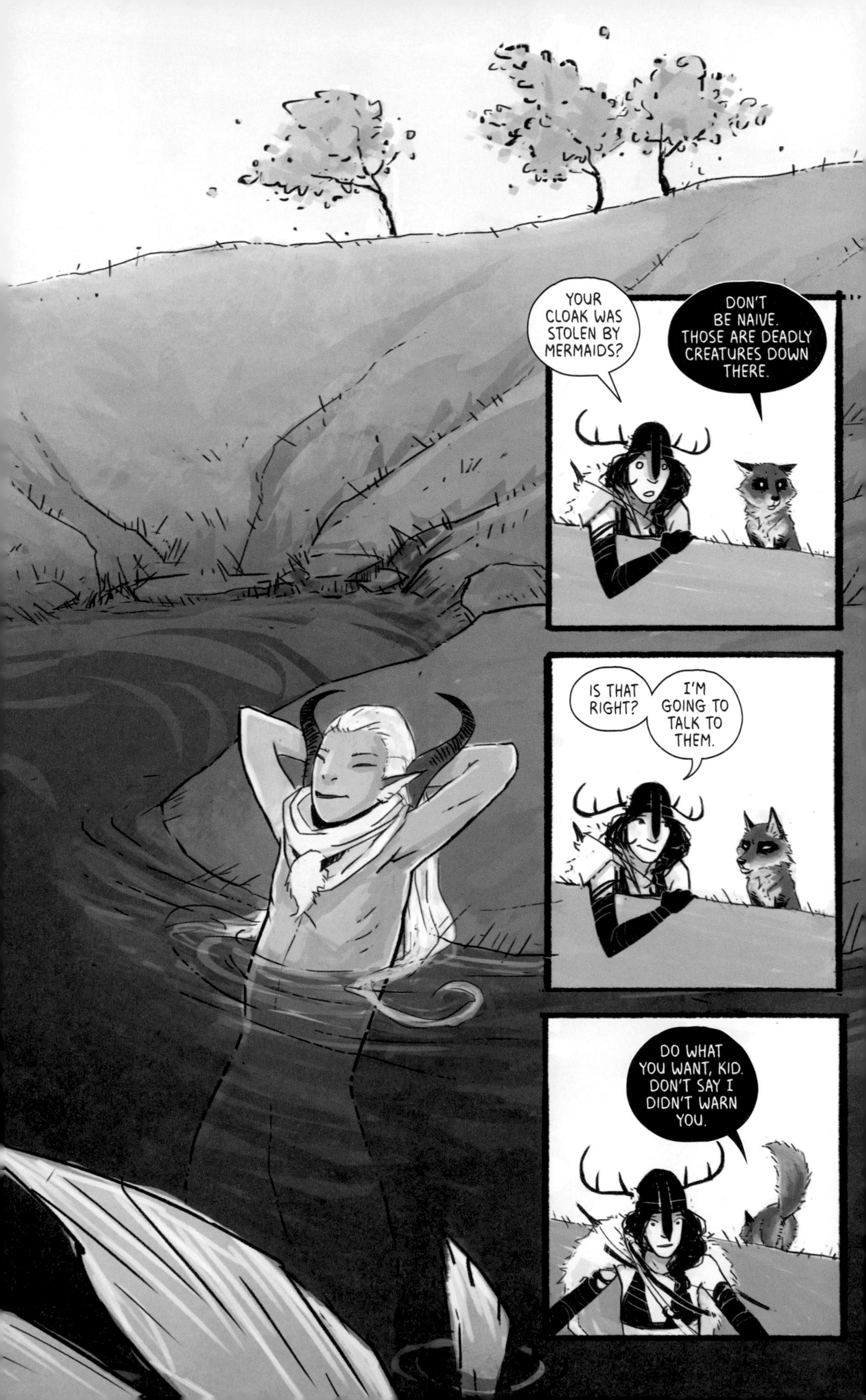
YOUR CLOAK WAS STOLEN BY MERMAIDS?
DON'T BE NAIVE. THOSE ARE DEADLY CREATURES DOWN THERE.
IS THAT RIGHT?
I'M GOING TO TALK TO THEM.
DO WHAT YOU WANT, KID. DON'T SAY I DIDN'T WARN YOU.

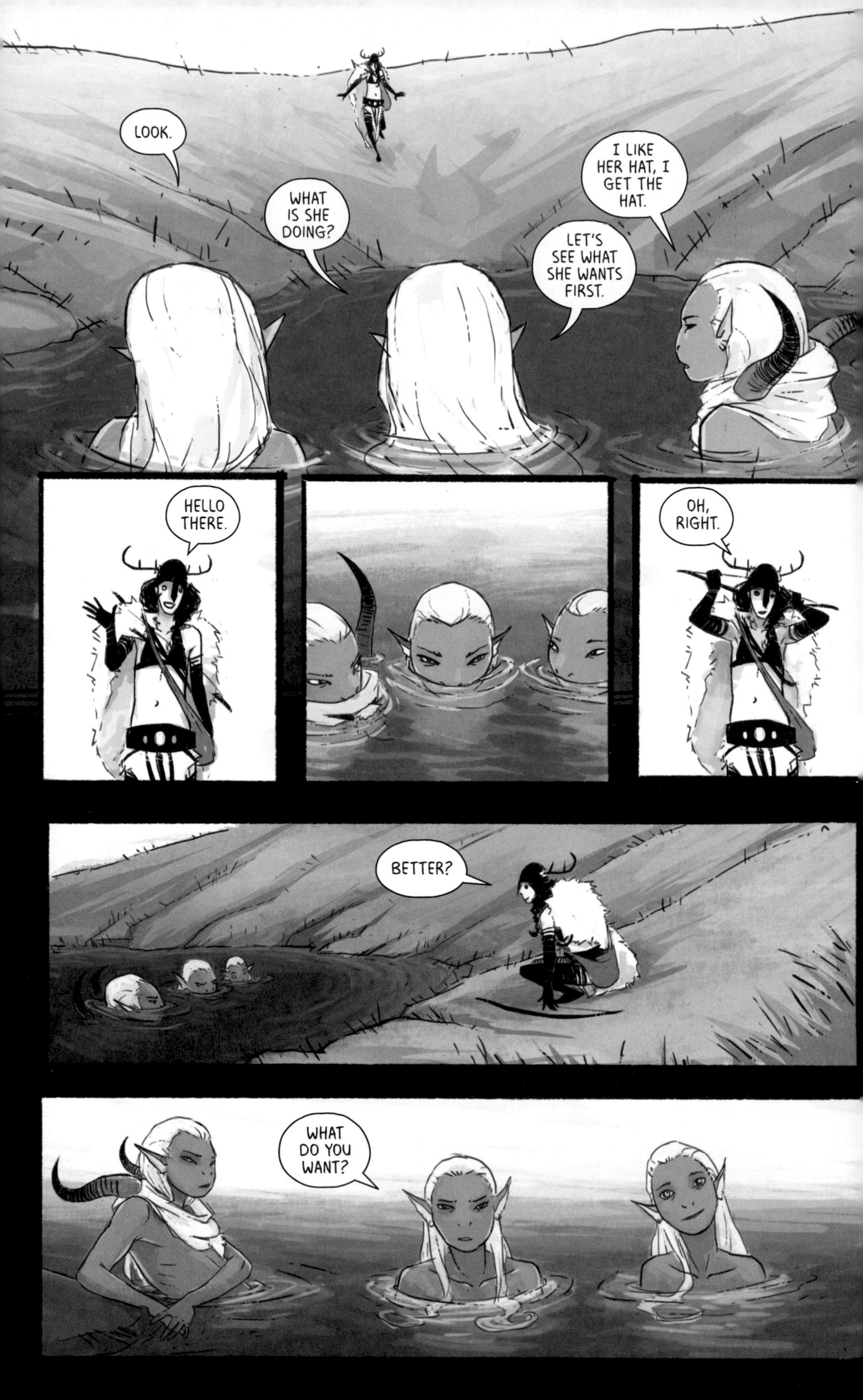
LOOK.
WHAT IS SHE DOING?
LET'S SEE WHAT SHE WANTS FIRST.
I LIKE HER HAT, I GET THE HAT.
HELLO THERE.
OH, RIGHT.
BETTER?
WHAT DO YOU WANT?

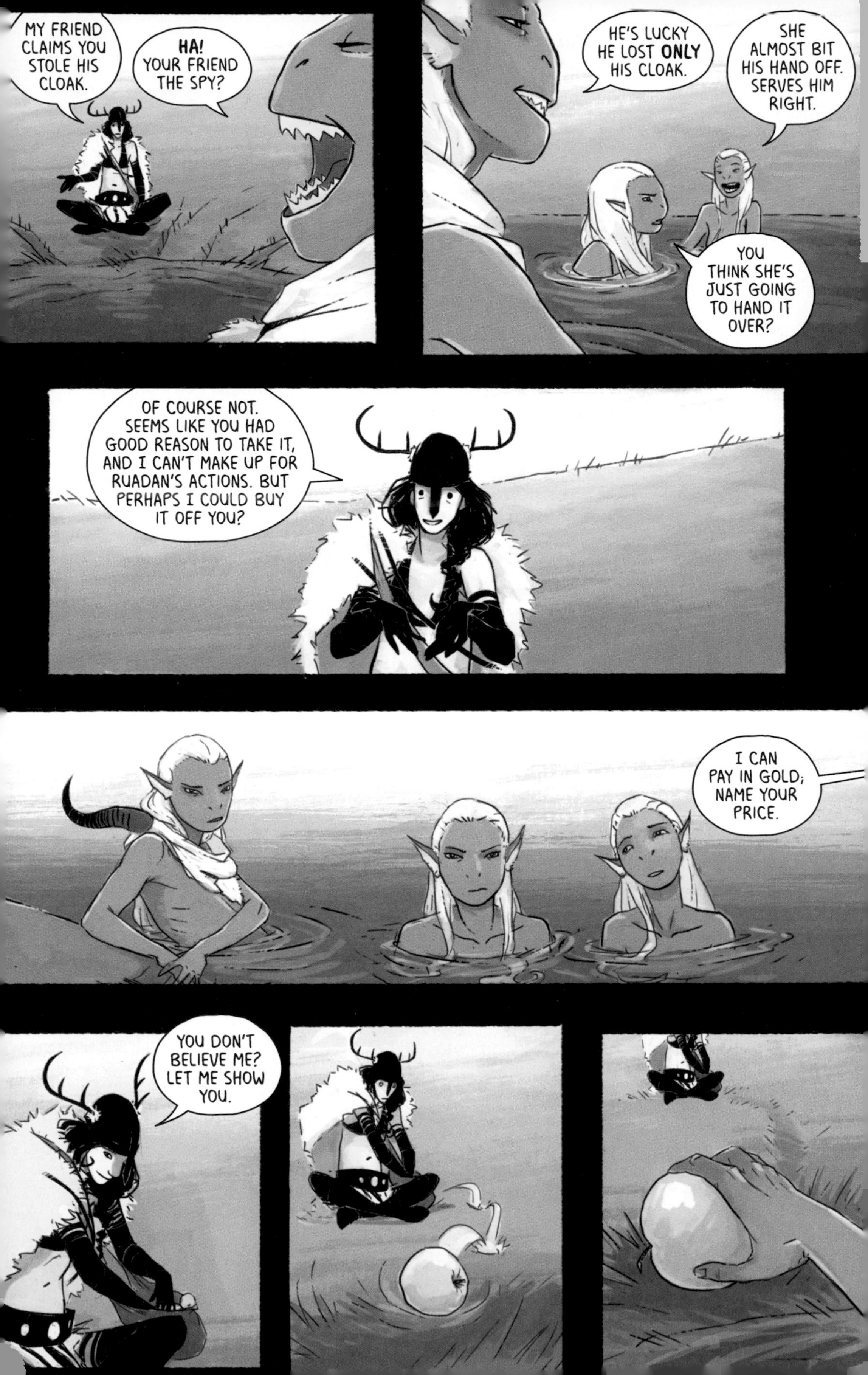
MY FRIEND CLAIMS YOU STOLE HIS CLOAK.
HA! YOUR FRIEND THE SPY?
HE'S LUCKY HE LOST **ONLY** HIS CLOAK.
SHE ALMOST BIT HIS HAND OFF. SERVES HIM RIGHT.
YOU THINK SHE'S JUST GOING TO HAND IT OVER?
OF COURSE NOT. SEEMS LIKE YOU HAD GOOD REASON TO TAKE IT, AND I CAN'T MAKE UP FOR RUADAN'S ACTIONS. BUT PERHAPS I COULD BUY IT OFF YOU?
I CAN PAY IN GOLD; NAME YOUR PRICE.
YOU DON'T BELIEVE ME? LET ME SHOW YOU.

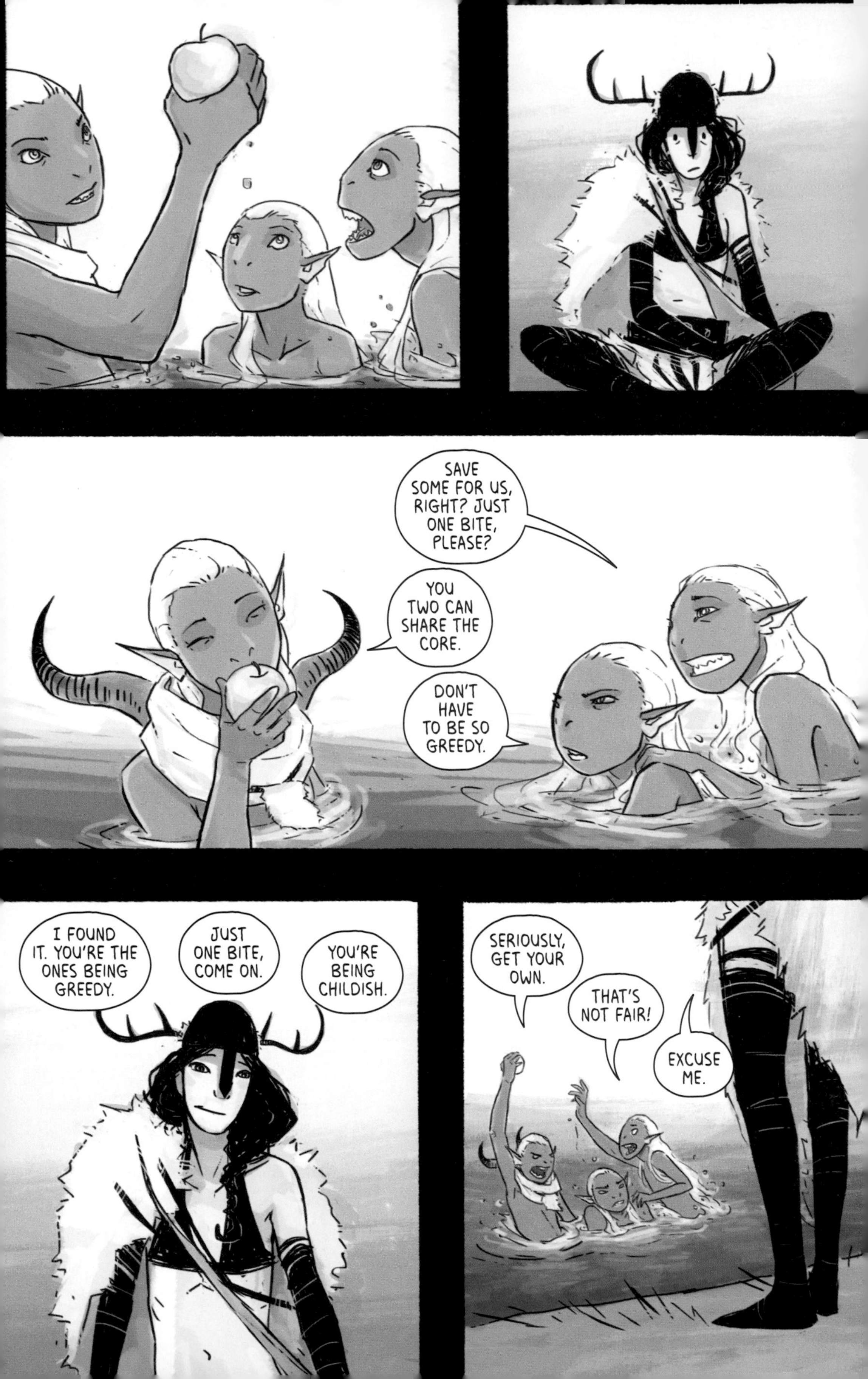
SAVE SOME FOR US, RIGHT? JUST ONE BITE, PLEASE?
YOU TWO CAN SHARE THE CORE.
DON'T HAVE TO BE SO GREEDY.
I FOUND IT. YOU'RE THE ONES BEING GREEDY.
JUST ONE BITE, COME ON.
YOU'RE BEING CHILDISH.
SERIOUSLY, GET YOUR OWN.
THAT'S NOT FAIR!
EXCUSE ME.

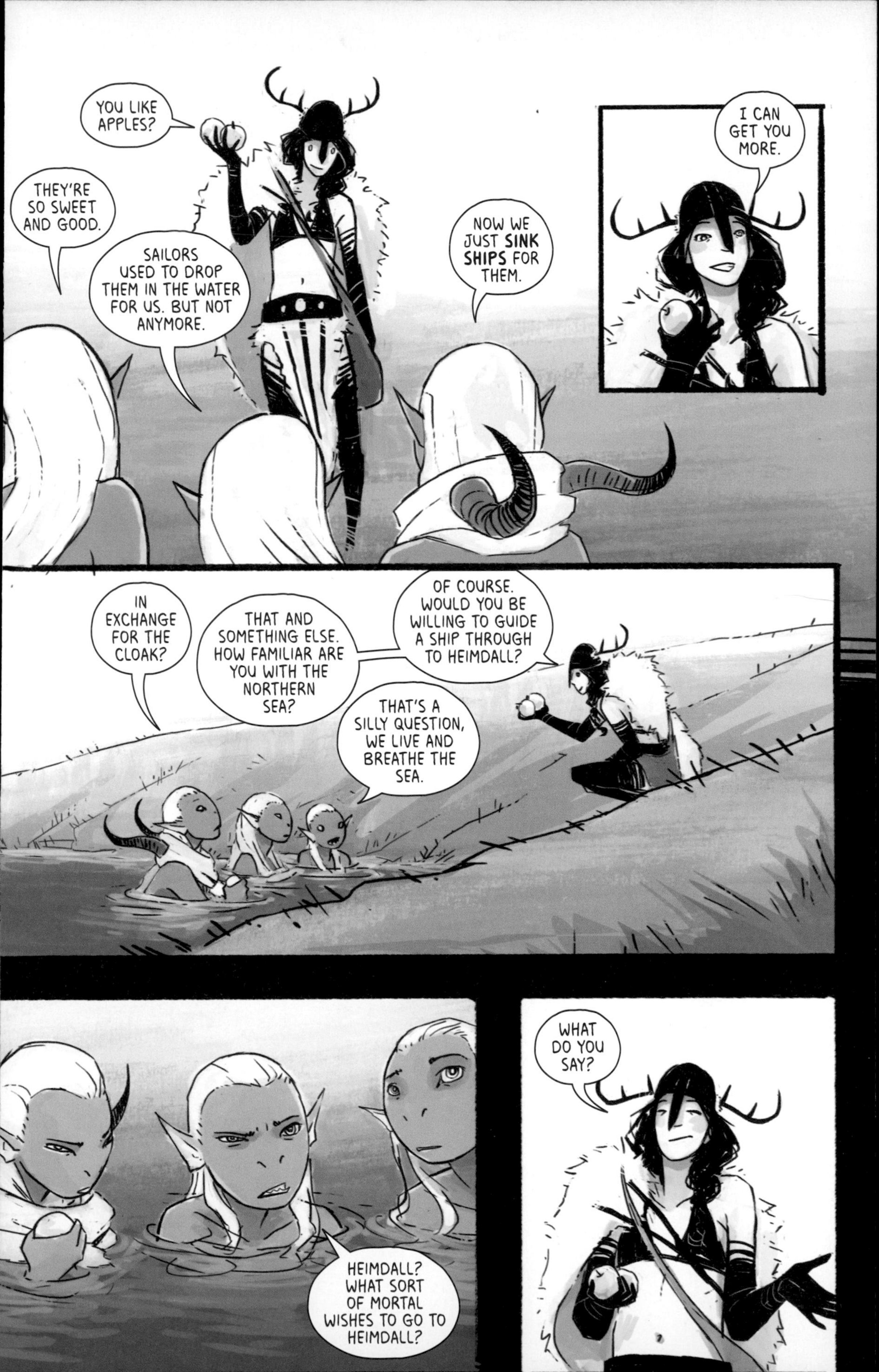
YOU LIKE APPLES?
THEY'RE SO SWEET AND GOOD.
SAILORS USED TO DROP THEM IN THE WATER FOR US. BUT NOT ANYMORE.
NOW WE JUST **SINK SHIPS** FOR THEM.
I CAN GET YOU MORE.
IN EXCHANGE FOR THE CLOAK?
THAT AND SOMETHING ELSE. HOW FAMILIAR ARE YOU WITH THE NORTHERN SEA?
THAT'S A SILLY QUESTION, WE LIVE AND BREATHE THE SEA.
OF COURSE. WOULD YOU BE WILLING TO GUIDE A SHIP THROUGH TO HEIMDALL?
HEIMDALL? WHAT SORT OF MORTAL WISHES TO GO TO HEIMDALL?
WHAT DO YOU SAY?

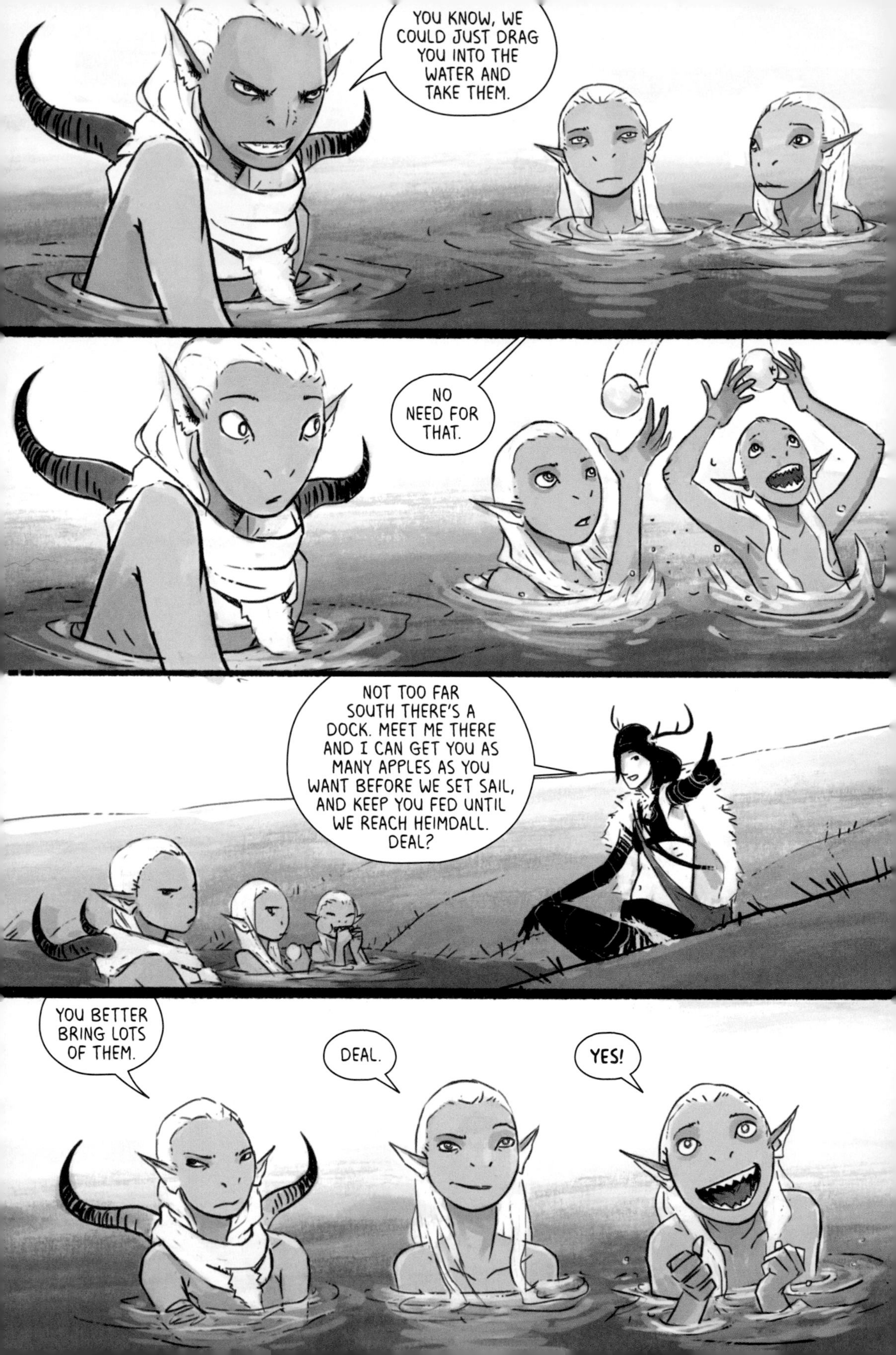
YOU KNOW, WE COULD JUST DRAG YOU INTO THE WATER AND TAKE THEM.
NO NEED FOR THAT.
NOT TOO FAR SOUTH THERE'S A DOCK. MEET ME THERE AND I CAN GET YOU AS MANY APPLES AS YOU WANT BEFORE WE SET SAIL, AND KEEP YOU FED UNTIL WE REACH HEIMDALL. DEAL?
YOU BETTER BRING LOTS OF THEM.
DEAL.
YES!

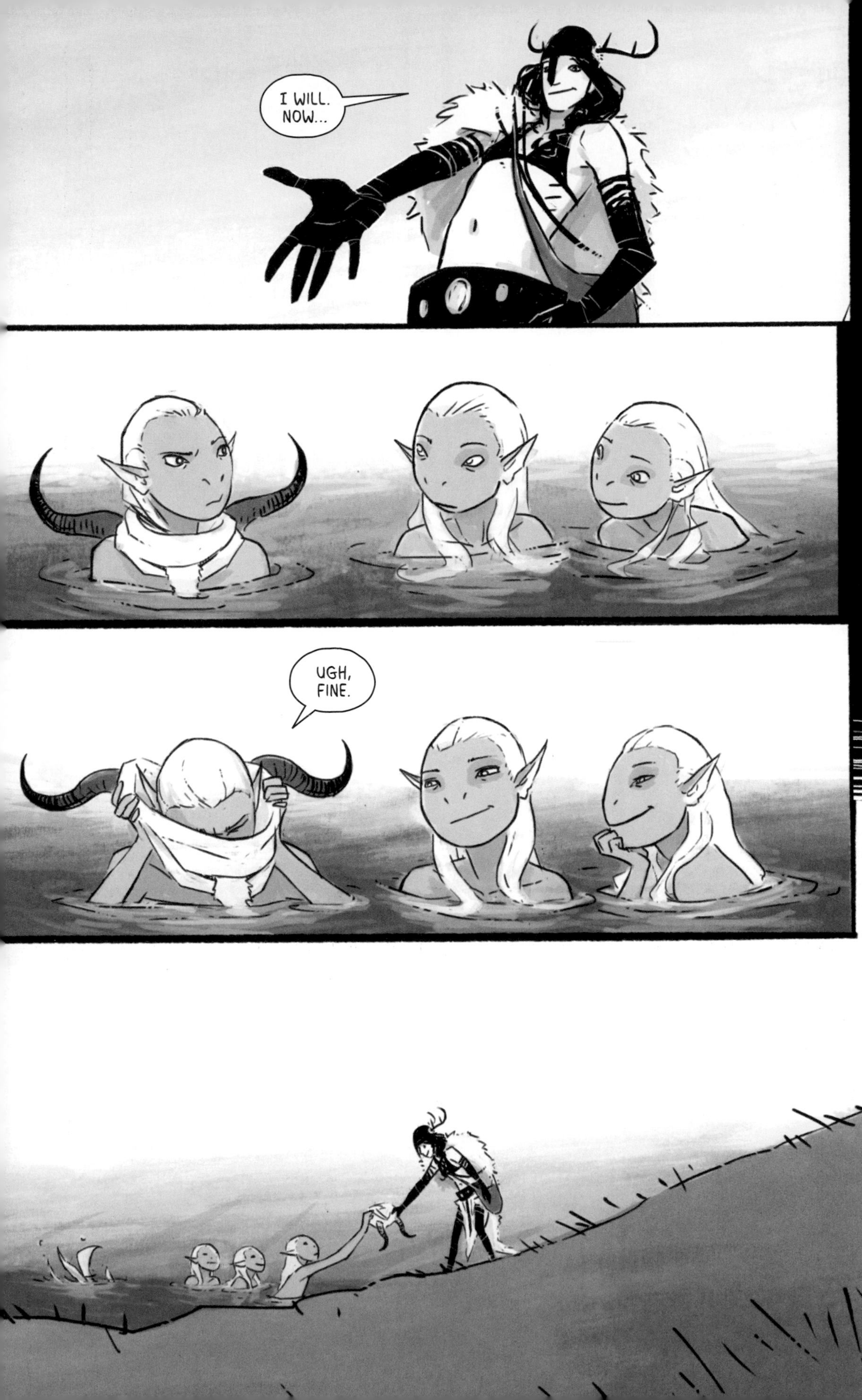
I WILL. NOW...
UGH, FINE.

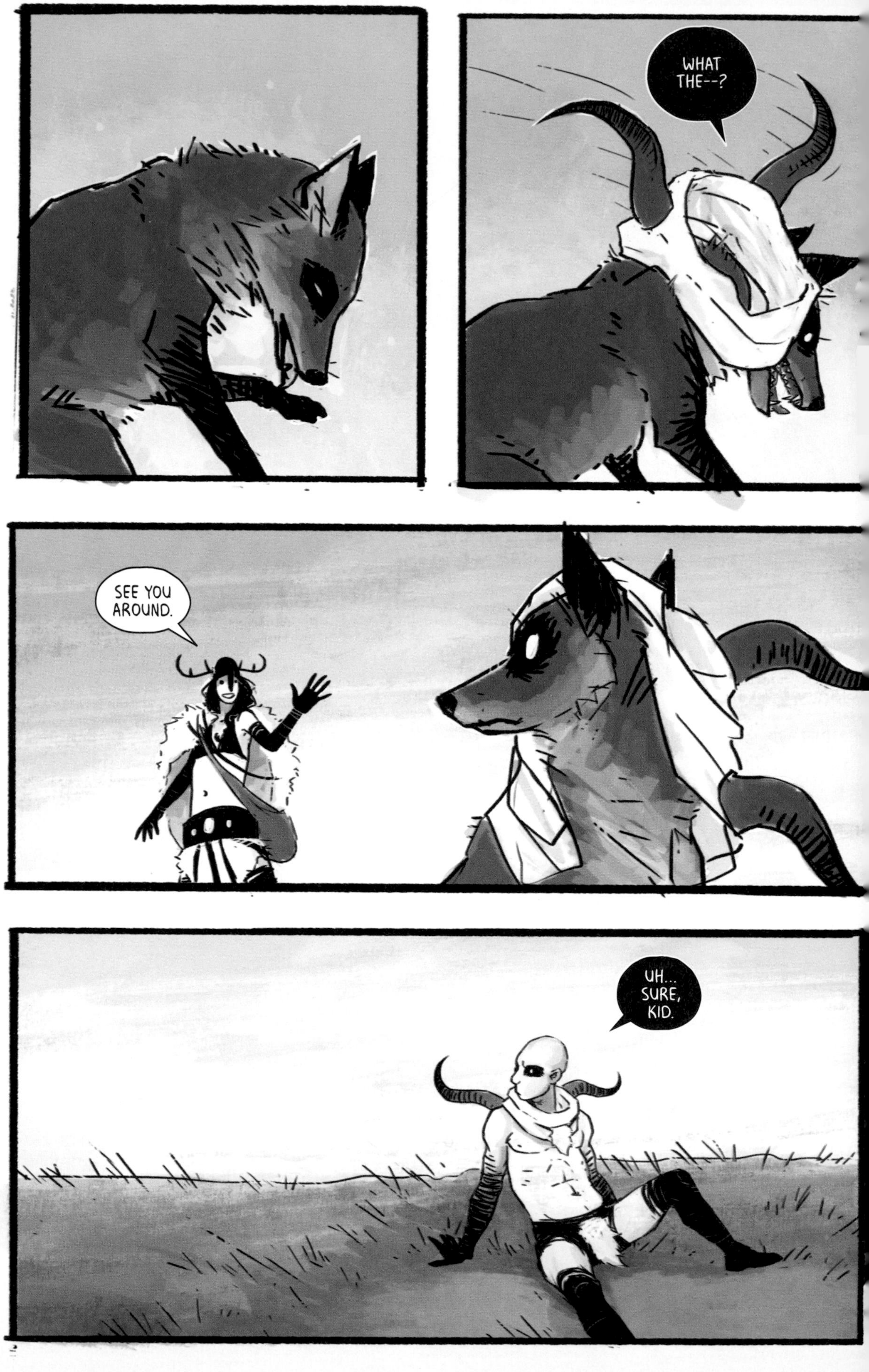
WHAT THE--?
SEE YOU AROUND.
UH... SURE, KID.

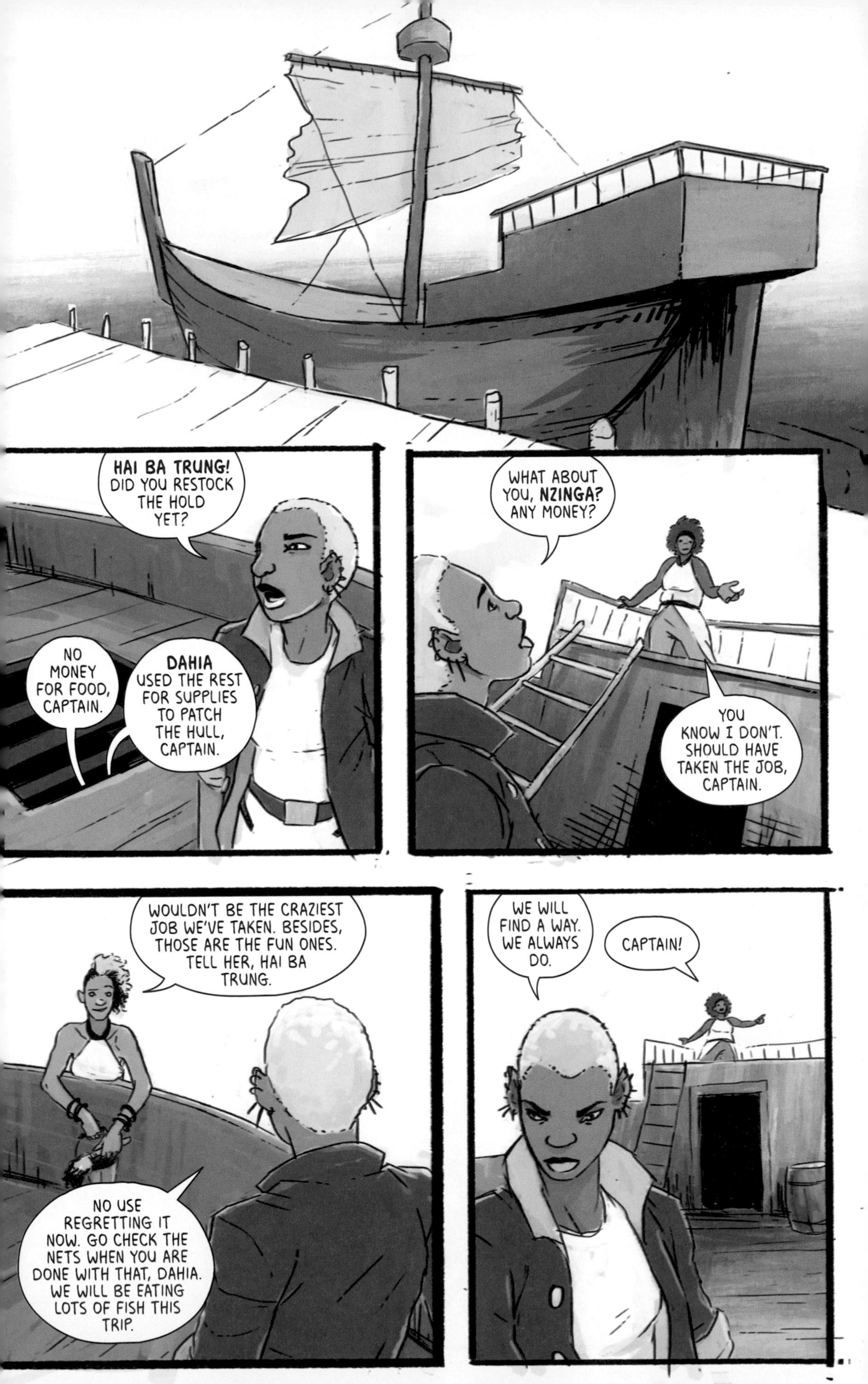
HAI BA TRUNG! DID YOU RESTOCK THE HOLD YET?
NO MONEY FOR FOOD, CAPTAIN.
DAHIA USED THE REST FOR SUPPLIES TO PATCH THE HULL, CAPTAIN.
WHAT ABOUT YOU, NZINGA? ANY MONEY?
YOU KNOW I DON'T. SHOULD HAVE TAKEN THE JOB, CAPTAIN.
WOULDN'T BE THE CRAZIEST JOB WE'VE TAKEN. BESIDES, THOSE ARE THE FUN ONES. TELL HER, HAI BA TRUNG.
NO USE REGRETTING IT NOW. GO CHECK THE NETS WHEN YOU ARE DONE WITH THAT, DAHIA. WE WILL BE EATING LOTS OF FISH THIS TRIP.
WE WILL FIND A WAY. WE ALWAYS DO.
CAPTAIN!

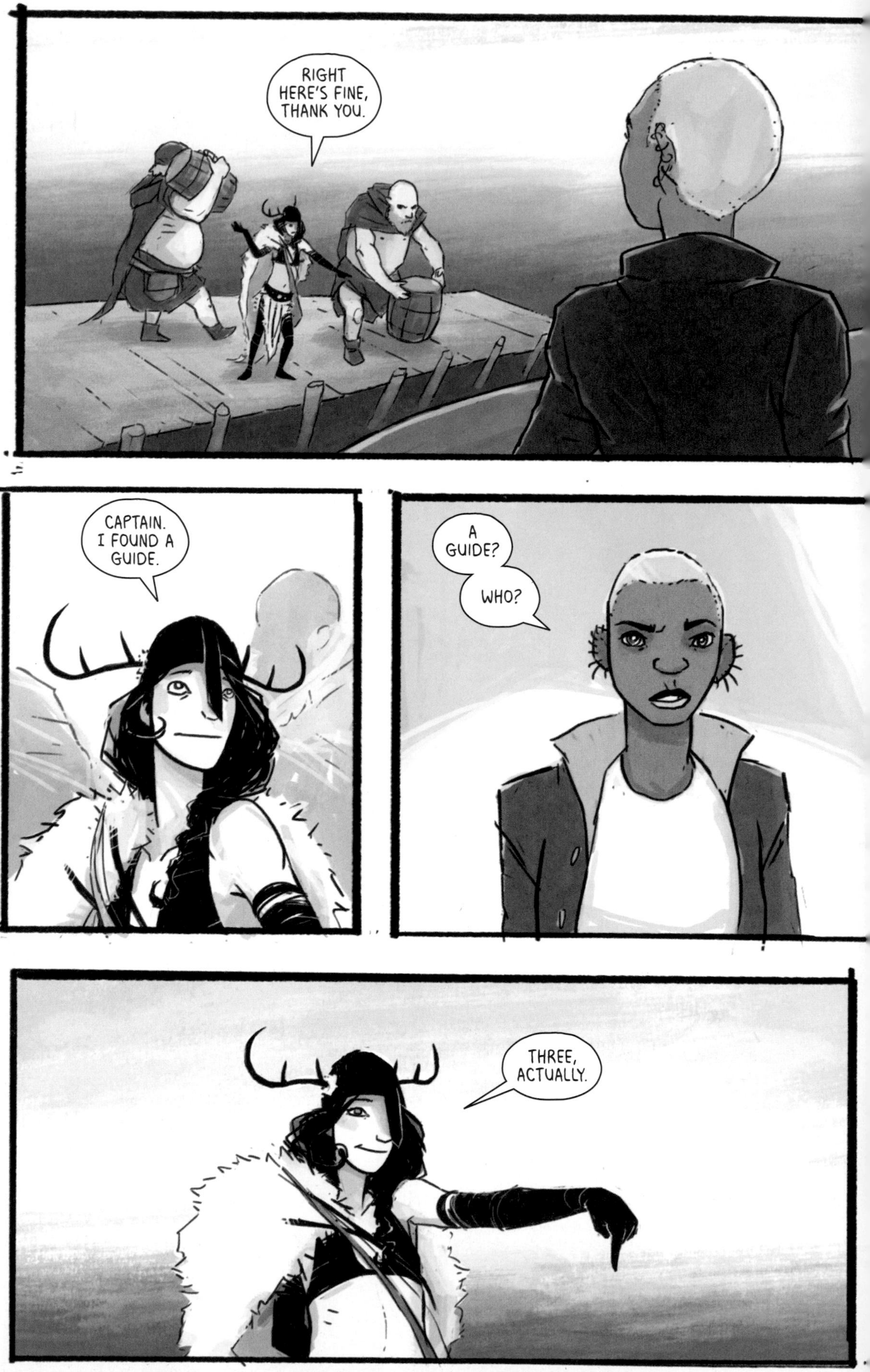
RIGHT HERE'S FINE, THANK YOU.
CAPTAIN. I FOUND A GUIDE.
A GUIDE?
WHO?
THREE, ACTUALLY.

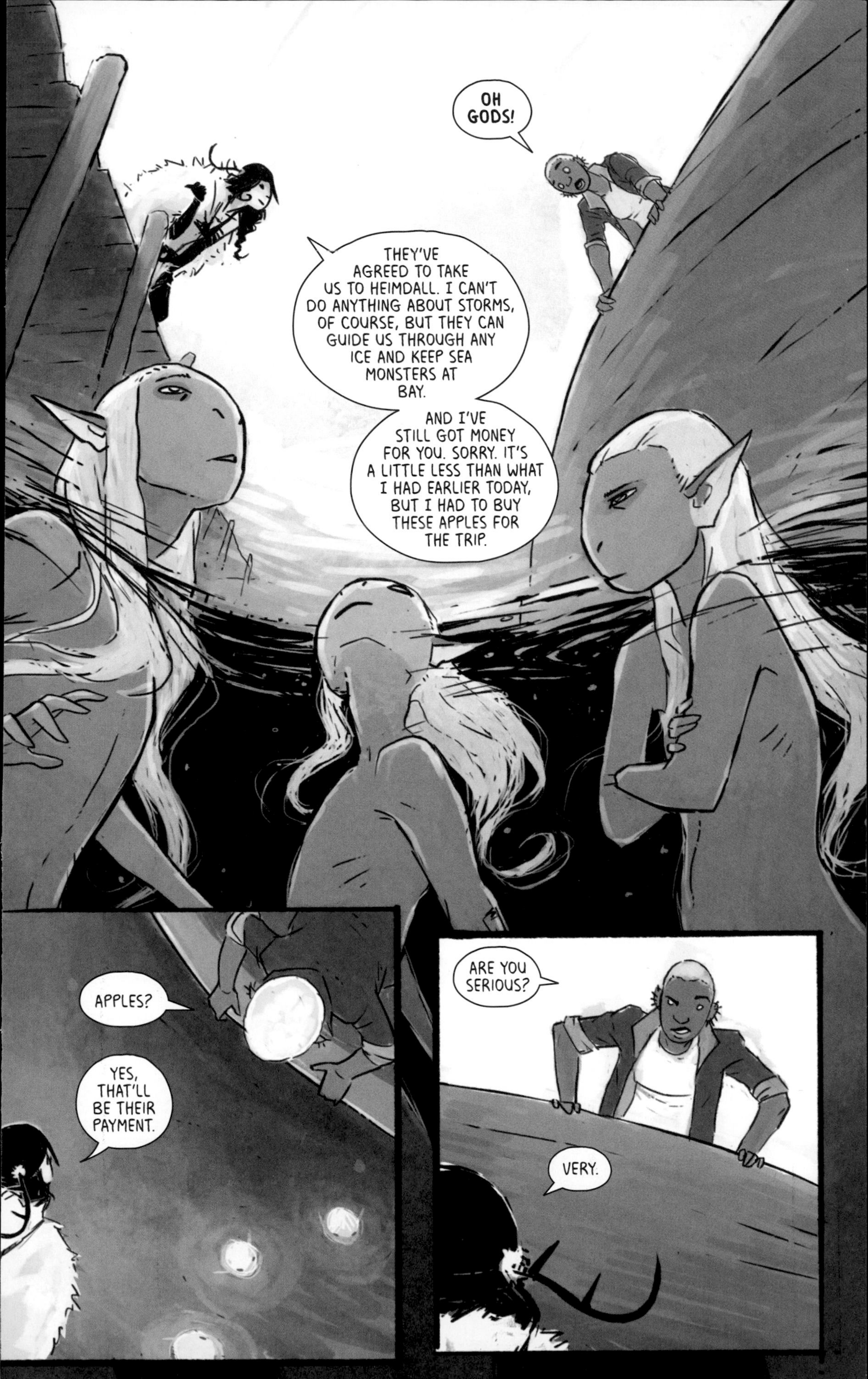
OH GODS!
THEY'VE AGREED TO TAKE US TO HEIMDALL. I CAN'T DO ANYTHING ABOUT STORMS, OF COURSE, BUT THEY CAN GUIDE US THROUGH ANY ICE AND KEEP SEA MONSTERS AT BAY.
AND I'VE STILL GOT MONEY FOR YOU. SORRY. IT'S A LITTLE LESS THAN WHAT I HAD EARLIER TODAY, BUT I HAD TO BUY THESE APPLES FOR THE TRIP.
APPLES?
YES, THAT'LL BE THEIR PAYMENT.
ARE YOU SERIOUS?
VERY.

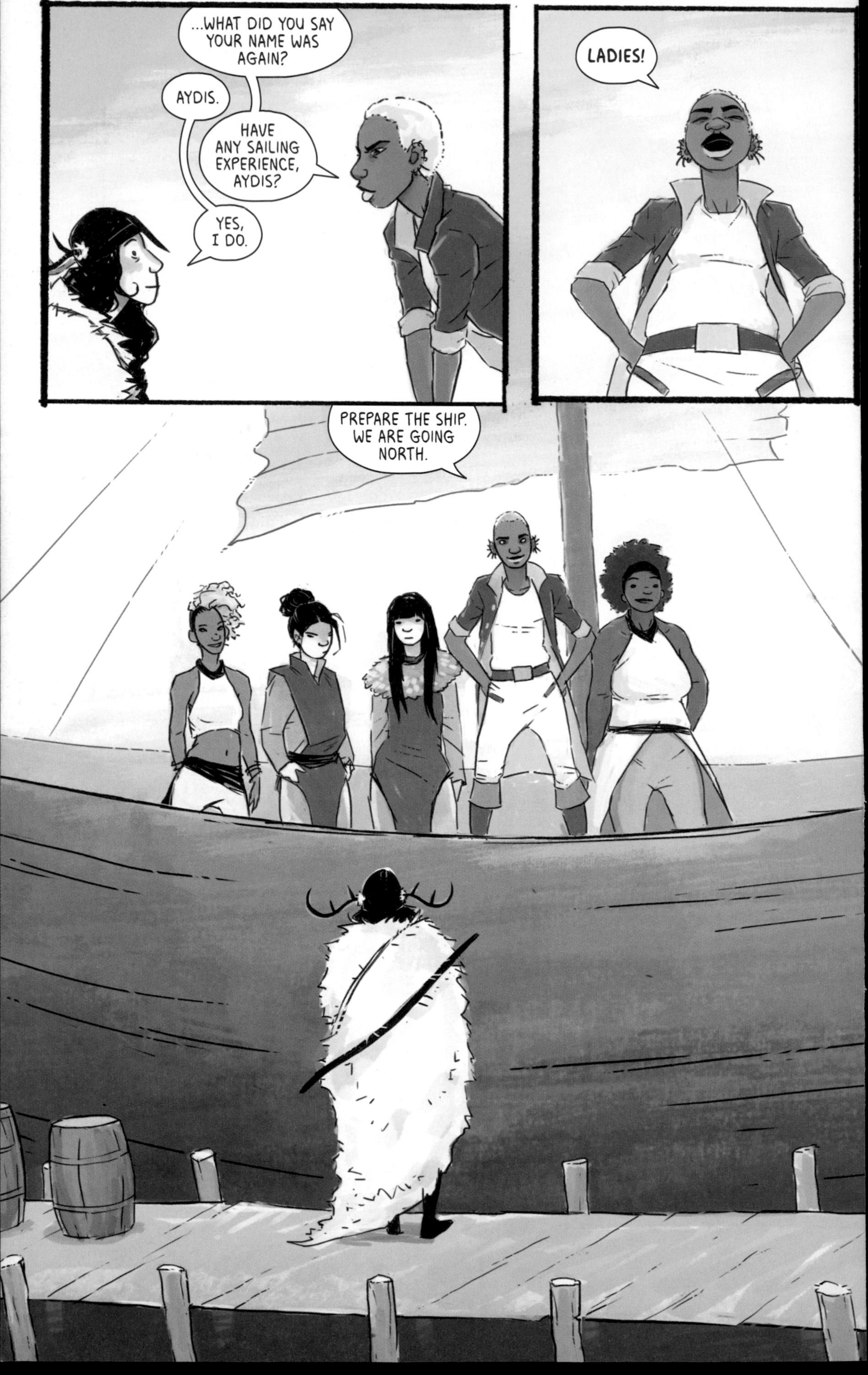
...WHAT DID YOU SAY YOUR NAME WAS AGAIN?
AYDIS.
HAVE ANY SAILING EXPERIENCE, AYDIS?
YES, I DO.
LADIES!
PREPARE THE SHIP. WE ARE GOING NORTH.

CHAPTER 6

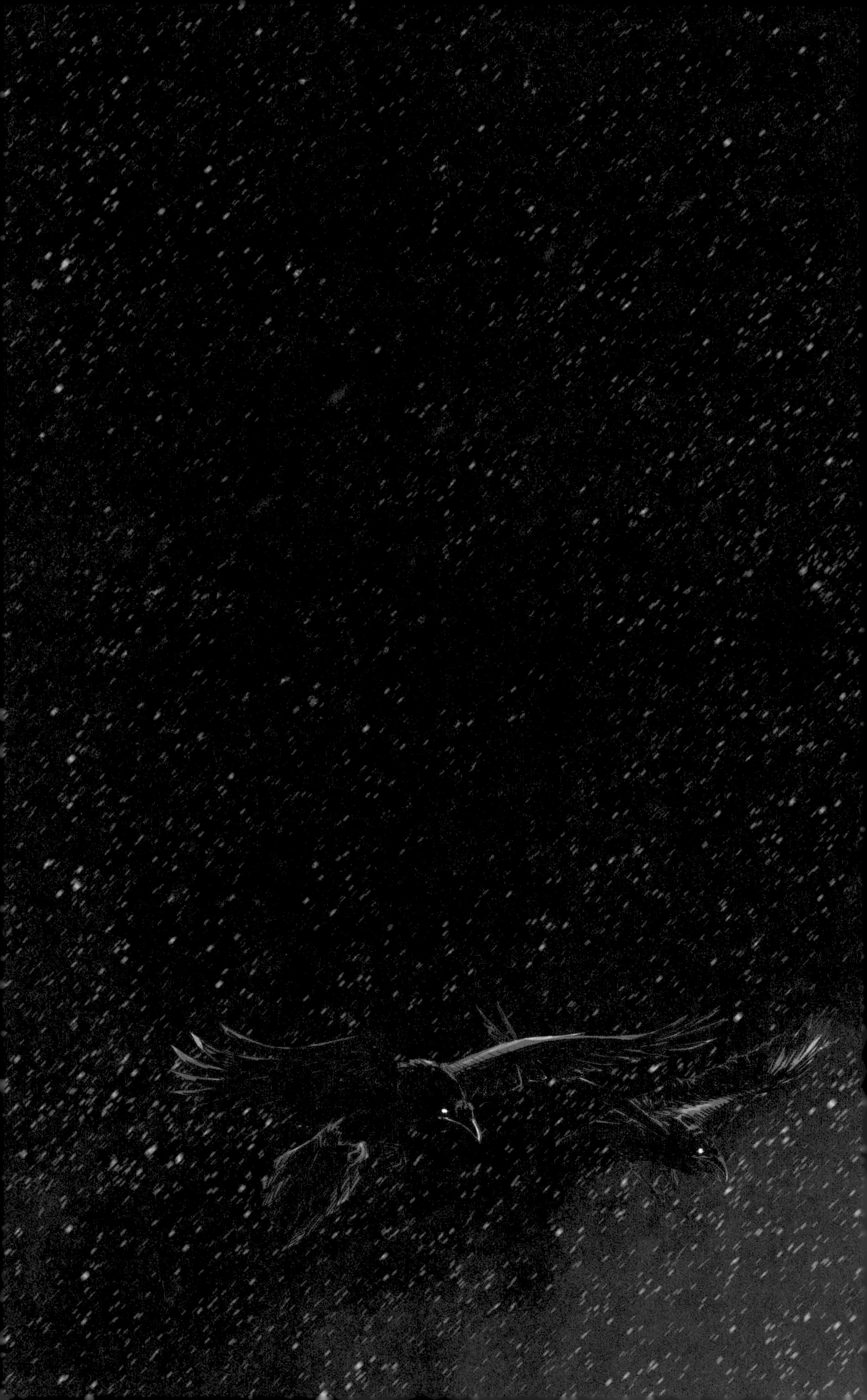

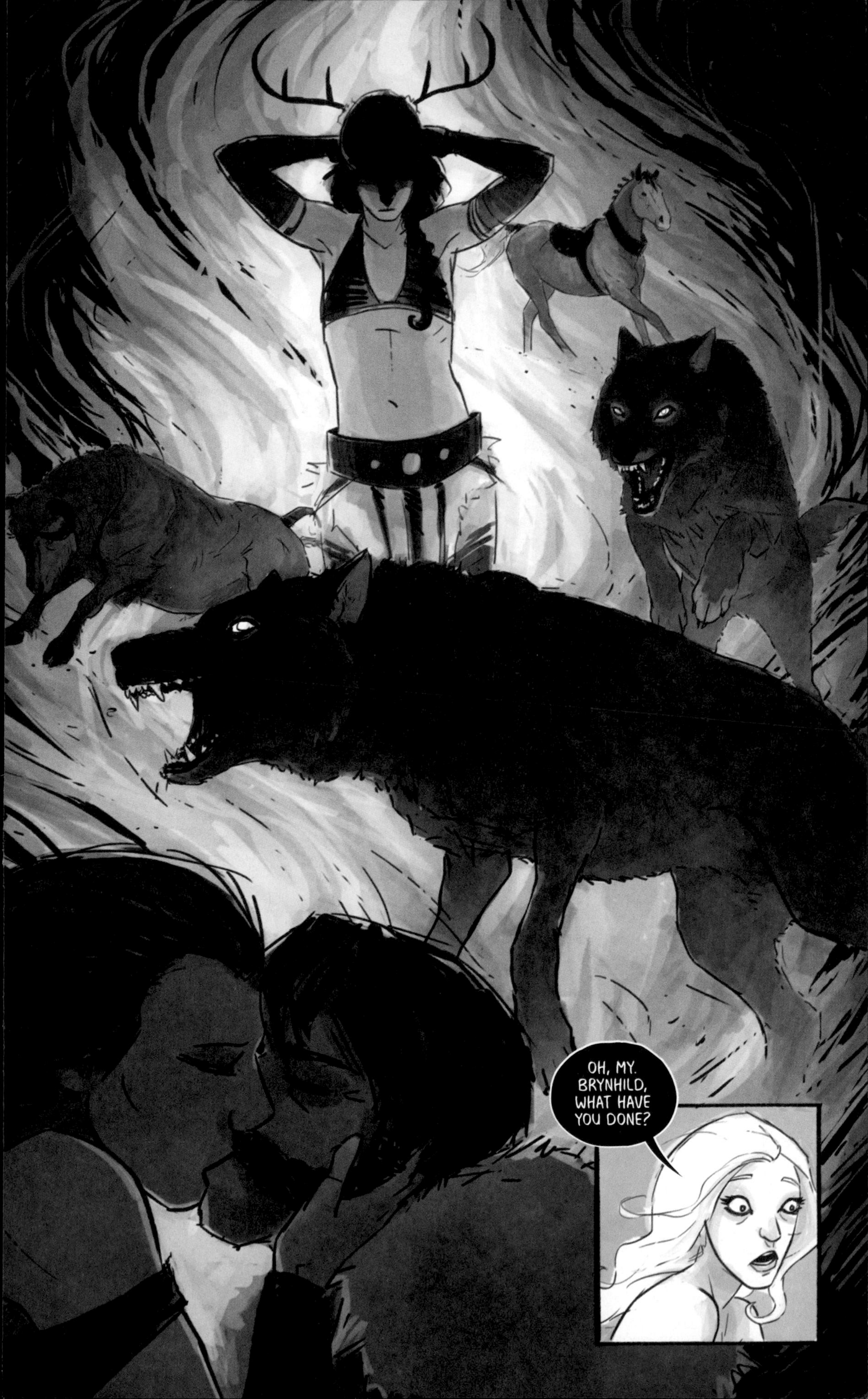
OH, MY. BRYNHILD, WHAT HAVE YOU DONE?

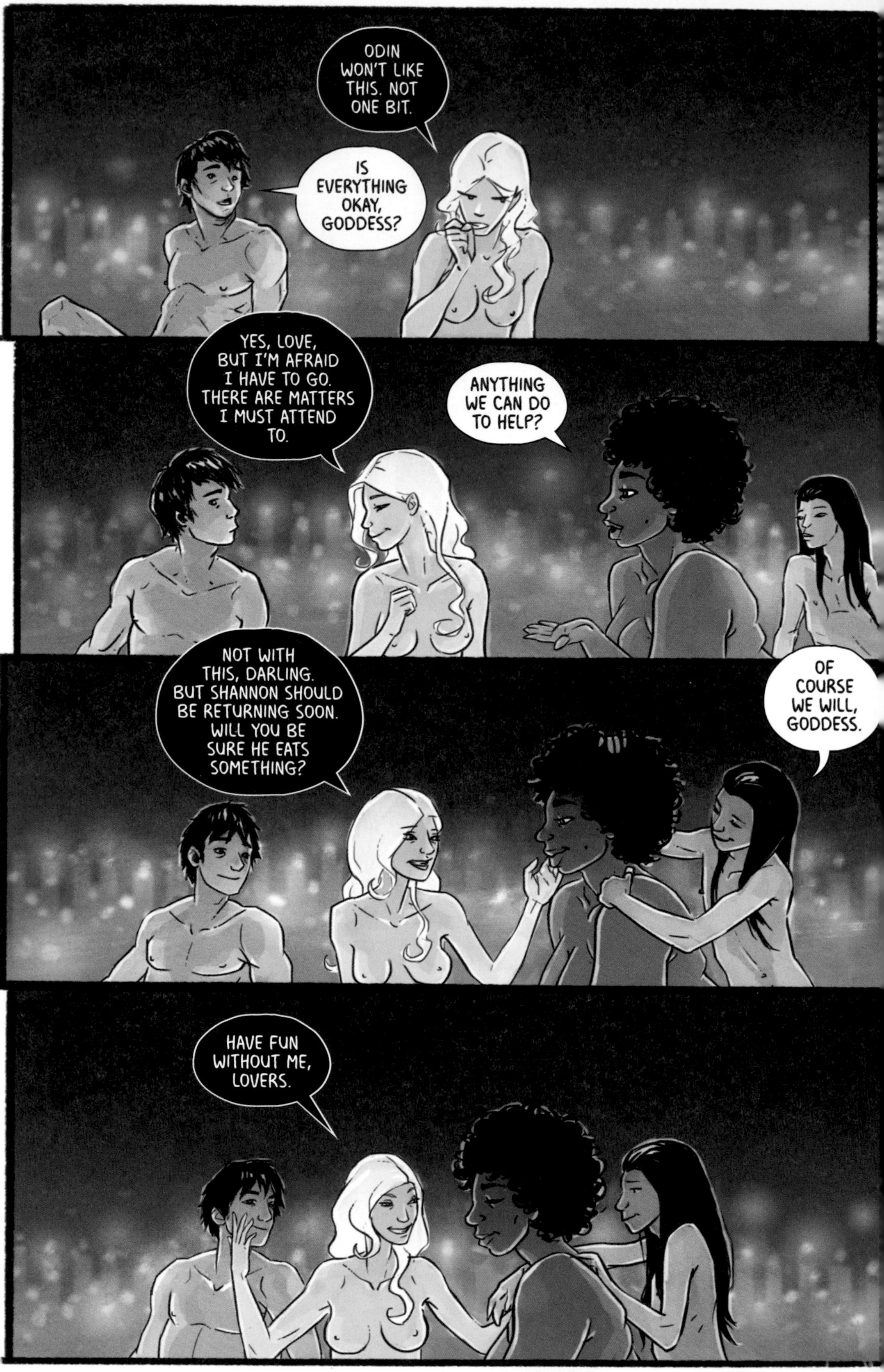
ODIN WON'T LIKE THIS. NOT ONE BIT.
IS EVERYTHING OKAY, GODDESS?
YES, LOVE, BUT I'M AFRAID I HAVE TO GO. THERE ARE MATTERS I MUST ATTEND TO.
ANYTHING WE CAN DO TO HELP?
NOT WITH THIS, DARLING. BUT SHANNON SHOULD BE RETURNING SOON. WILL YOU BE SURE HE EATS SOMETHING?
OF COURSE WE WILL, GODDESS.
HAVE FUN WITHOUT ME, LOVERS.

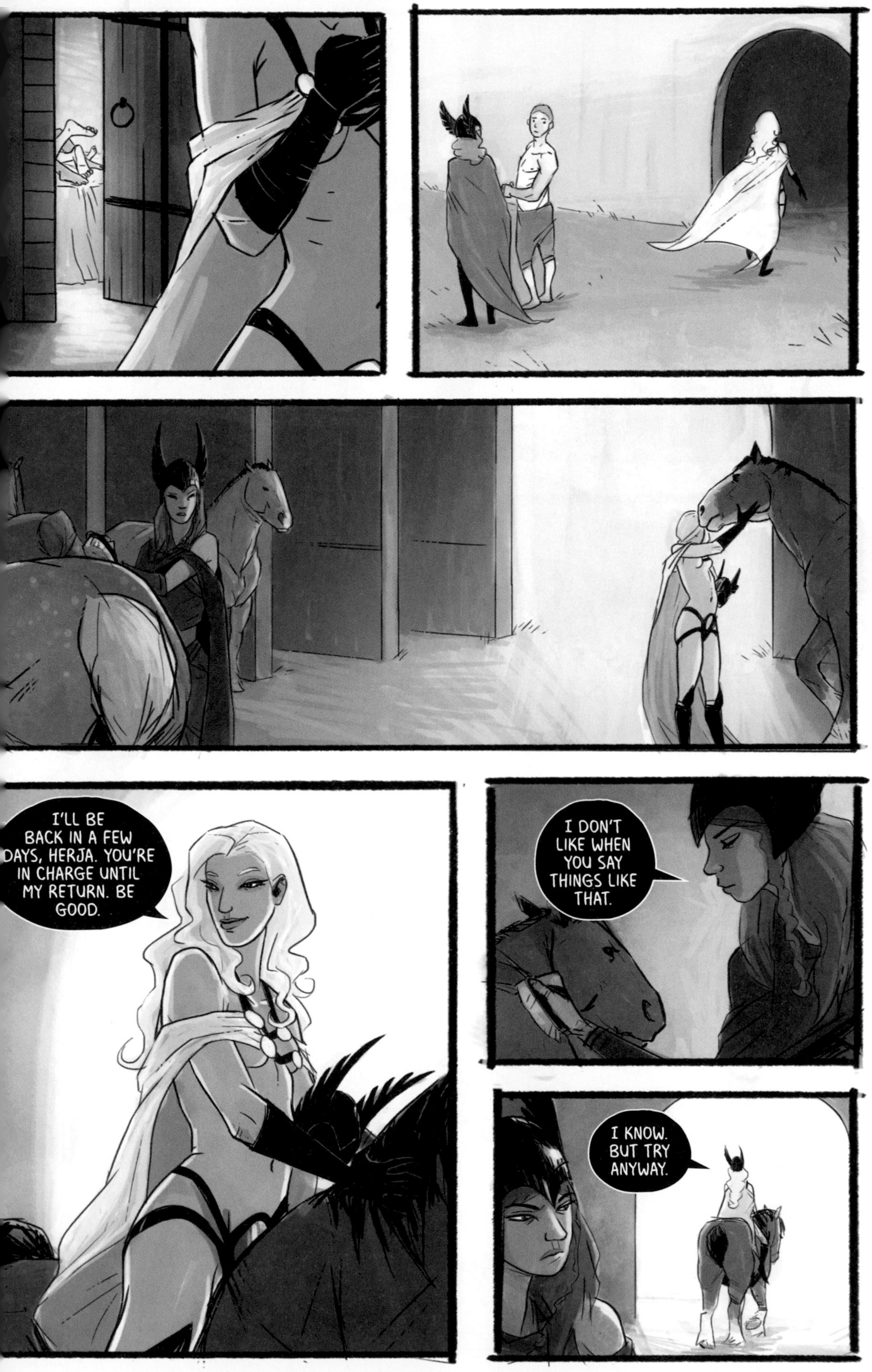

I'LL BE BACK IN A FEW DAYS, HERJA. YOU'RE IN CHARGE UNTIL MY RETURN. BE GOOD.
I DON'T LIKE WHEN YOU SAY THINGS LIKE THAT.
I KNOW. BUT TRY ANYWAY.

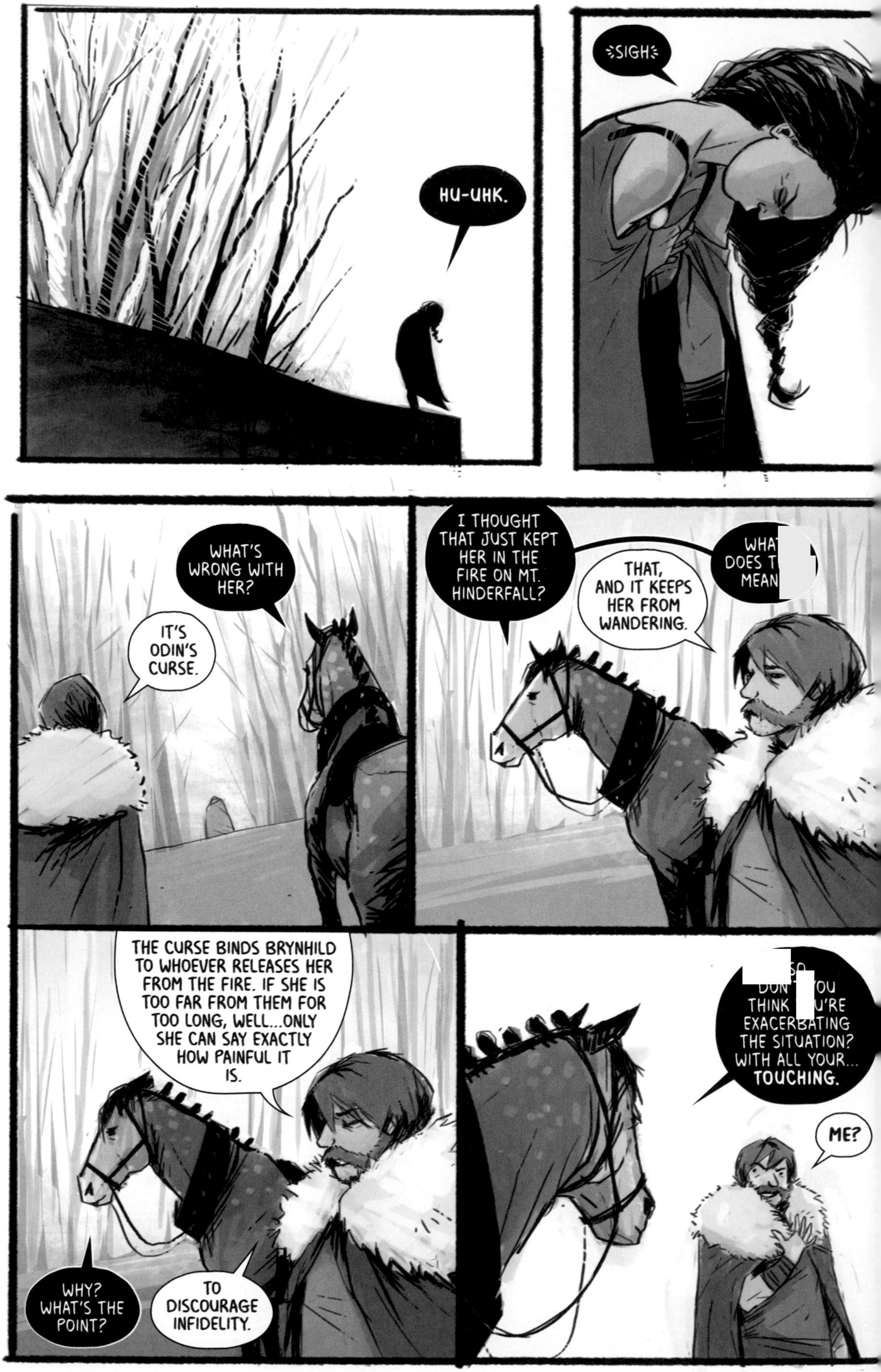
HU-UHK.
SIGH
WHAT'S WRONG WITH HER?
IT'S ODIN'S CURSE.
I THOUGHT THAT JUST KEPT HER IN THE FIRE ON MT. HINDERFALL?
THAT, AND IT KEEPS HER FROM WANDERING.
WHA DOES T MEAN
THE CURSE BINDS BRYNHILD TO WHOEVER RELEASES HER FROM THE FIRE. IF SHE IS TOO FAR FROM THEM FOR TOO LONG, WELL...ONLY SHE CAN SAY EXACTLY HOW PAINFUL IT IS.
WHY? WHAT'S THE POINT?
TO DISCOURAGE INFIDELITY.
SO DON OU THINK U'RE EXACERBATING THE SITUATION? WITH ALL YOUR... **TOUCHING.**
ME?

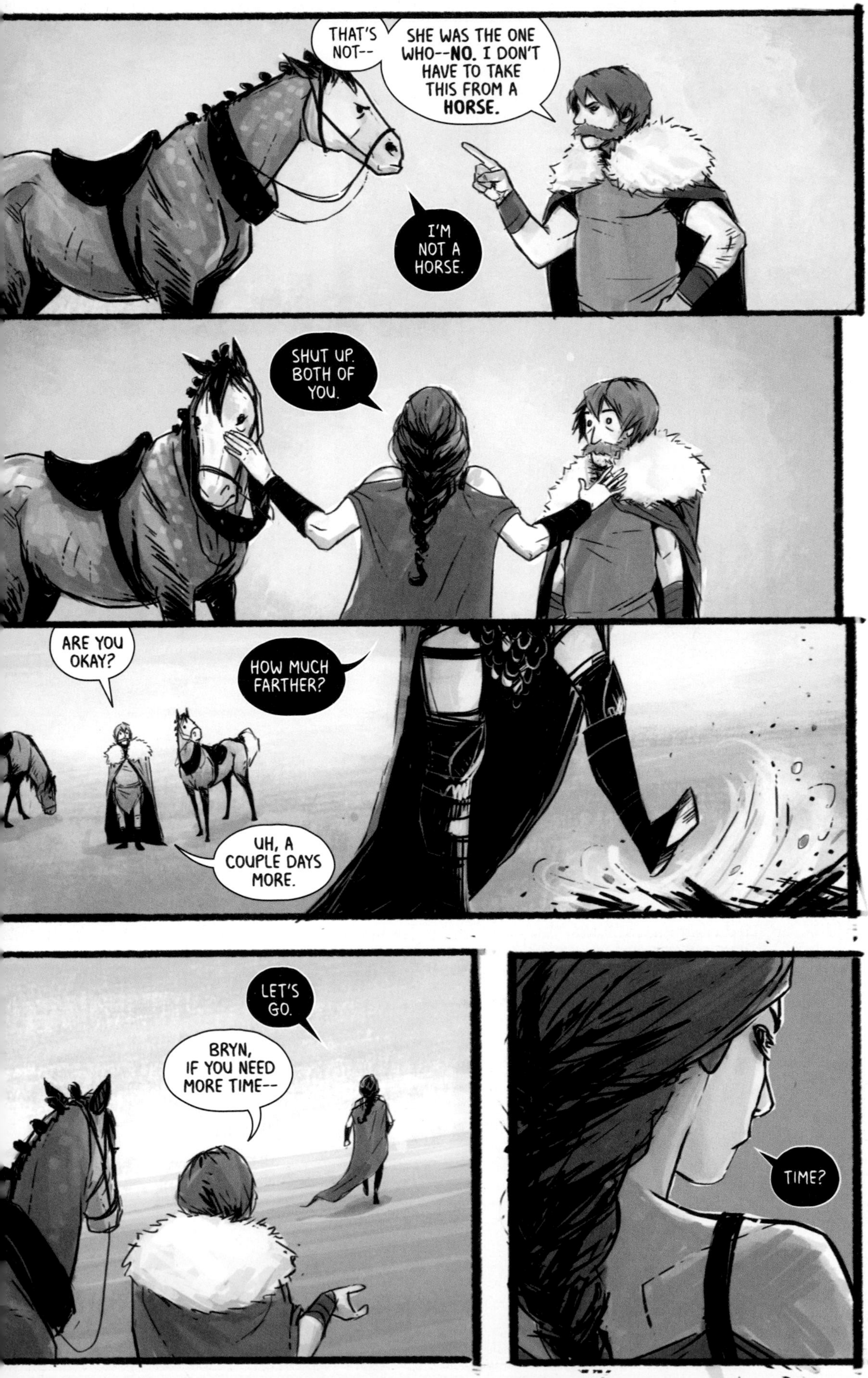

THAT'S NOT--
SHE WAS THE ONE WHO--**NO.** I DON'T HAVE TO TAKE THIS FROM A **HORSE.**
I'M NOT A HORSE.
SHUT UP. BOTH OF YOU.
ARE YOU OKAY?
HOW MUCH FARTHER?
UH, A COUPLE DAYS MORE.
LET'S GO.
BRYN, IF YOU NEED MORE TIME--
TIME?

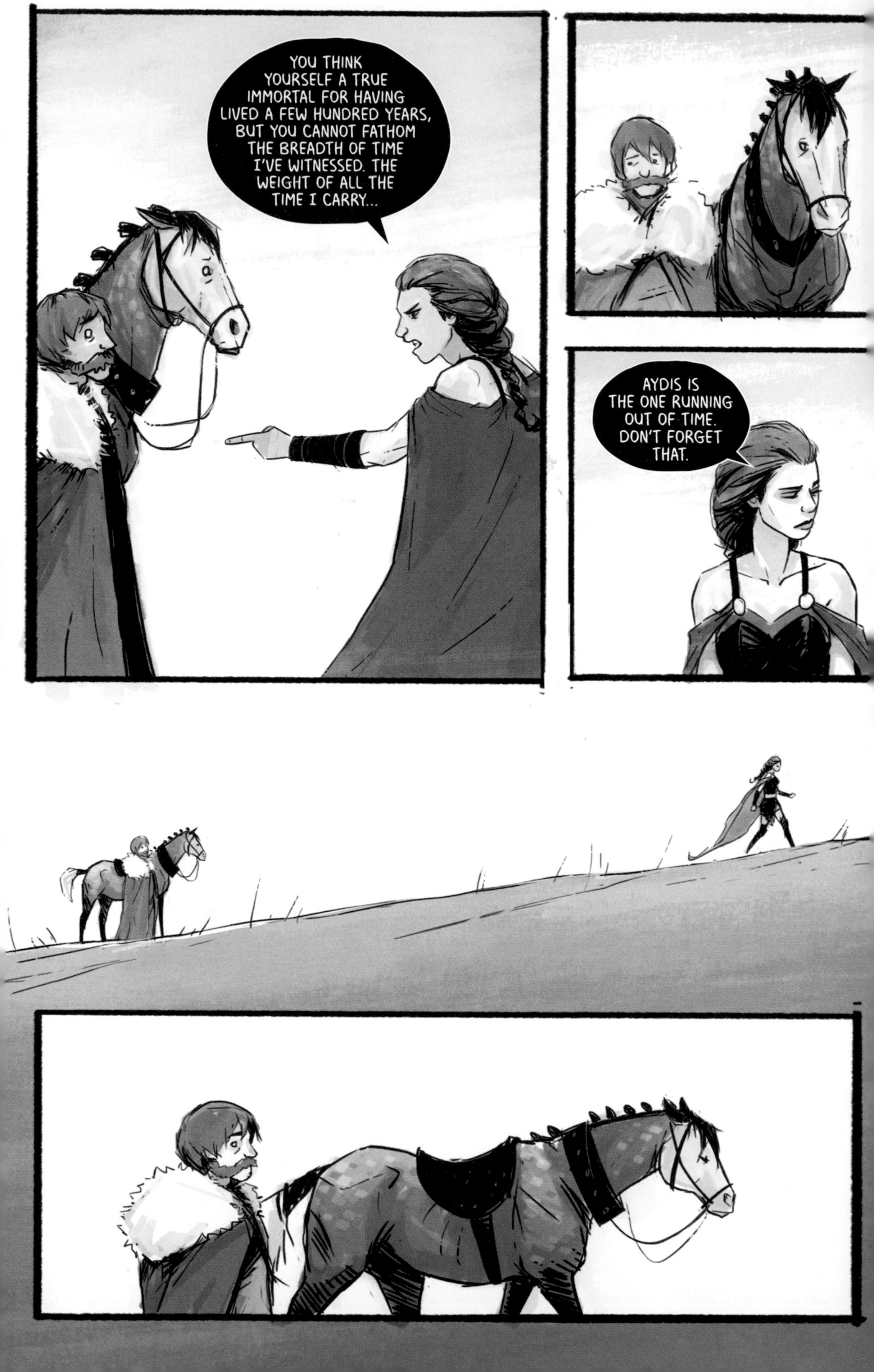
YOU THINK YOURSELF A TRUE IMMORTAL FOR HAVING LIVED A FEW HUNDRED YEARS, BUT YOU CANNOT FATHOM THE BREADTH OF TIME I'VE WITNESSED. THE WEIGHT OF ALL THE TIME I CARRY...
AYDIS IS THE ONE RUNNING OUT OF TIME. DON'T FORGET THAT.

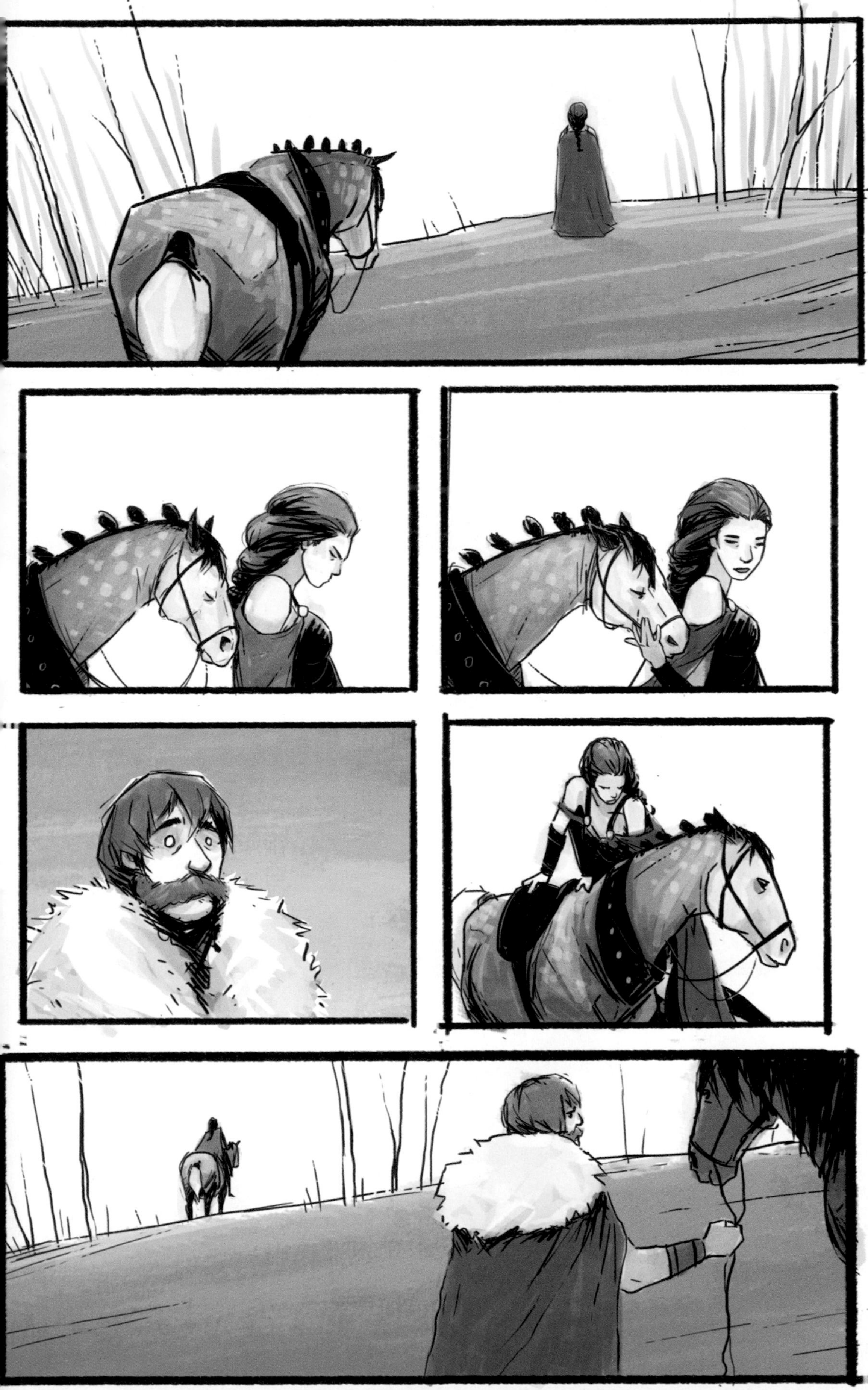

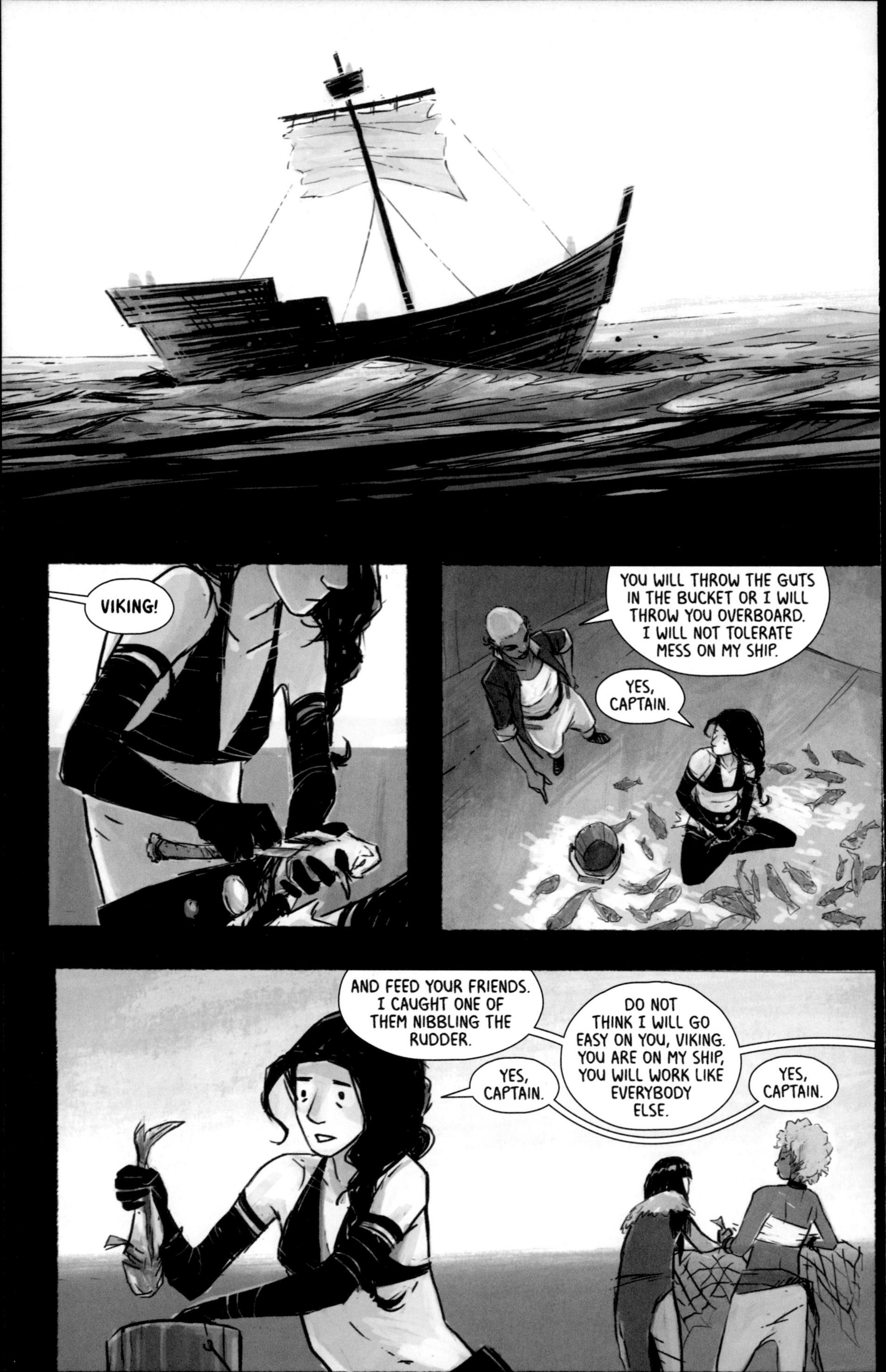
VIKING!
YOU WILL THROW THE GUTS IN THE BUCKET OR I WILL THROW YOU OVERBOARD. I WILL NOT TOLERATE MESS ON MY SHIP.
YES, CAPTAIN.
AND FEED YOUR FRIENDS. I CAUGHT ONE OF THEM NIBBLING THE RUDDER.
YES, CAPTAIN.
DO NOT THINK I WILL GO EASY ON YOU, VIKING. YOU ARE ON MY SHIP, YOU WILL WORK LIKE EVERYBODY ELSE.
YES, CAPTAIN.

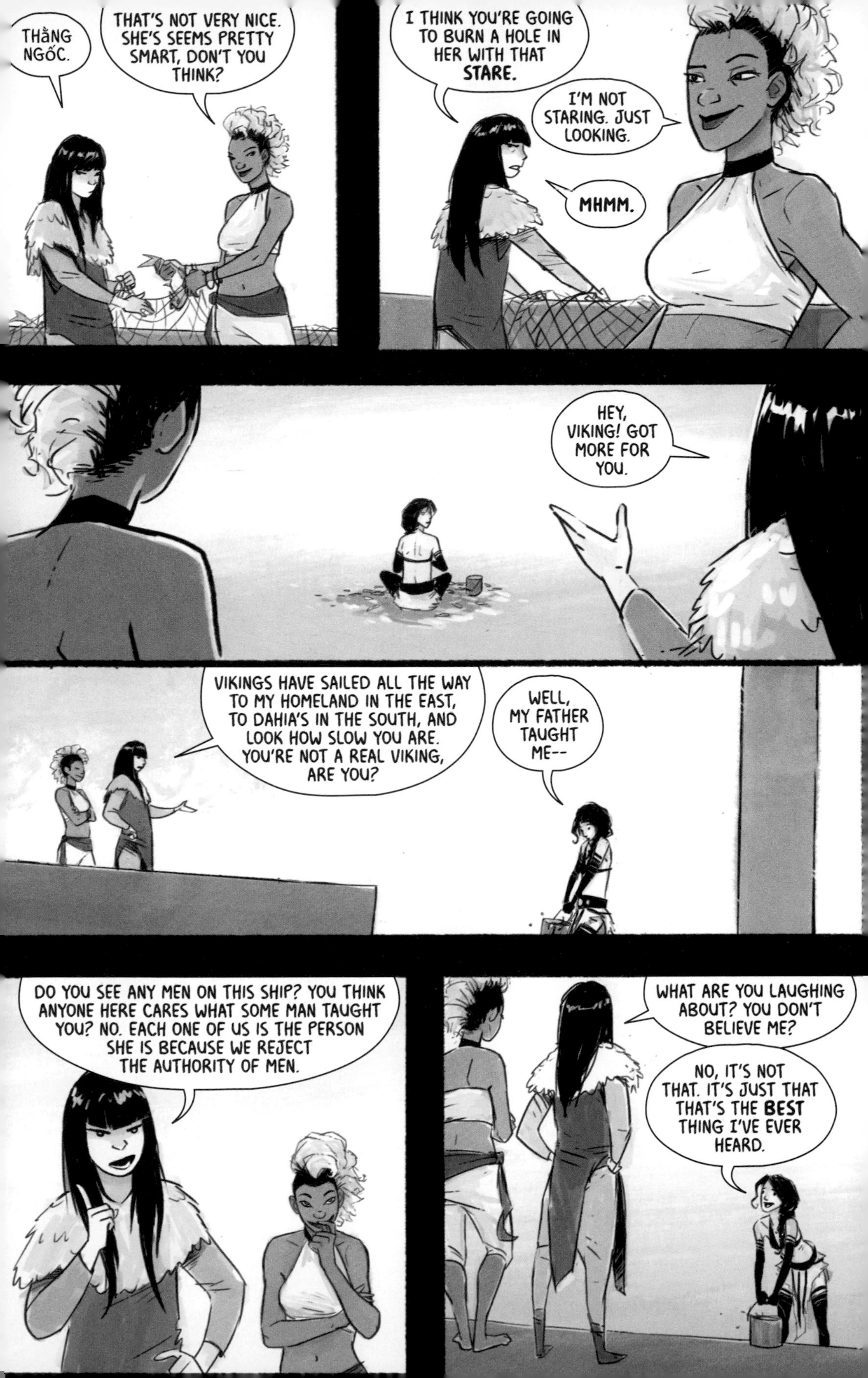
THẰNG NGỐC.
THAT'S NOT VERY NICE. SHE'S SEEMS PRETTY SMART, DON'T YOU THINK?
I THINK YOU'RE GOING TO BURN A HOLE IN HER WITH THAT **STARE.**
I'M NOT STARING. JUST LOOKING.
MHMM.
HEY, VIKING! GOT MORE FOR YOU.
VIKINGS HAVE SAILED ALL THE WAY TO MY HOMELAND IN THE EAST, TO DAHIA'S IN THE SOUTH, AND LOOK HOW SLOW YOU ARE. YOU'RE NOT A REAL VIKING, ARE YOU?
WELL, MY FATHER TAUGHT ME--
DO YOU SEE ANY MEN ON THIS SHIP? YOU THINK ANYONE HERE CARES WHAT SOME MAN TAUGHT YOU? NO. EACH ONE OF US IS THE PERSON SHE IS BECAUSE WE REJECT THE AUTHORITY OF MEN.
WHAT ARE YOU LAUGHING ABOUT? YOU DON'T BELIEVE ME?
NO, IT'S NOT THAT. IT'S JUST THAT THAT'S THE **BEST** THING I'VE EVER HEARD.

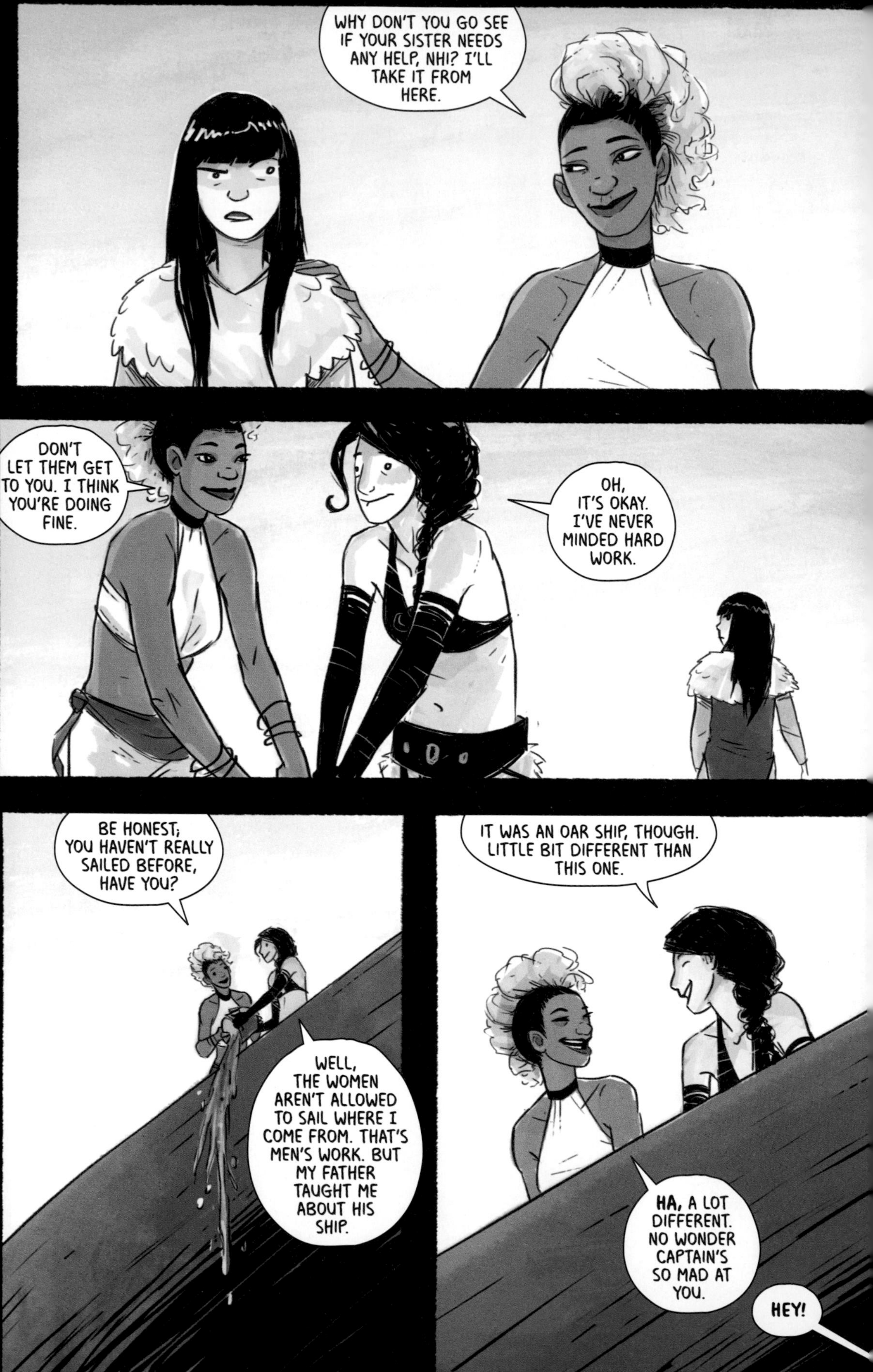
WHY DON'T YOU GO SEE IF YOUR SISTER NEEDS ANY HELP, NHI? I'LL TAKE IT FROM HERE.
DON'T LET THEM GET TO YOU. I THINK YOU'RE DOING FINE.
OH, IT'S OKAY. I'VE NEVER MINDED HARD WORK.
BE HONEST; YOU HAVEN'T REALLY SAILED BEFORE, HAVE YOU?
WELL, THE WOMEN AREN'T ALLOWED TO SAIL WHERE I COME FROM. THAT'S MEN'S WORK. BUT MY FATHER TAUGHT ME ABOUT HIS SHIP.
IT WAS AN OAR SHIP, THOUGH. LITTLE BIT DIFFERENT THAN THIS ONE.
HA, A LOT DIFFERENT. NO WONDER CAPTAIN'S SO MAD AT YOU.
HEY!

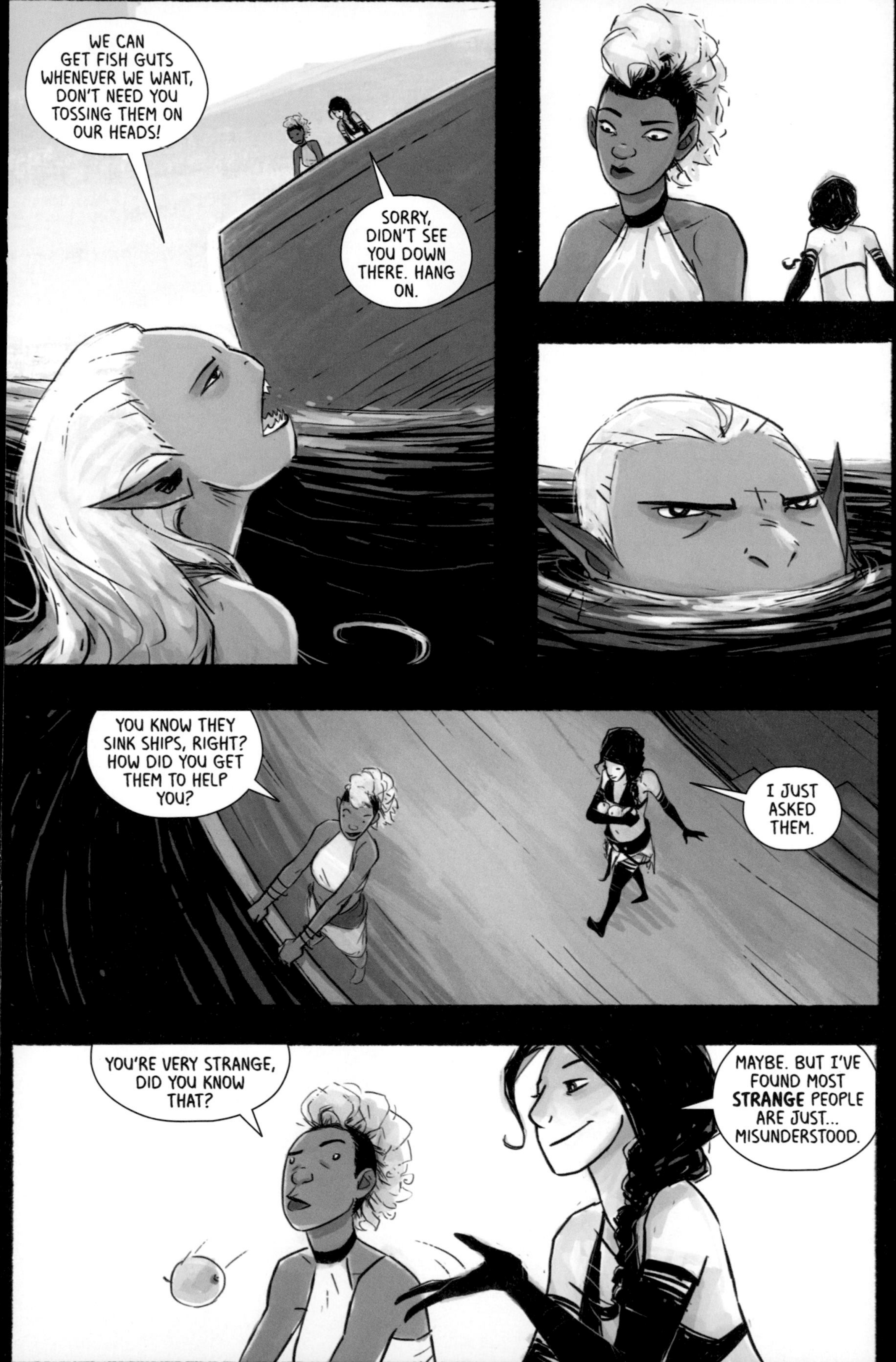
WE CAN GET FISH GUTS WHENEVER WE WANT, DON'T NEED YOU TOSSING THEM ON OUR HEADS!
SORRY, DIDN'T SEE YOU DOWN THERE. HANG ON.
YOU KNOW THEY SINK SHIPS, RIGHT? HOW DID YOU GET THEM TO HELP YOU?
I JUST ASKED THEM.
YOU'RE VERY STRANGE, DID YOU KNOW THAT?
MAYBE. BUT I'VE FOUND MOST **STRANGE** PEOPLE ARE JUST... MISUNDERSTOOD.

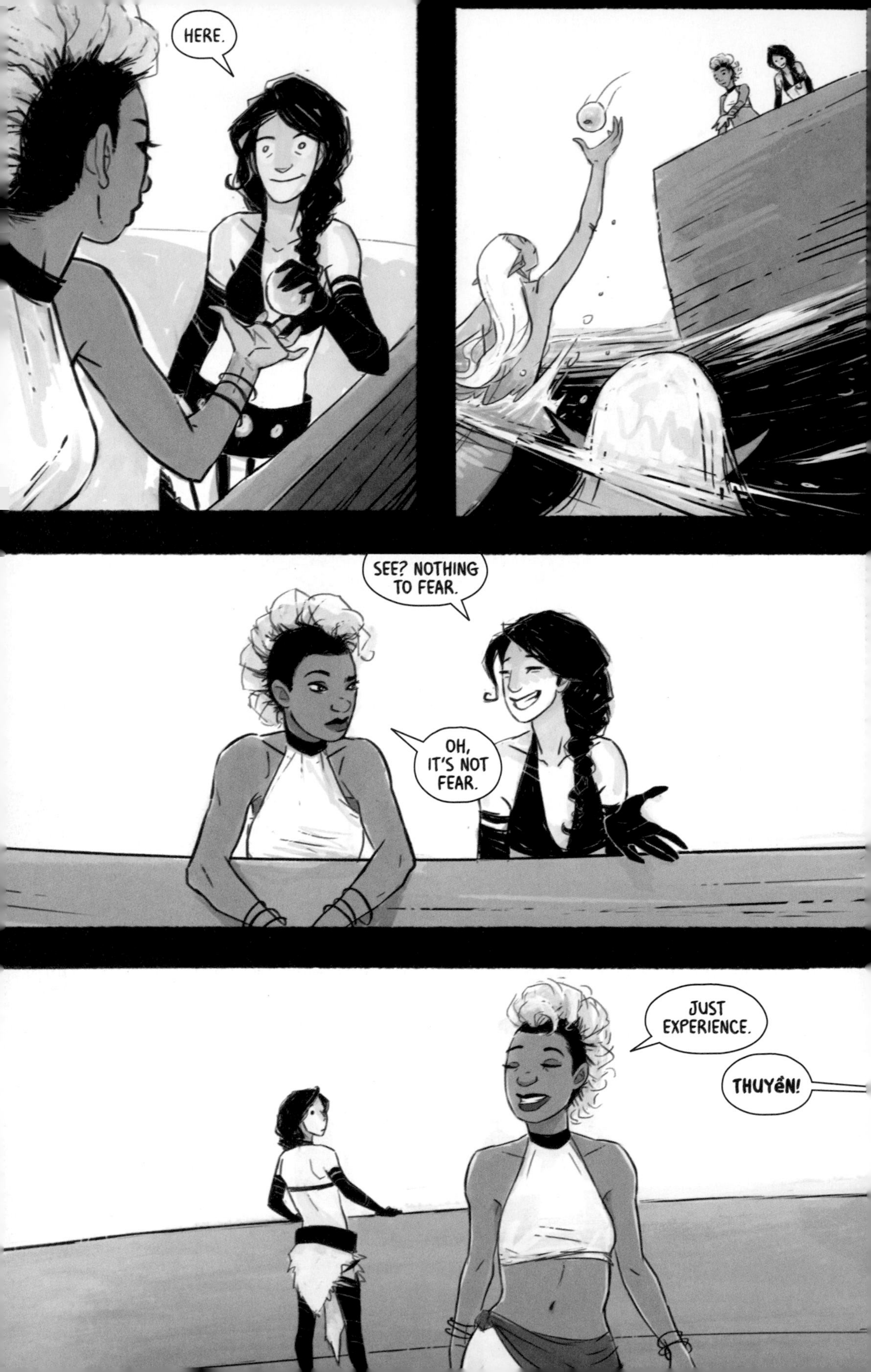
HERE.
SEE? NOTHING TO FEAR.
OH, IT'S NOT FEAR.
JUST EXPERIENCE.
THUYỀN!

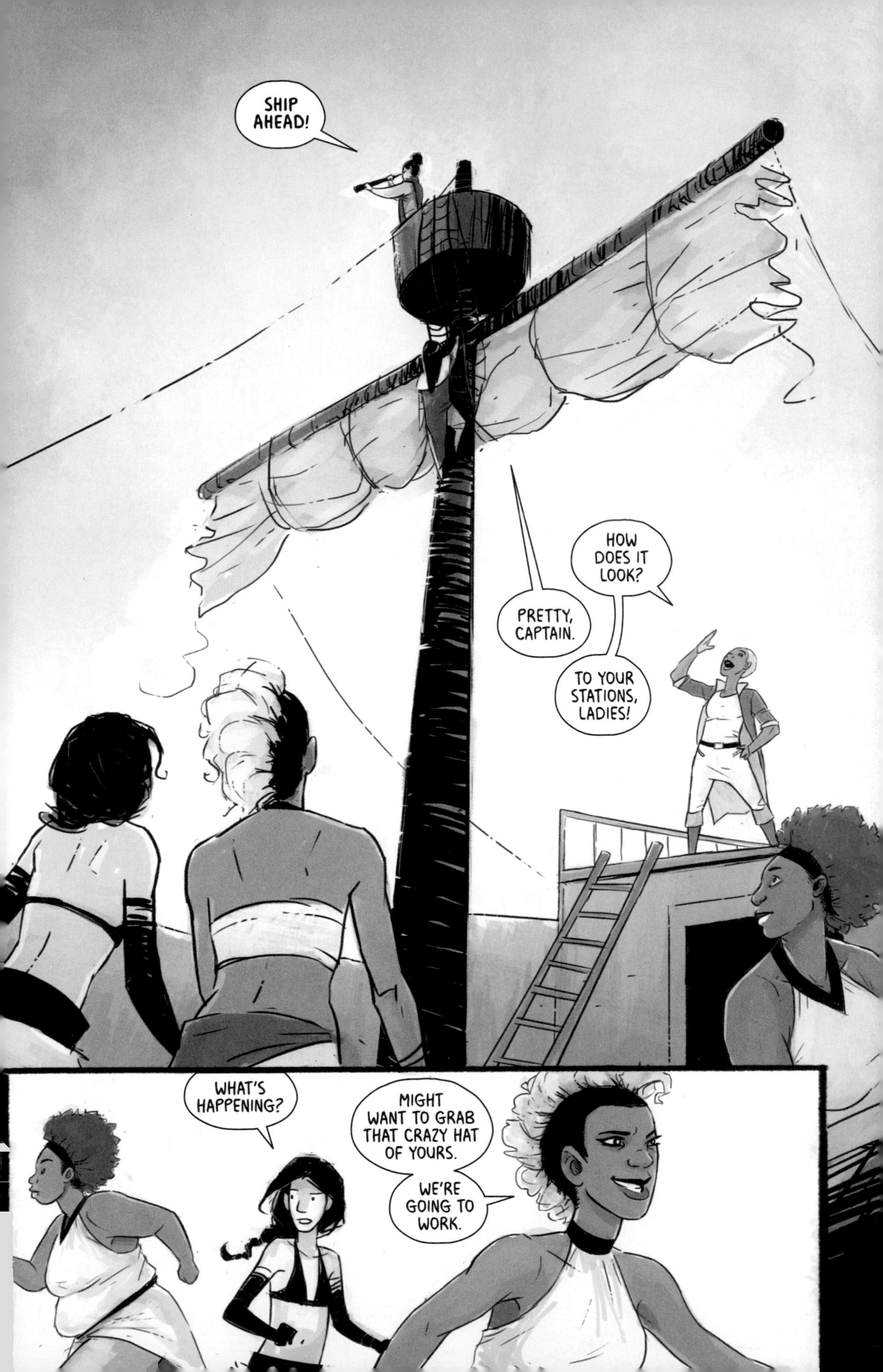
SHIP AHEAD!
HOW DOES IT LOOK?
PRETTY, CAPTAIN.
TO YOUR STATIONS, LADIES!
WHAT'S HAPPENING?
MIGHT WANT TO GRAB THAT CRAZY HAT OF YOURS.
WE'RE GOING TO WORK.

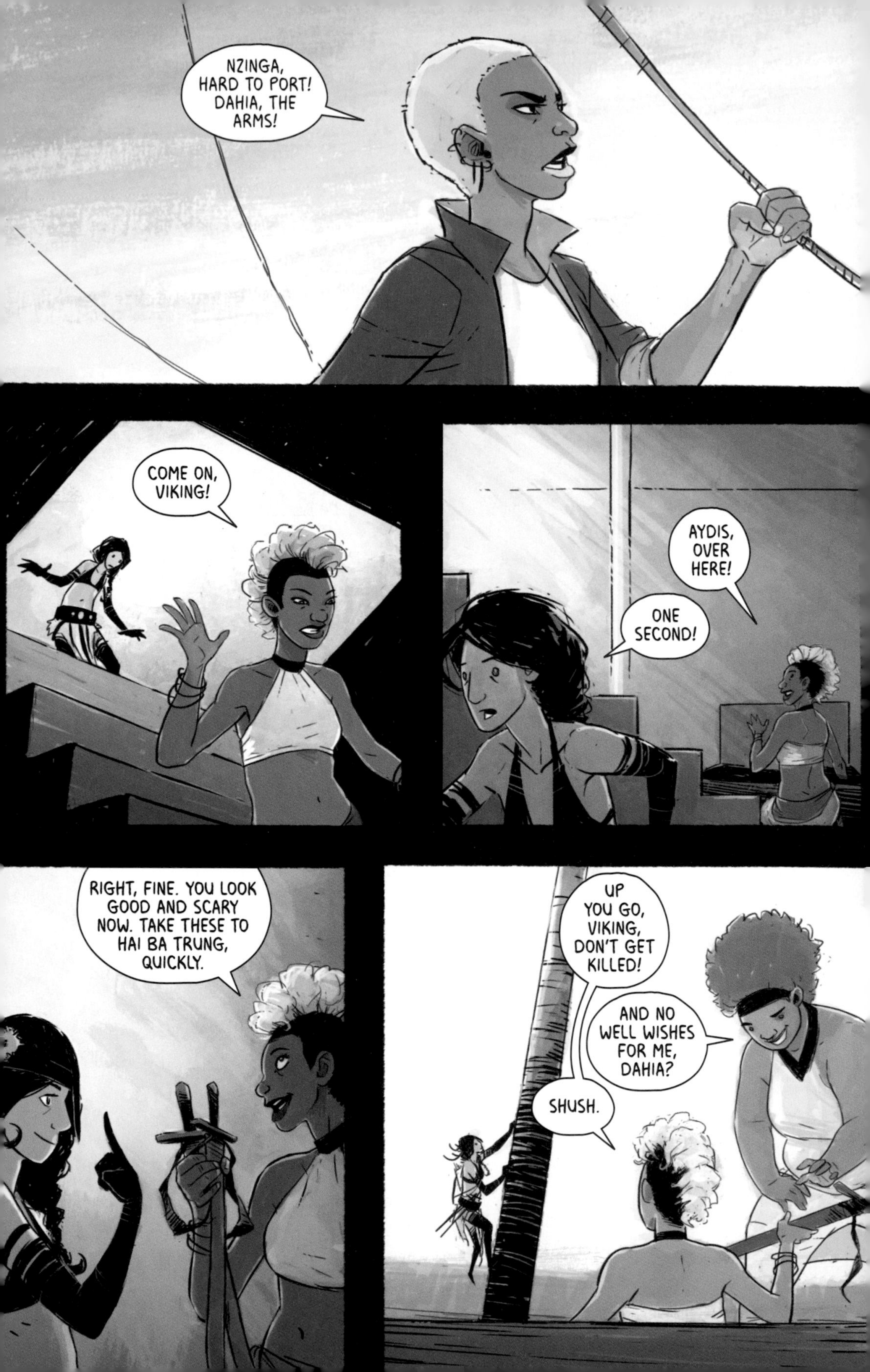
NZINGA, HARD TO PORT! DAHIA, THE ARMS!
COME ON, VIKING!
AYDIS, OVER HERE!
ONE SECOND!
RIGHT, FINE. YOU LOOK GOOD AND SCARY NOW. TAKE THESE TO HAI BA TRUNG, QUICKLY.
UP YOU GO, VIKING, DON'T GET KILLED!
AND NO WELL WISHES FOR ME, DAHIA?
SHUSH.

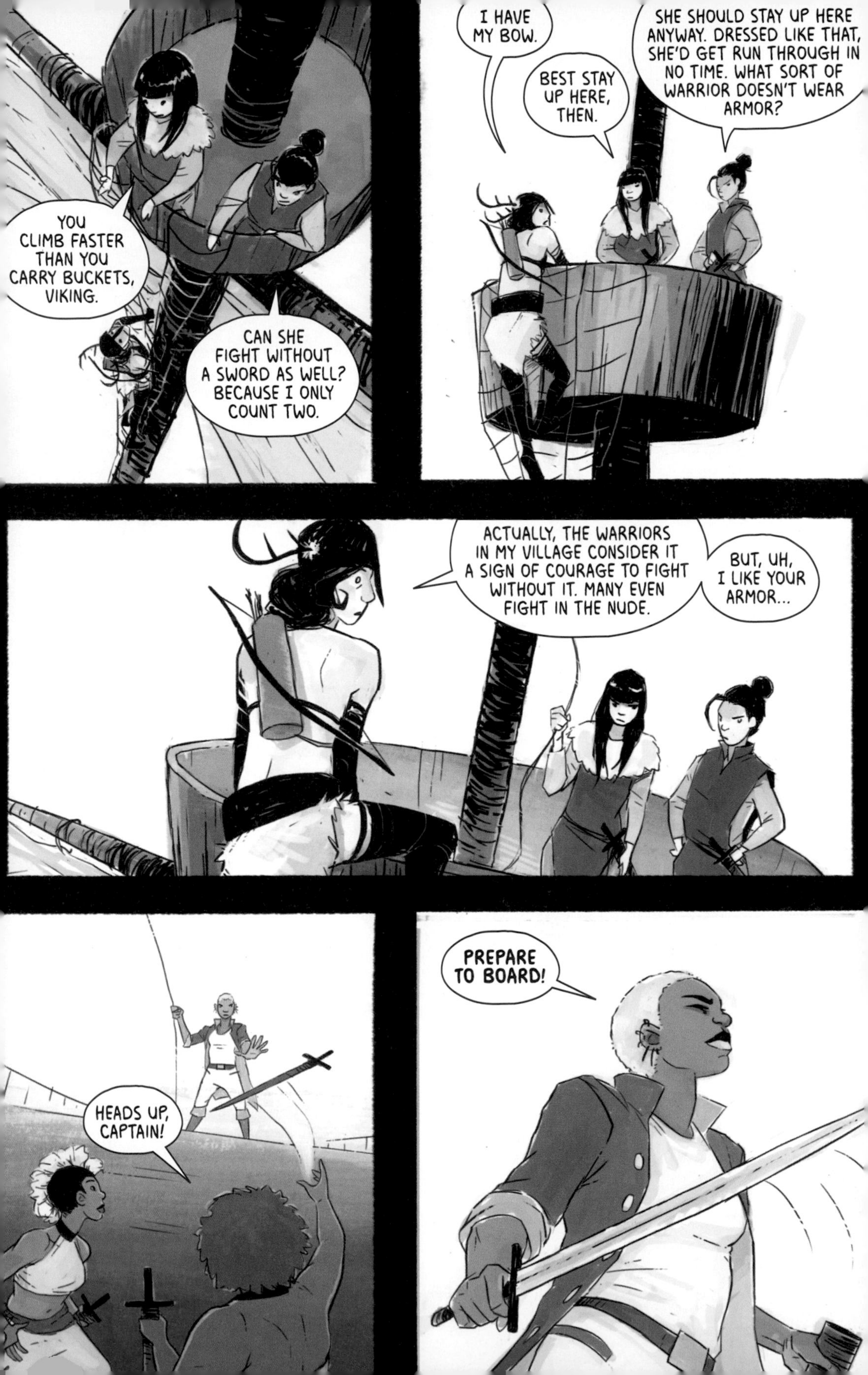
YOU CLIMB FASTER THAN YOU CARRY BUCKETS, VIKING.
CAN SHE FIGHT WITHOUT A SWORD AS WELL? BECAUSE I ONLY COUNT TWO.
I HAVE MY BOW.
BEST STAY UP HERE, THEN.
SHE SHOULD STAY UP HERE ANYWAY. DRESSED LIKE THAT, SHE'D GET RUN THROUGH IN NO TIME. WHAT SORT OF WARRIOR DOESN'T WEAR ARMOR?
ACTUALLY, THE WARRIORS IN MY VILLAGE CONSIDER IT A SIGN OF COURAGE TO FIGHT WITHOUT IT. MANY EVEN FIGHT IN THE NUDE.
BUT, UH, I LIKE YOUR ARMOR...
HEADS UP, CAPTAIN!
PREPARE TO BOARD!

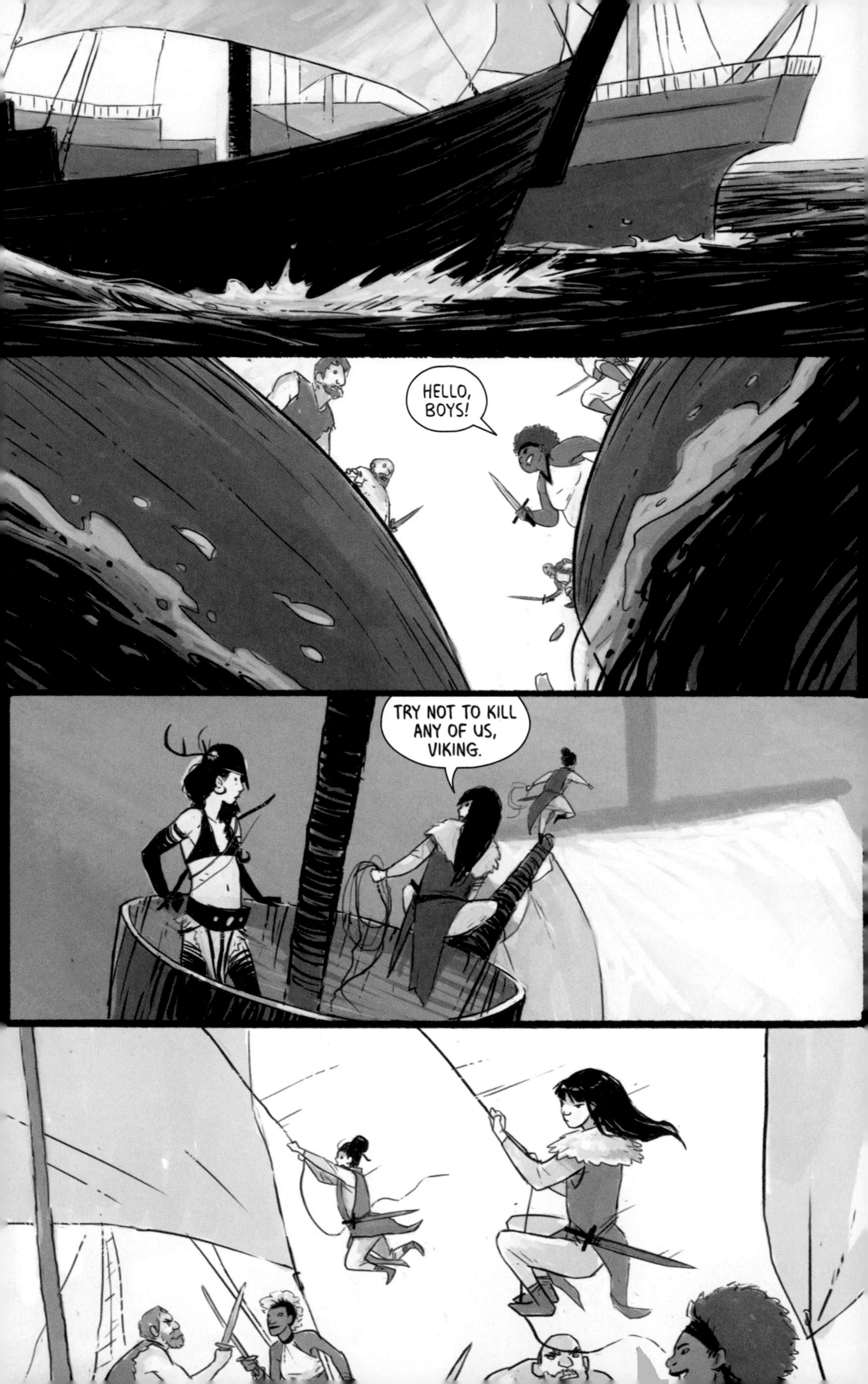
HELLO, BOYS!
TRY NOT TO KILL ANY OF US, VIKING.

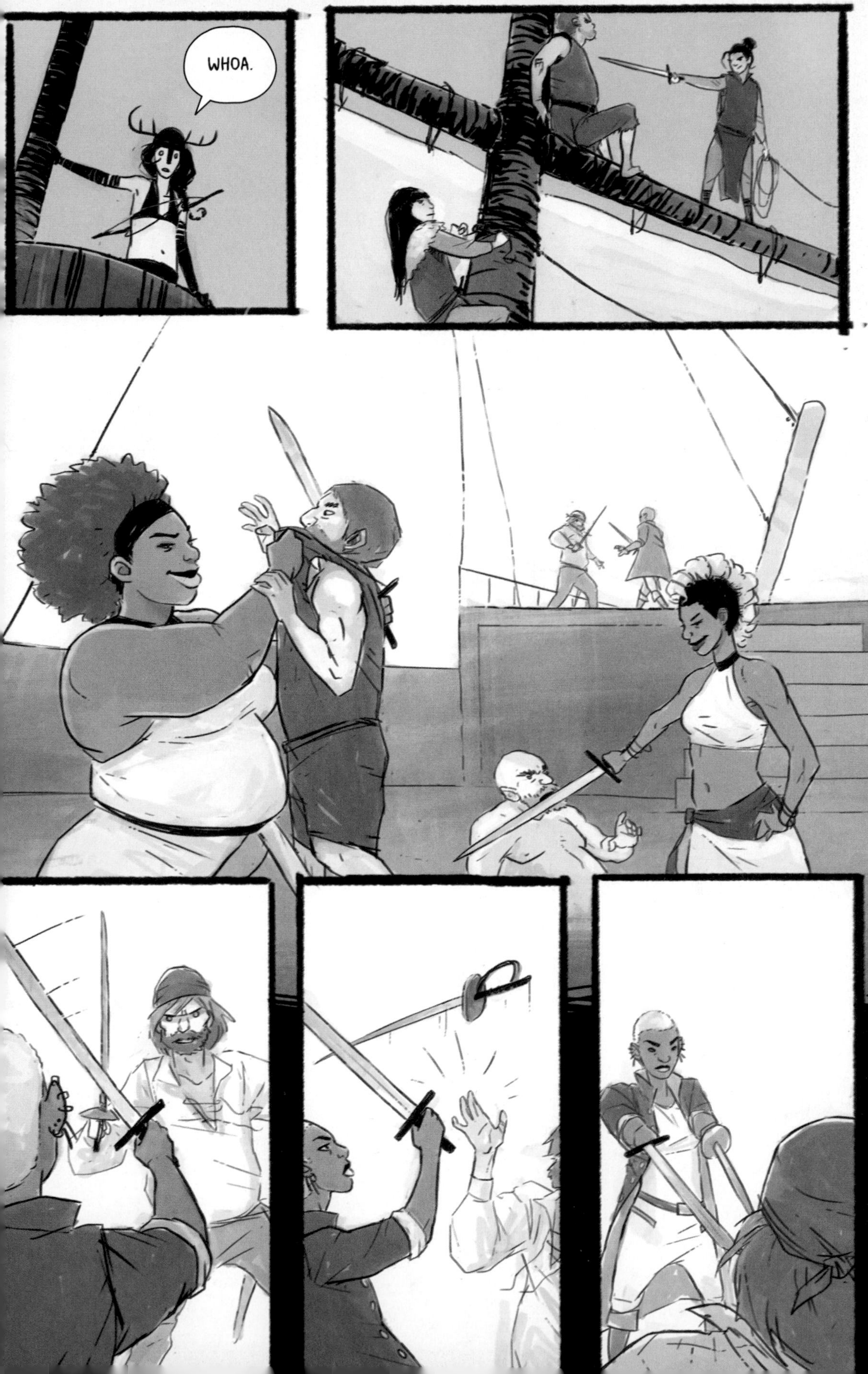
WHOA.

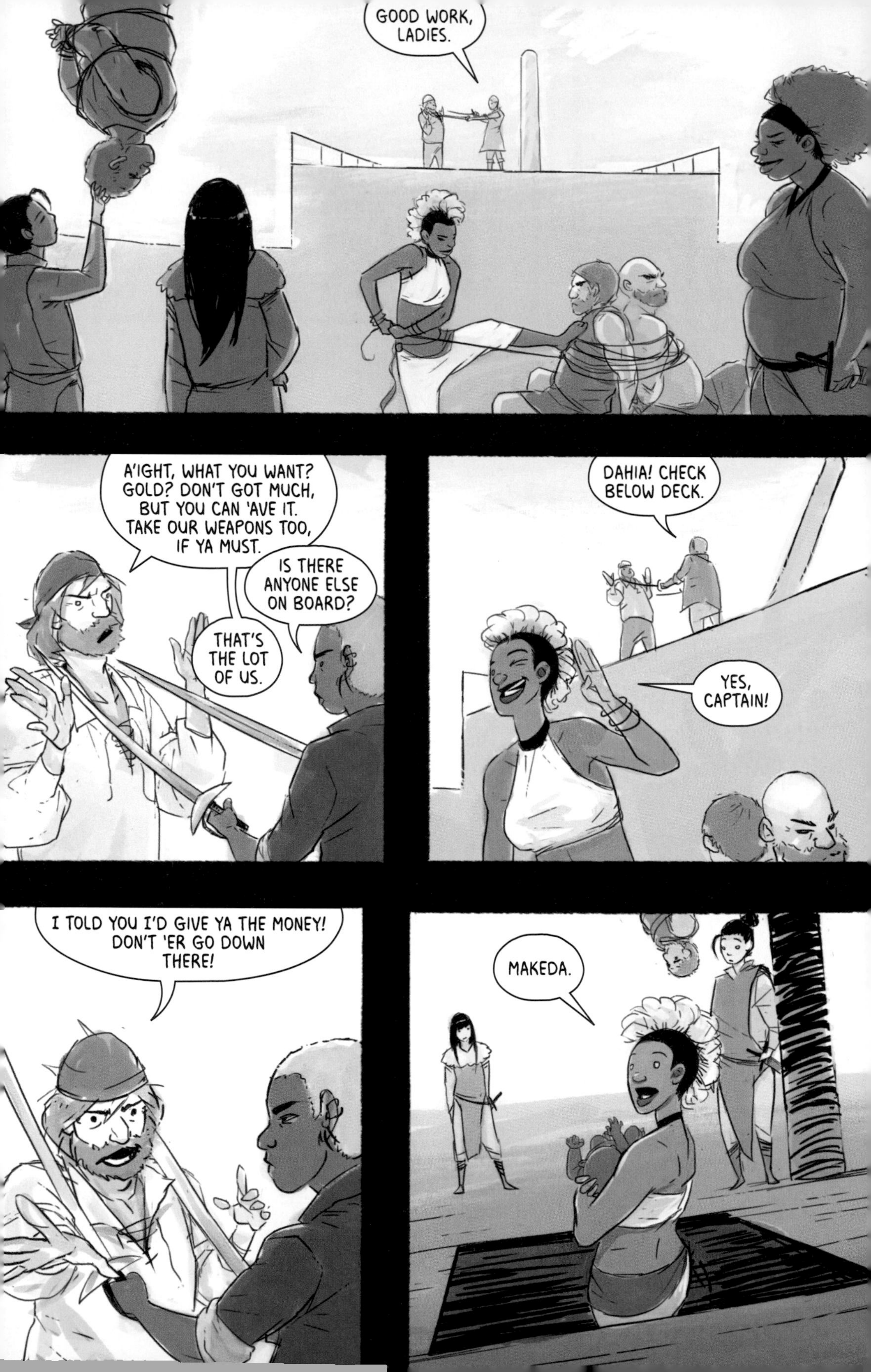

GOOD WORK, LADIES.
A'IGHT, WHAT YOU WANT? GOLD? DON'T GOT MUCH, BUT YOU CAN 'AVE IT. TAKE OUR WEAPONS TOO, IF YA MUST.
IS THERE ANYONE ELSE ON BOARD?
THAT'S THE LOT OF US.
DAHIA! CHECK BELOW DECK.
YES, CAPTAIN!
I TOLD YOU I'D GIVE YA THE MONEY! DON'T 'ER GO DOWN THERE!
MAKEDA.

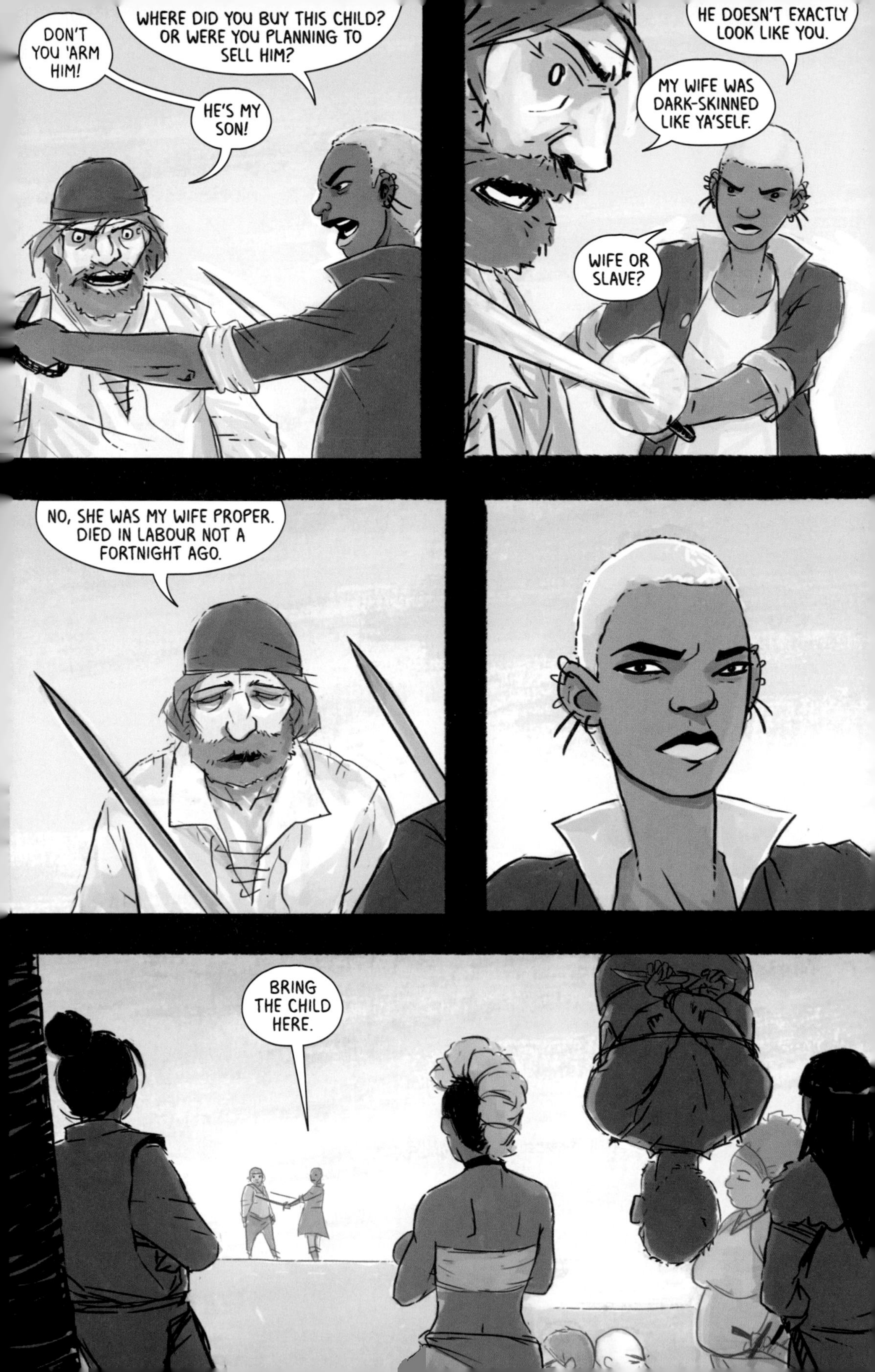
WHERE DID YOU BUY THIS CHILD? OR WERE YOU PLANNING TO SELL HIM?
DON'T YOU 'ARM HIM!
HE'S MY SON!
HE DOESN'T EXACTLY LOOK LIKE YOU.
MY WIFE WAS DARK-SKINNED LIKE YA'SELF.
WIFE OR SLAVE?
NO, SHE WAS MY WIFE PROPER. DIED IN LABOUR NOT A FORTNIGHT AGO.
BRING THE CHILD HERE.

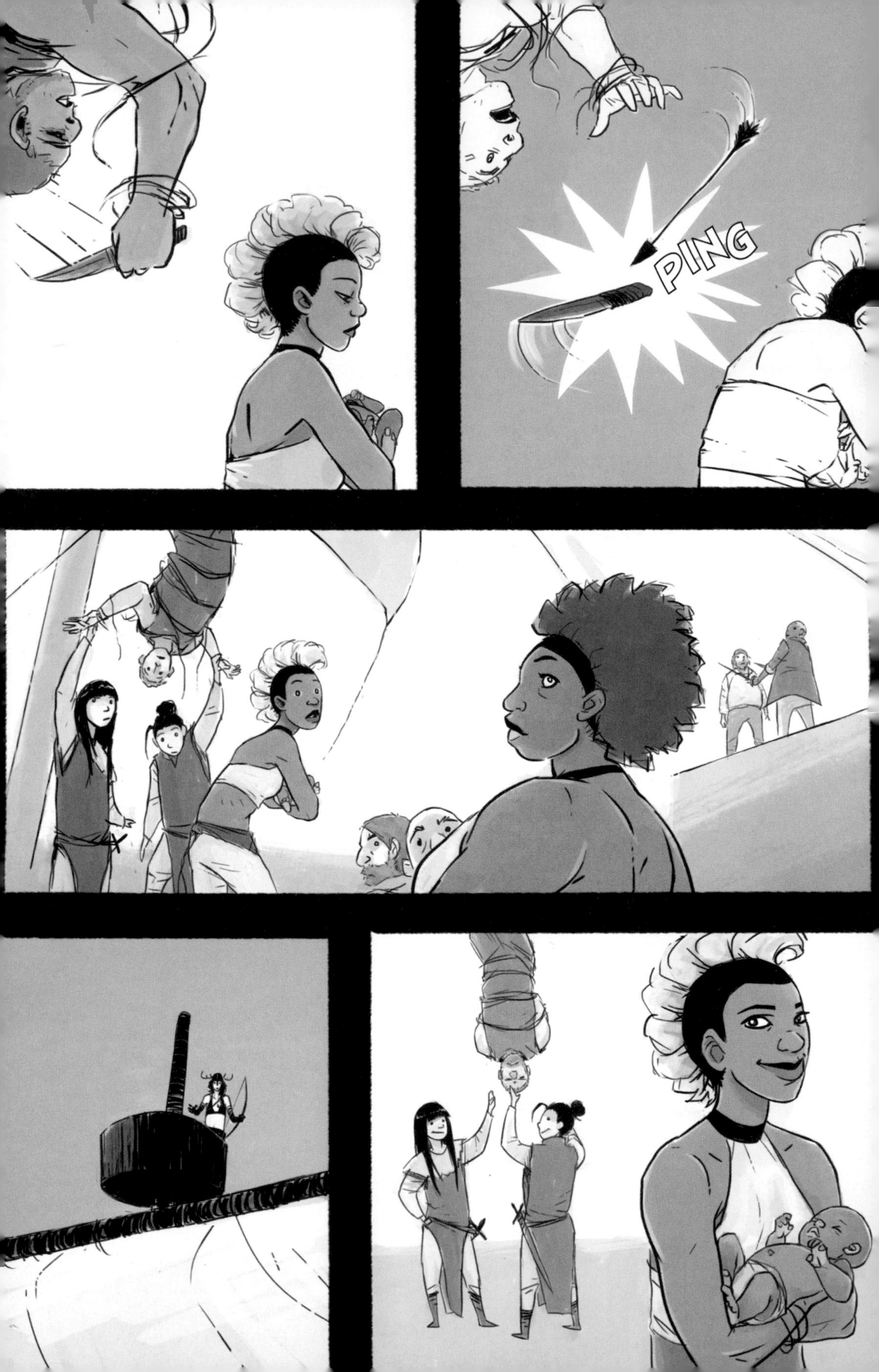
PING

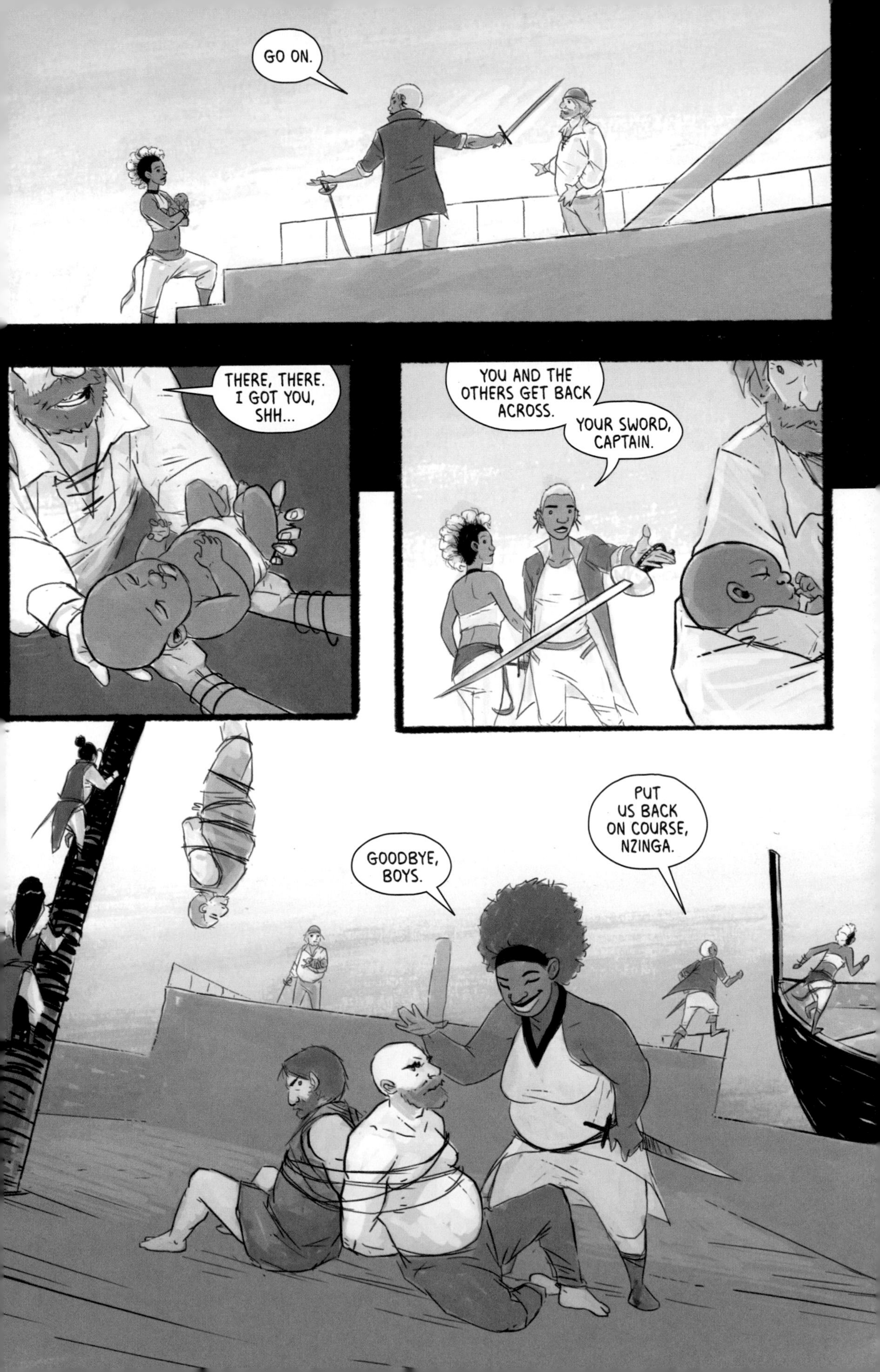
GO ON.
THERE, THERE. I GOT YOU, SHH...
YOU AND THE OTHERS GET BACK ACROSS.
YOUR SWORD, CAPTAIN.
GOODBYE, BOYS.
PUT US BACK ON COURSE, NZINGA.

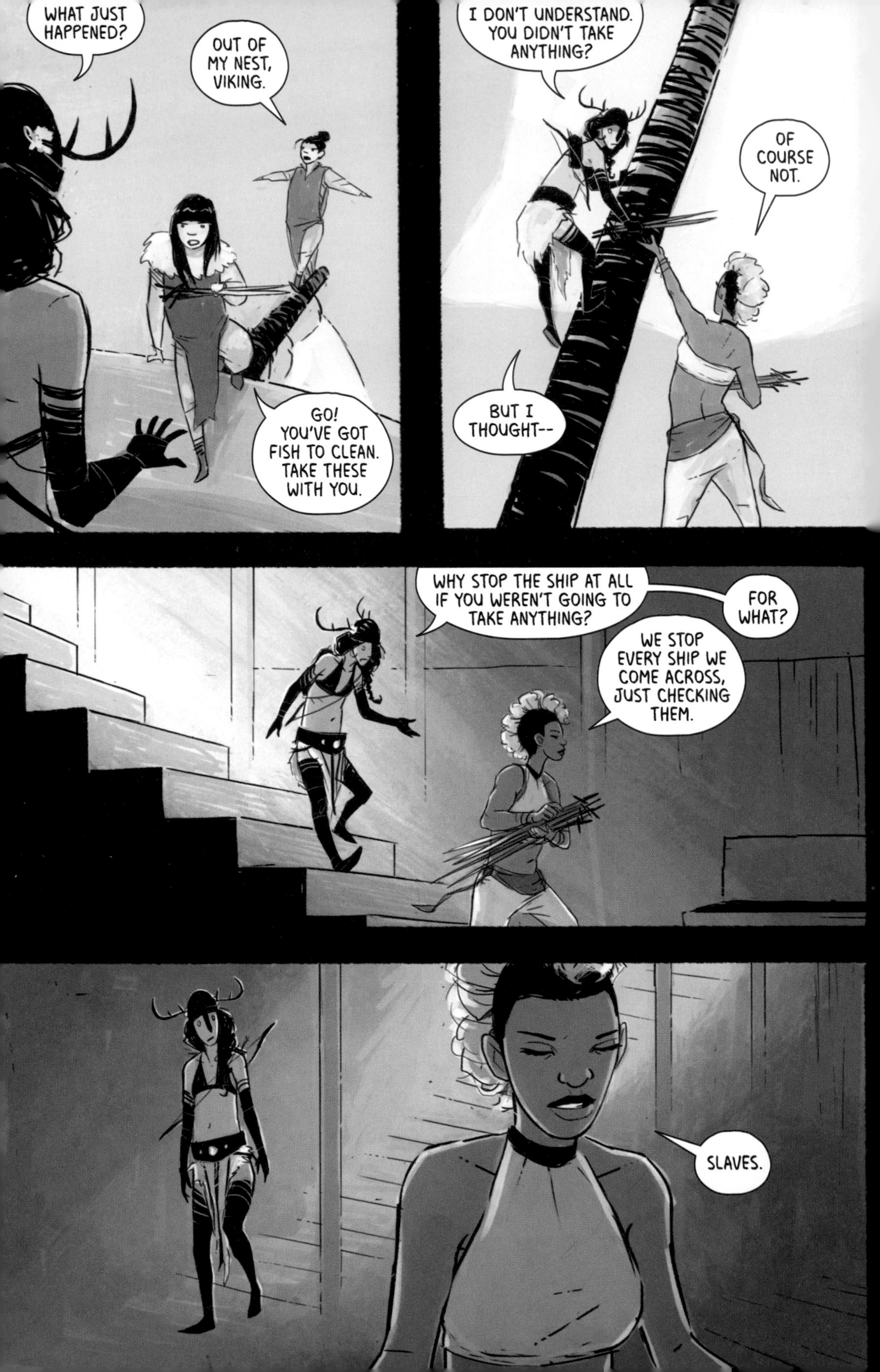
WHAT JUST HAPPENED?
OUT OF MY NEST, VIKING.
GO! YOU'VE GOT FISH TO CLEAN. TAKE THESE WITH YOU.
I DON'T UNDERSTAND. YOU DIDN'T TAKE ANYTHING?
OF COURSE NOT.
BUT I THOUGHT--
WHY STOP THE SHIP AT ALL IF YOU WEREN'T GOING TO TAKE ANYTHING?
WE STOP EVERY SHIP WE COME ACROSS, JUST CHECKING THEM.
FOR WHAT?
SLAVES.

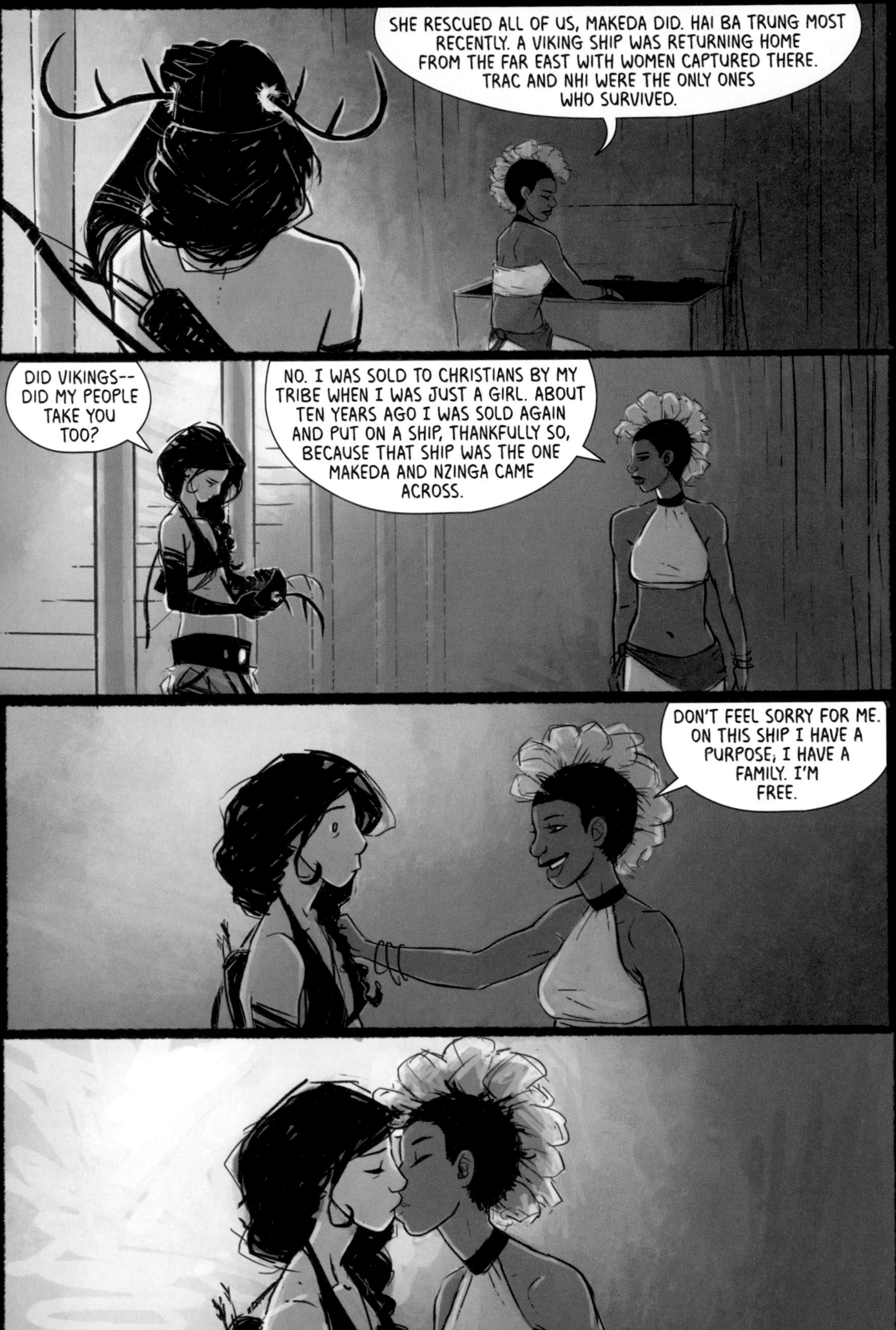
SHE RESCUED ALL OF US, MAKEDA DID. HAI BA TRUNG MOST RECENTLY. A VIKING SHIP WAS RETURNING HOME FROM THE FAR EAST WITH WOMEN CAPTURED THERE. TRAC AND NHI WERE THE ONLY ONES WHO SURVIVED.
DID VIKINGS-- DID MY PEOPLE TAKE YOU TOO?
NO. I WAS SOLD TO CHRISTIANS BY MY TRIBE WHEN I WAS JUST A GIRL. ABOUT TEN YEARS AGO I WAS SOLD AGAIN AND PUT ON A SHIP, THANKFULLY SO, BECAUSE THAT SHIP WAS THE ONE MAKEDA AND NZINGA CAME ACROSS.
DON'T FEEL SORRY FOR ME. ON THIS SHIP I HAVE A PURPOSE; I HAVE A FAMILY. I'M FREE.

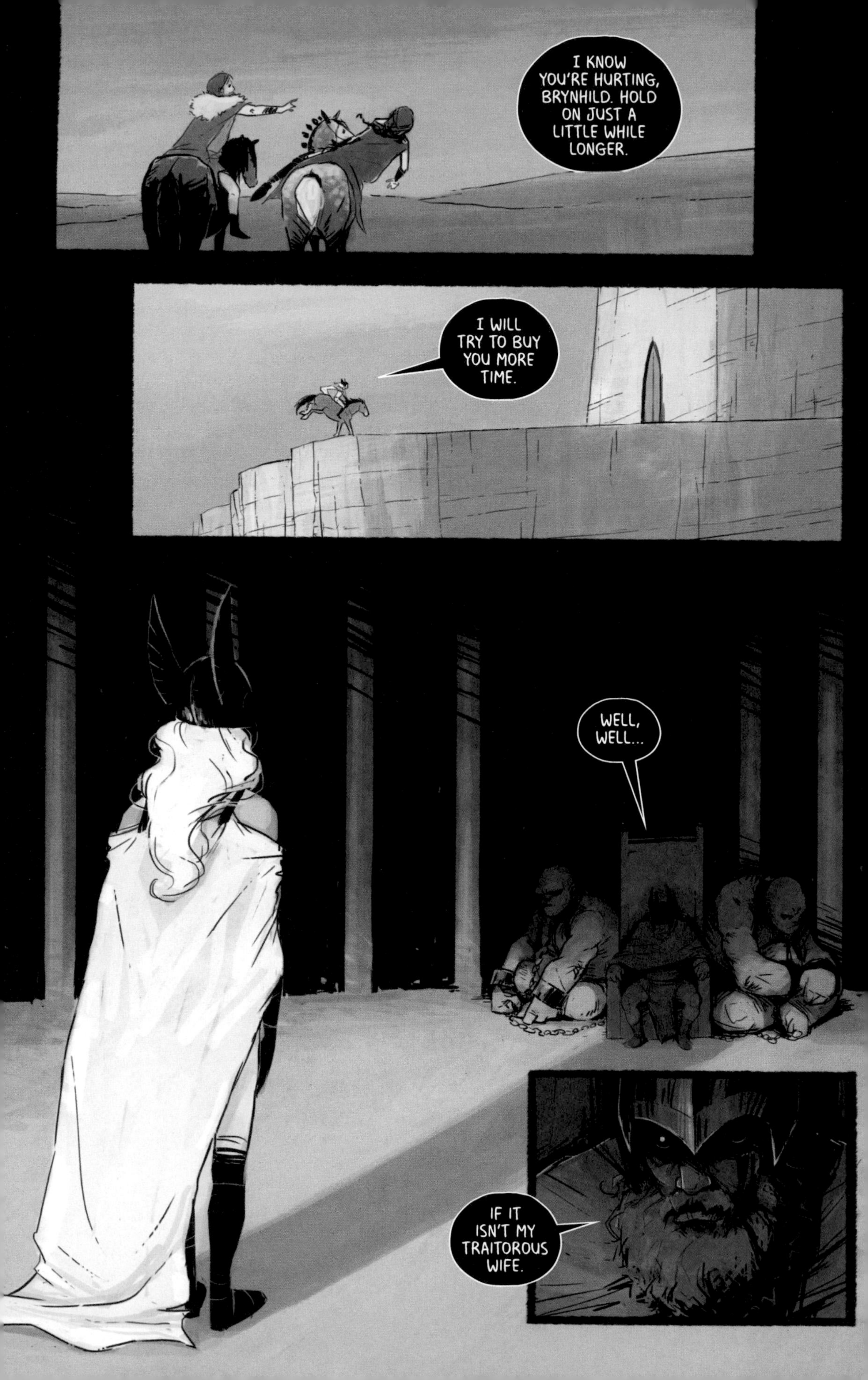
I KNOW YOU'RE HURTING, BRYNHILD. HOLD ON JUST A LITTLE WHILE LONGER.
I WILL TRY TO BUY YOU MORE TIME.
WELL, WELL...
IF IT ISN'T MY TRAITOROUS WIFE.

CHAPTER 7

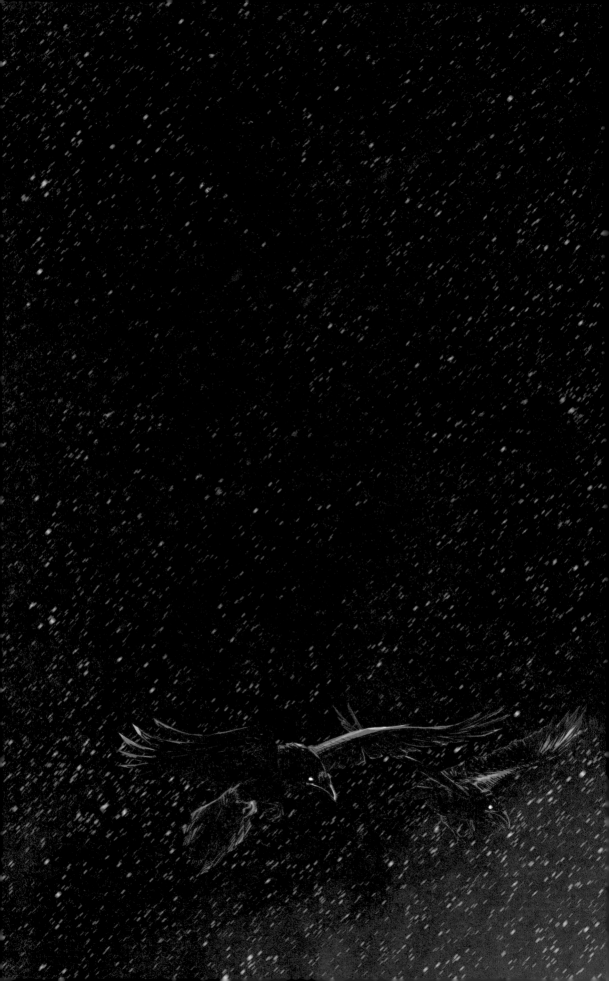

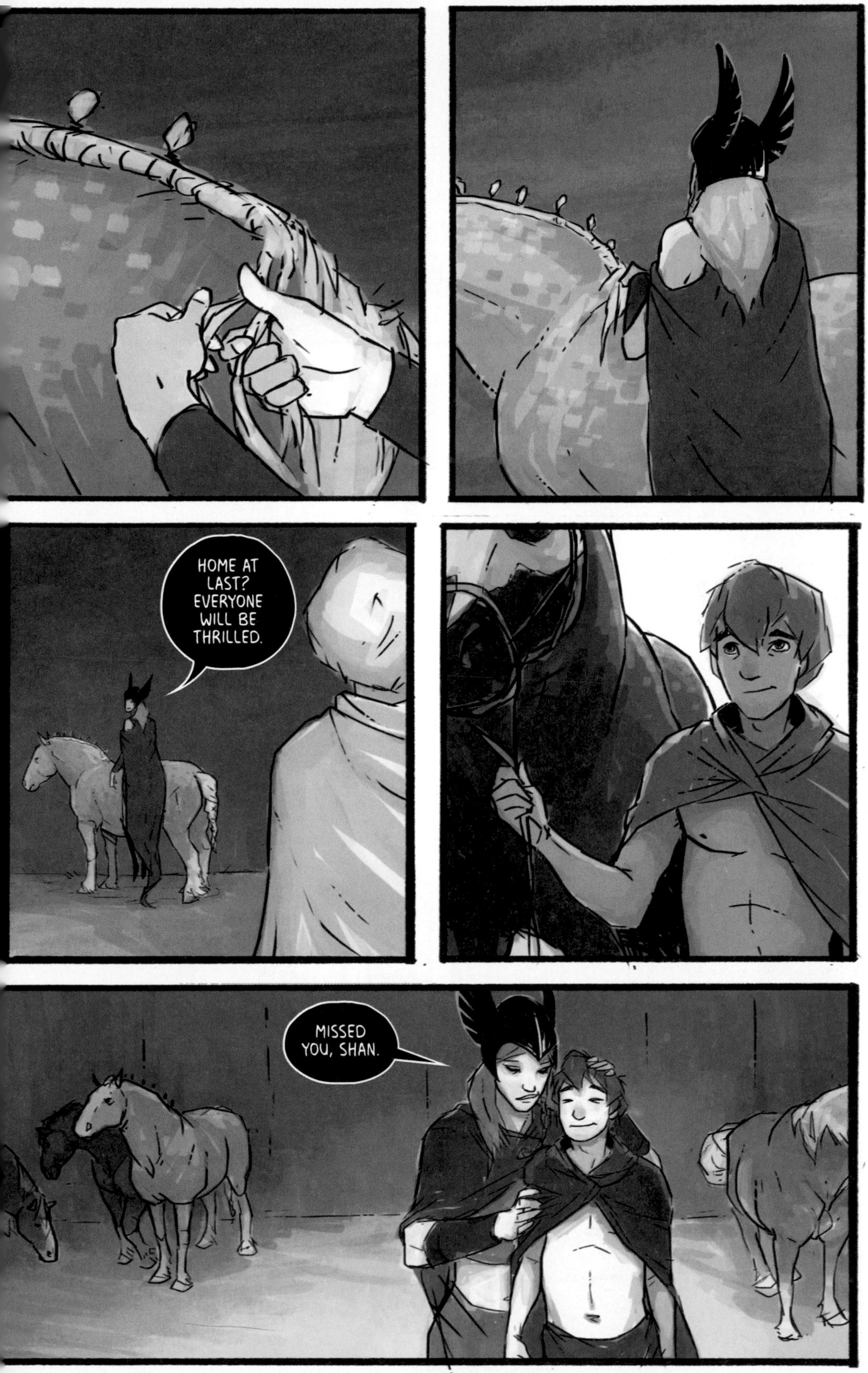
HOME AT LAST? EVERYONE WILL BE THRILLED.
MISSED YOU, SHAN.

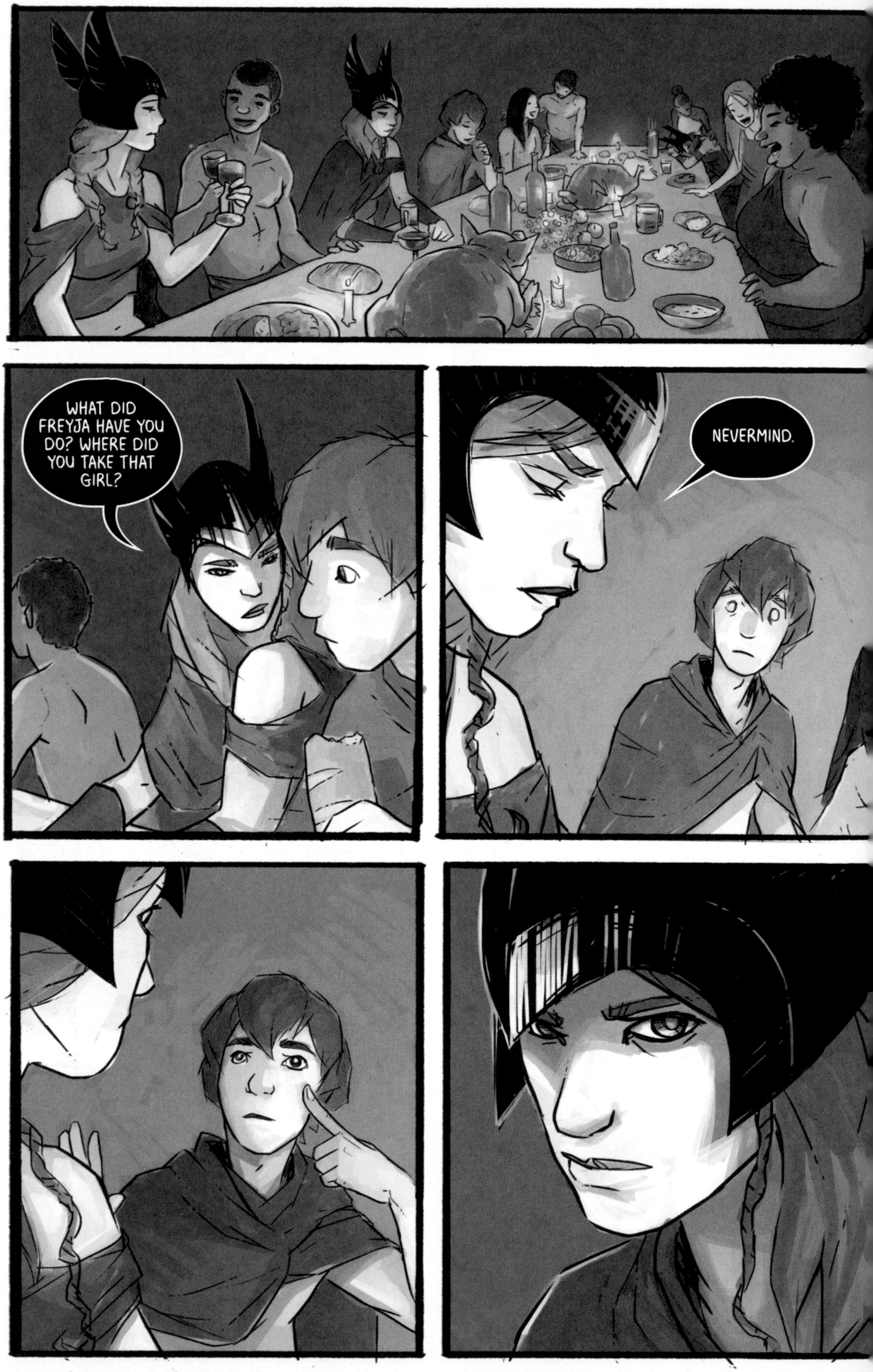
WHAT DID FREYJA HAVE YOU DO? WHERE DID YOU TAKE THAT GIRL?
NEVERMIND.

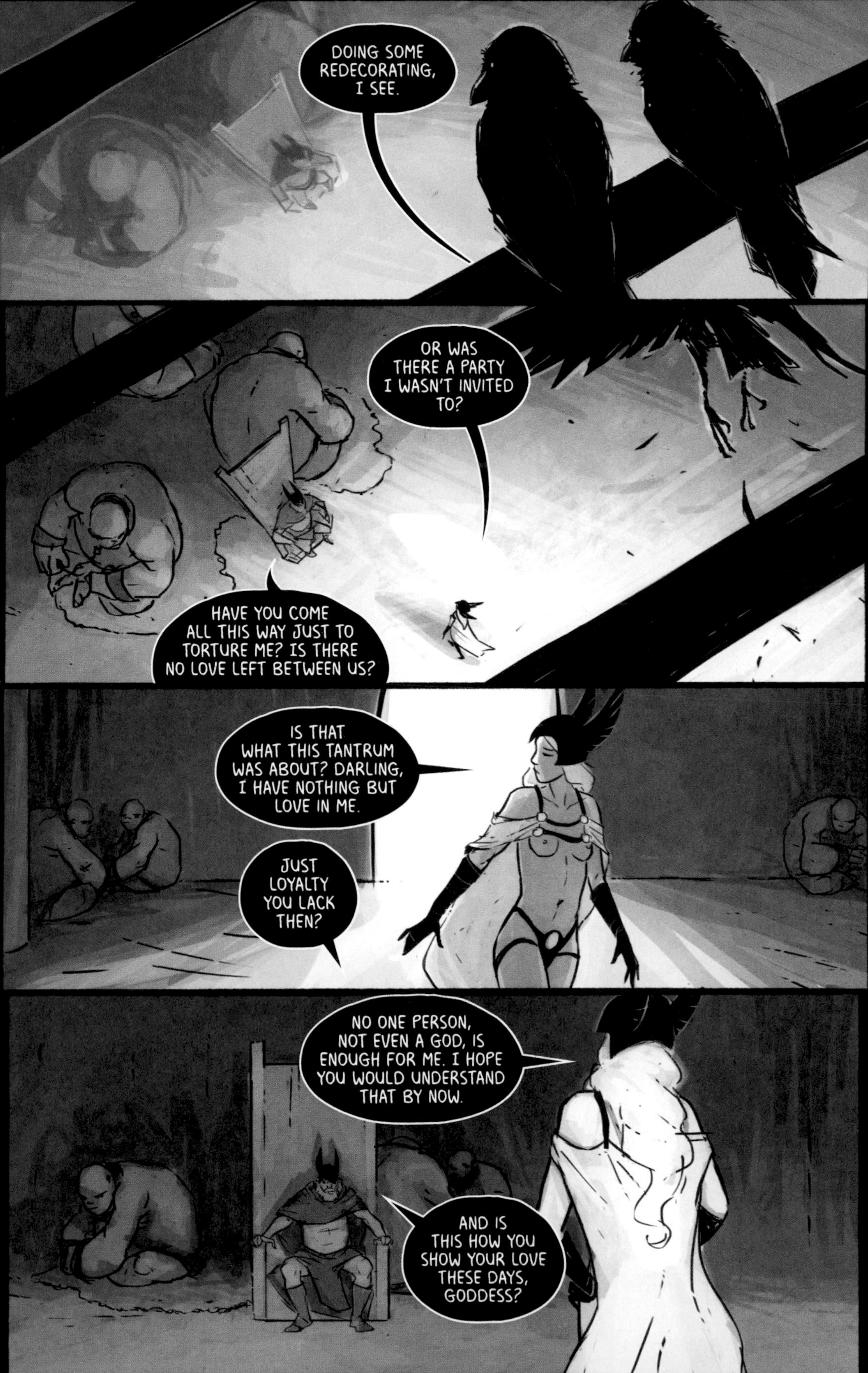
DOING SOME REDECORATING, I SEE.
OR WAS THERE A PARTY I WASN'T INVITED TO?
HAVE YOU COME ALL THIS WAY JUST TO TORTURE ME? IS THERE NO LOVE LEFT BETWEEN US?
IS THAT WHAT THIS TANTRUM WAS ABOUT? DARLING, I HAVE NOTHING BUT LOVE IN ME.
JUST LOYALTY YOU LACK THEN?
NO ONE PERSON, NOT EVEN A GOD, IS ENOUGH FOR ME. I HOPE YOU WOULD UNDERSTAND THAT BY NOW.
AND IS THIS HOW YOU SHOW YOUR LOVE THESE DAYS, GODDESS?

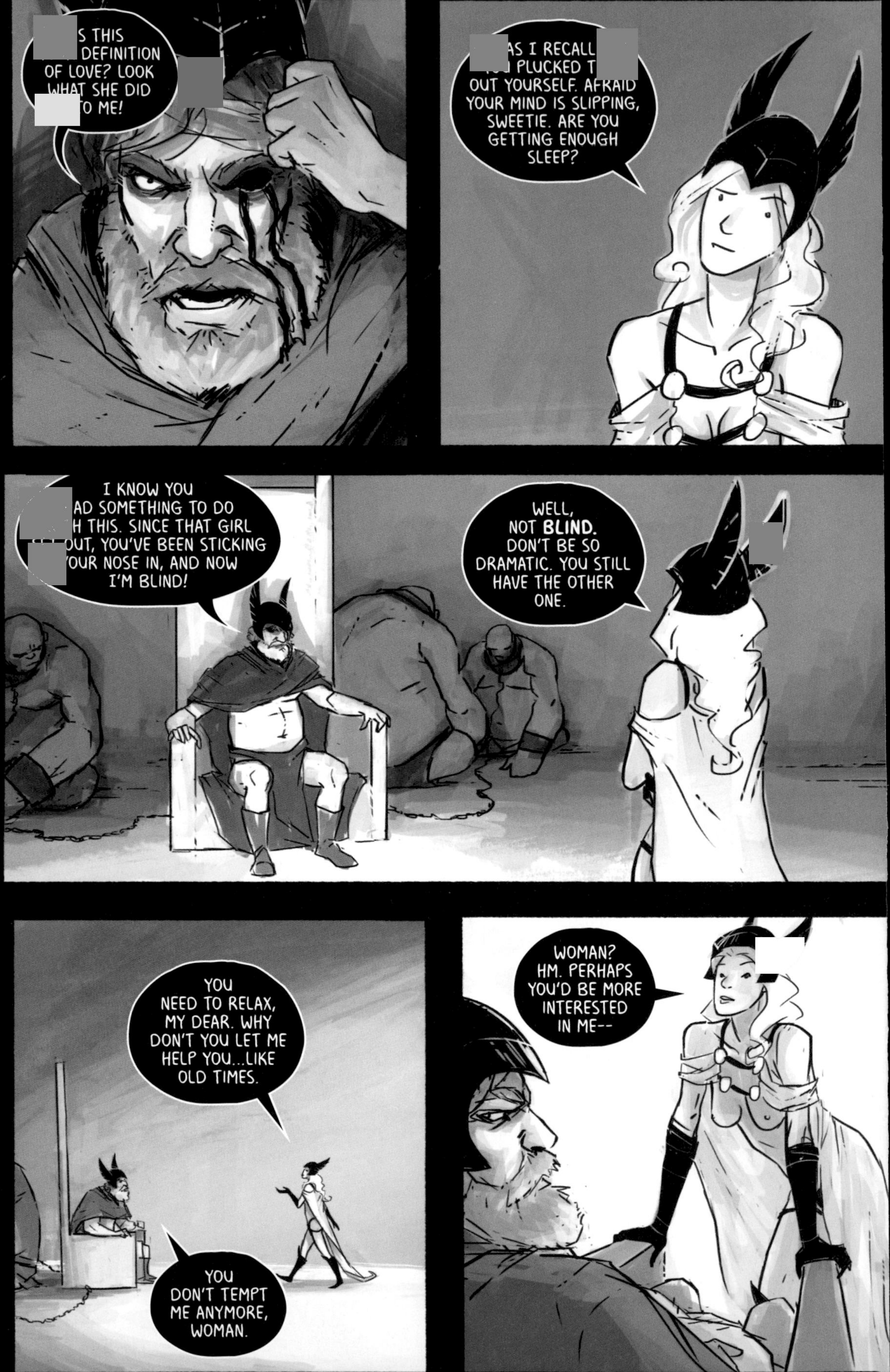
S THIS DEFINITION OF LOVE? LOOK WHAT SHE DID O ME!
AS I RECALL U PLUCKED T OUT YOURSELF. AFRAID YOUR MIND IS SLIPPING, SWEETIE. ARE YOU GETTING ENOUGH SLEEP?
I KNOW YOU AD SOMETHING TO DO H THIS. SINCE THAT GIRL OUT, YOU'VE BEEN STICKING OUR NOSE IN, AND NOW I'M BLIND!
WELL, NOT BLIND. DON'T BE SO DRAMATIC. YOU STILL HAVE THE OTHER ONE.
YOU NEED TO RELAX, MY DEAR. WHY DON'T YOU LET ME HELP YOU...LIKE OLD TIMES.
YOU DON'T TEMPT ME ANYMORE, WOMAN.
WOMAN? HM. PERHAPS YOU'D BE MORE INTERESTED IN ME--

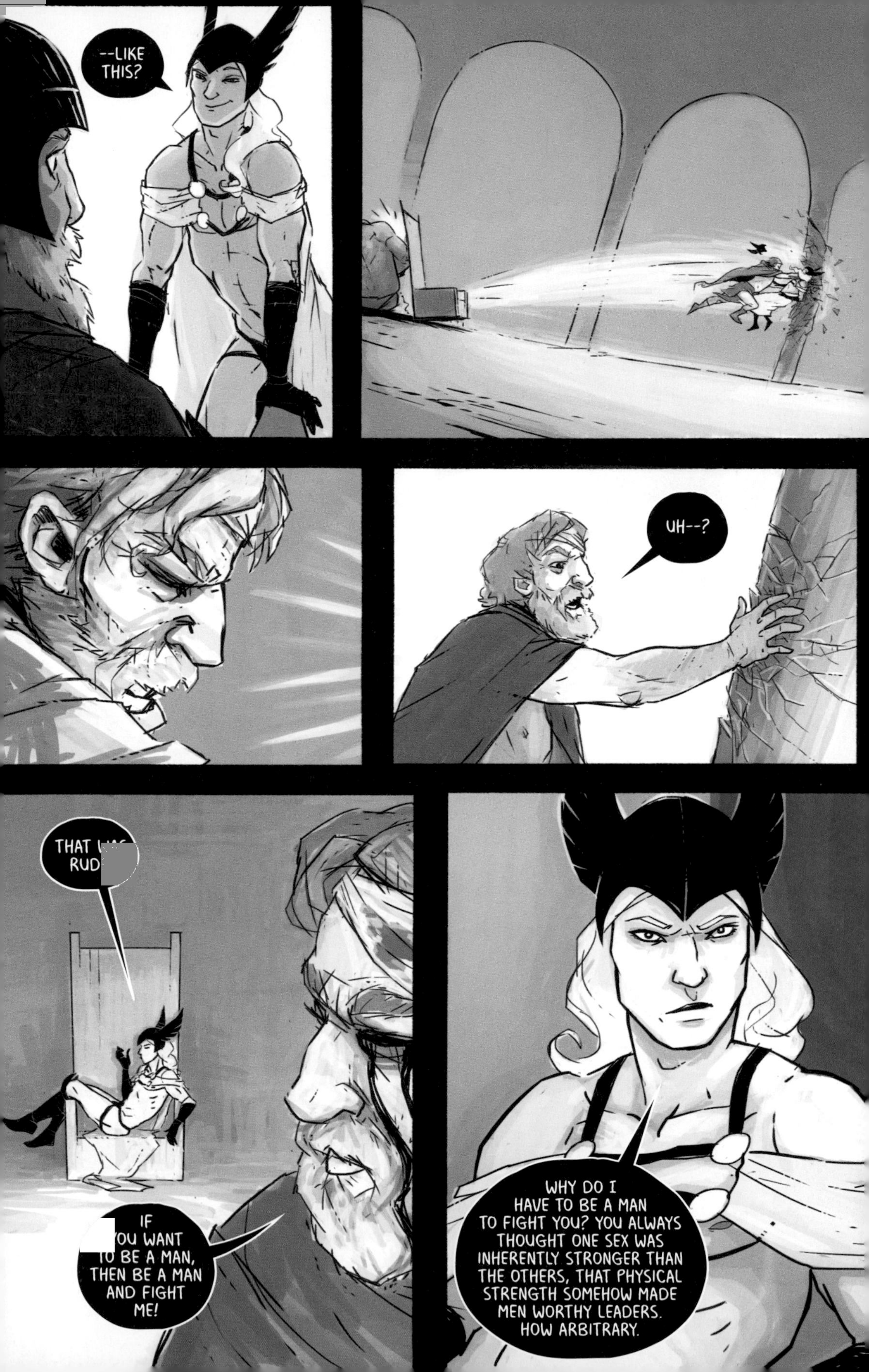
--LIKE THIS?
UH--?
THAT
IF YOU WANT TO BE A MAN, THEN BE A MAN AND FIGHT ME!
WHY DO I HAVE TO BE A MAN TO FIGHT YOU? YOU ALWAYS THOUGHT ONE SEX WAS INHERENTLY STRONGER THAN THE OTHERS, THAT PHYSICAL STRENGTH SOMEHOW MADE MEN WORTHY LEADERS. HOW ARBITRARY.

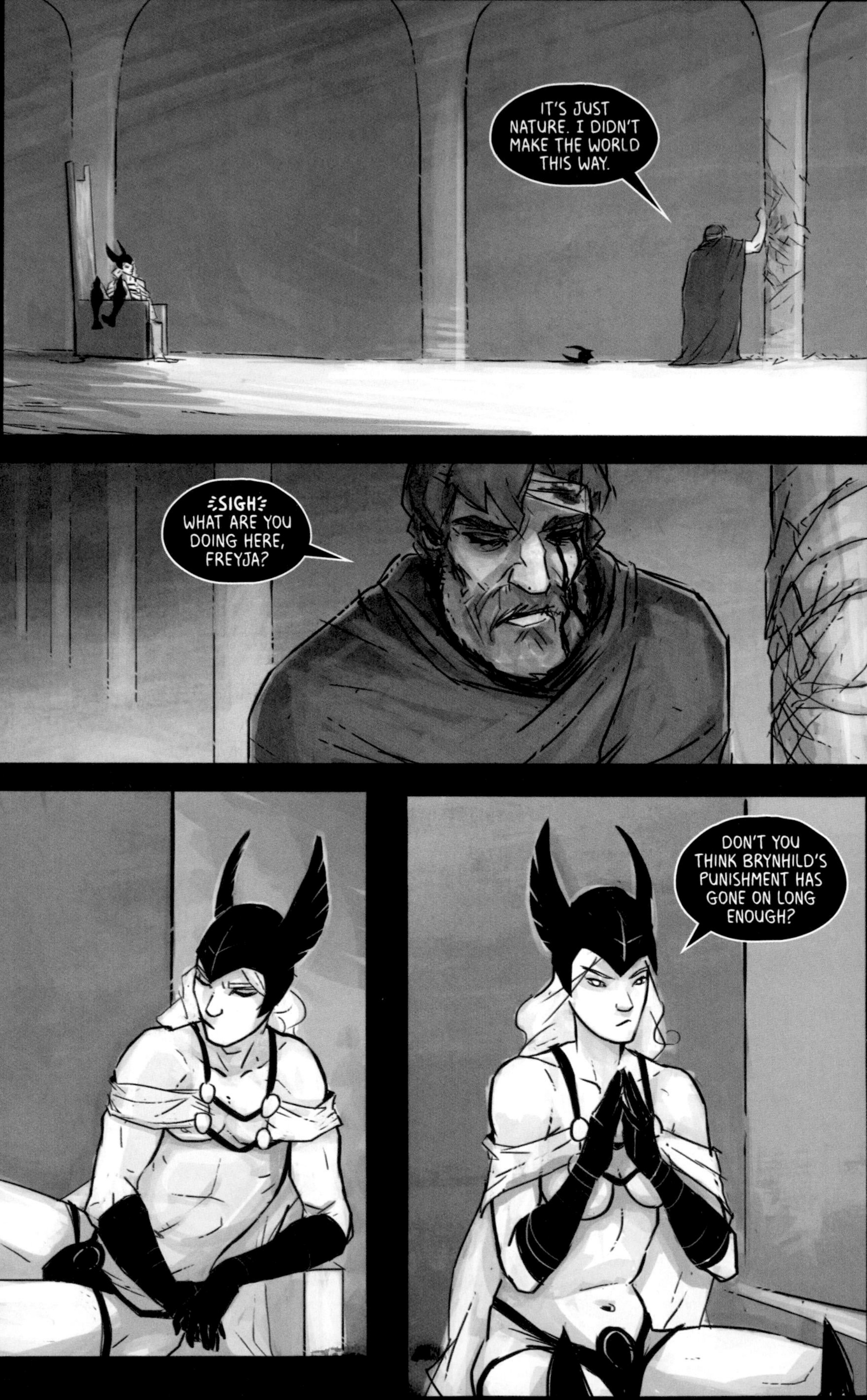
IT'S JUST NATURE. I DIDN'T MAKE THE WORLD THIS WAY.
SIGH
WHAT ARE YOU DOING HERE, FREYJA?
DON'T YOU THINK BRYNHILD'S PUNISHMENT HAS GONE ON LONG ENOUGH?

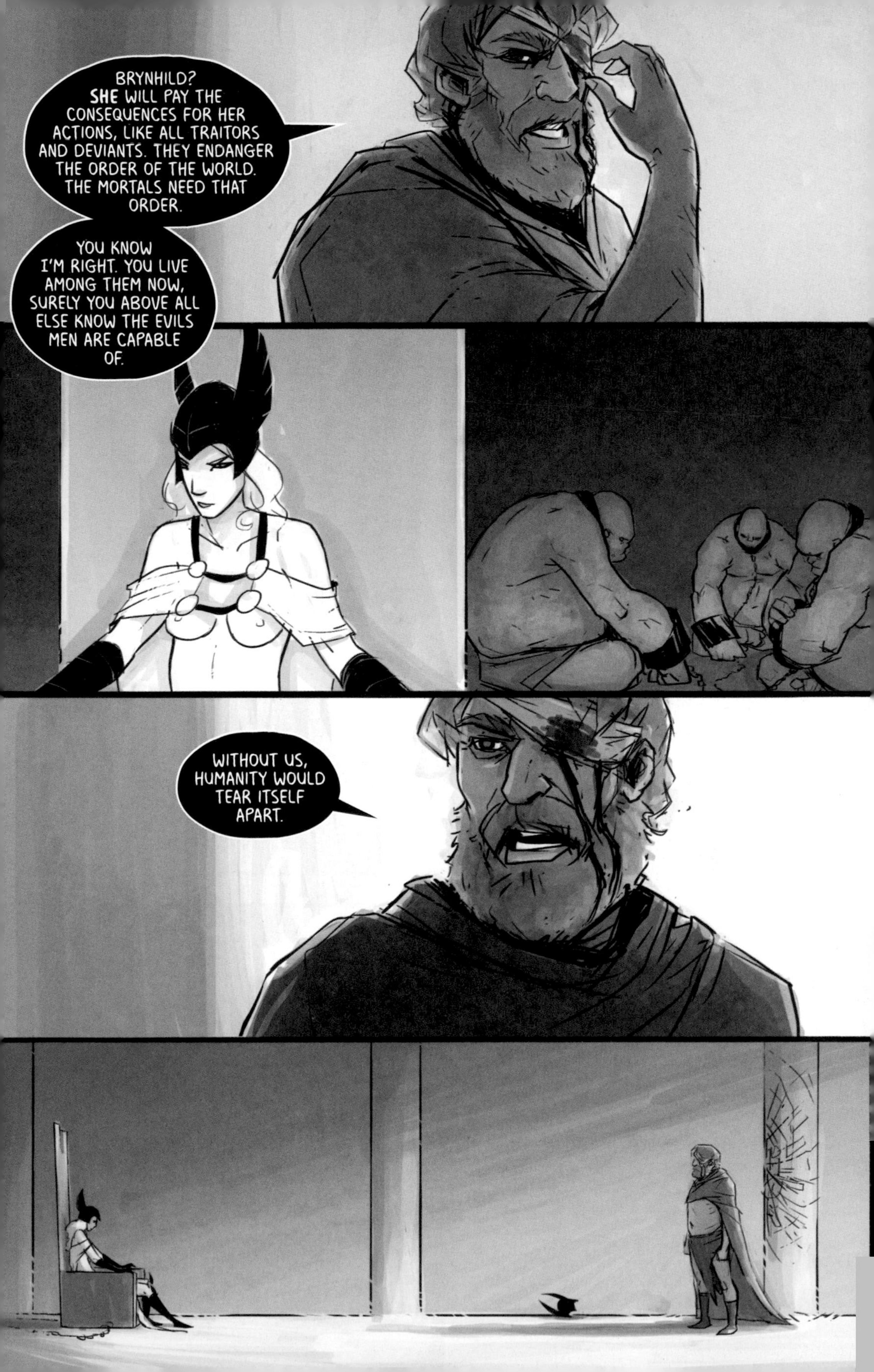
BRYNHILD? SHE WILL PAY THE CONSEQUENCES FOR HER ACTIONS, LIKE ALL TRAITORS AND DEVIANTS. THEY ENDANGER THE ORDER OF THE WORLD. THE MORTALS NEED THAT ORDER.
YOU KNOW I'M RIGHT. YOU LIVE AMONG THEM NOW, SURELY YOU ABOVE ALL ELSE KNOW THE EVILS MEN ARE CAPABLE OF.
WITHOUT US, HUMANITY WOULD TEAR ITSELF APART.

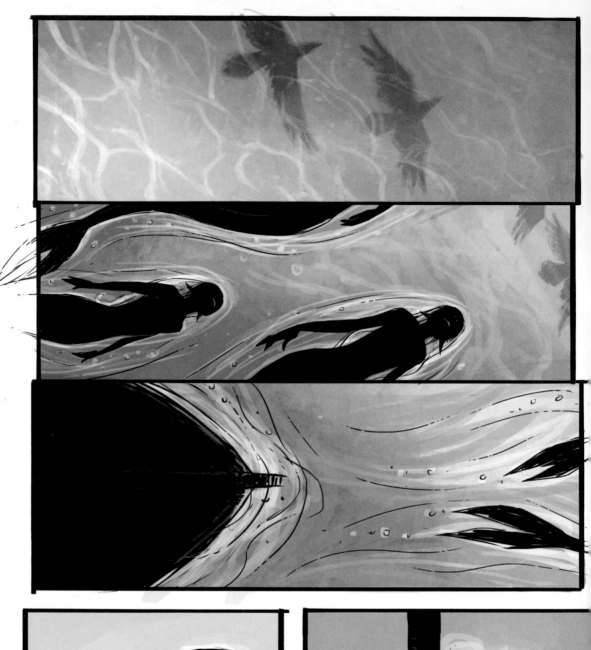

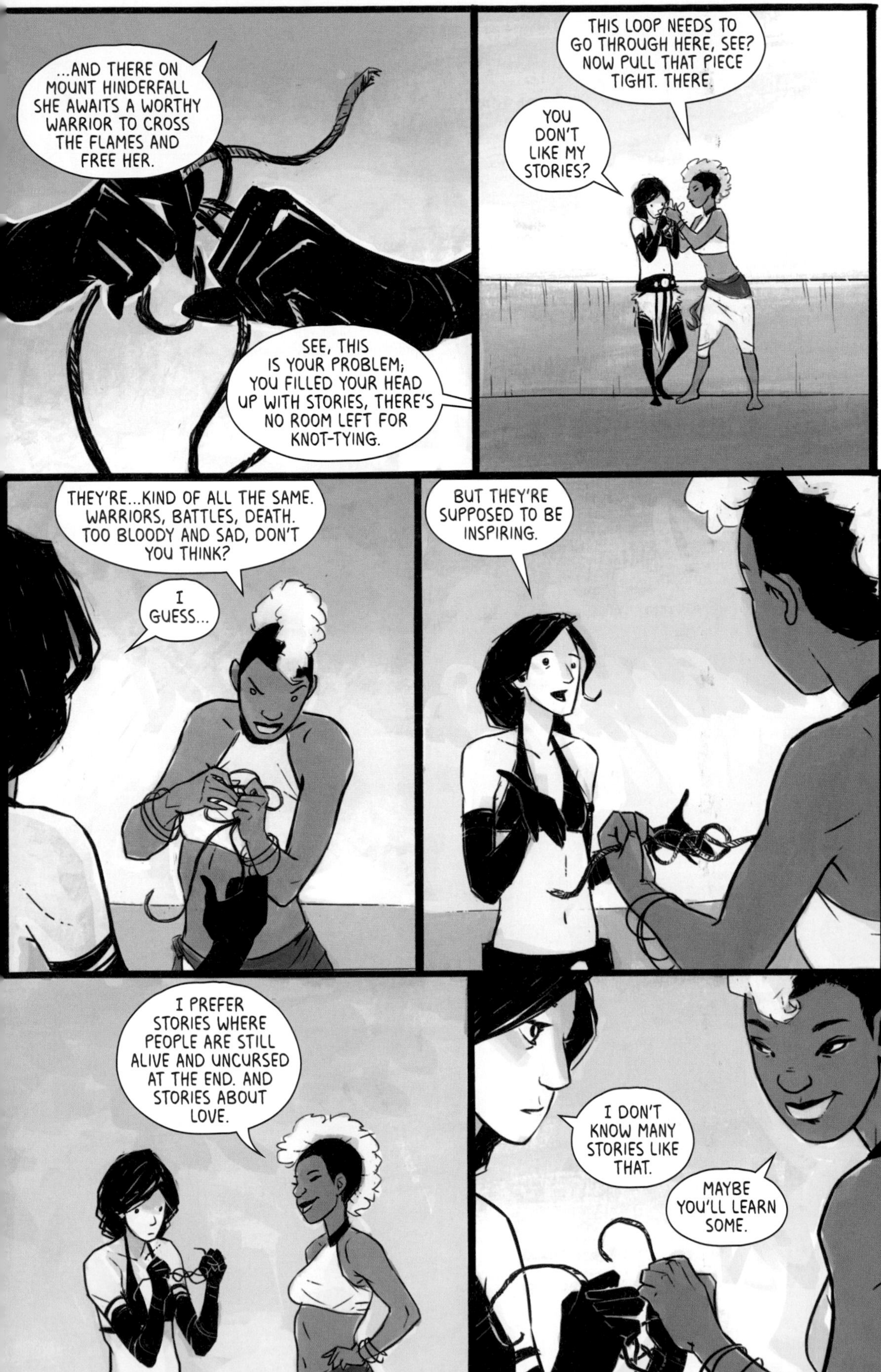
...AND THERE ON MOUNT HINDERFALL SHE AWAITS A WORTHY WARRIOR TO CROSS THE FLAMES AND FREE HER.
SEE, THIS IS YOUR PROBLEM; YOU FILLED YOUR HEAD UP WITH STORIES, THERE'S NO ROOM LEFT FOR KNOT-TYING.
THIS LOOP NEEDS TO GO THROUGH HERE, SEE? NOW PULL THAT PIECE TIGHT. THERE.
YOU DON'T LIKE MY STORIES?
THEY'RE...KIND OF ALL THE SAME. WARRIORS, BATTLES, DEATH. TOO BLOODY AND SAD, DON'T YOU THINK?
I GUESS...
BUT THEY'RE SUPPOSED TO BE INSPIRING.
I PREFER STORIES WHERE PEOPLE ARE STILL ALIVE AND UNCURSED AT THE END. AND STORIES ABOUT LOVE.
I DON'T KNOW MANY STORIES LIKE THAT.
MAYBE YOU'LL LEARN SOME.

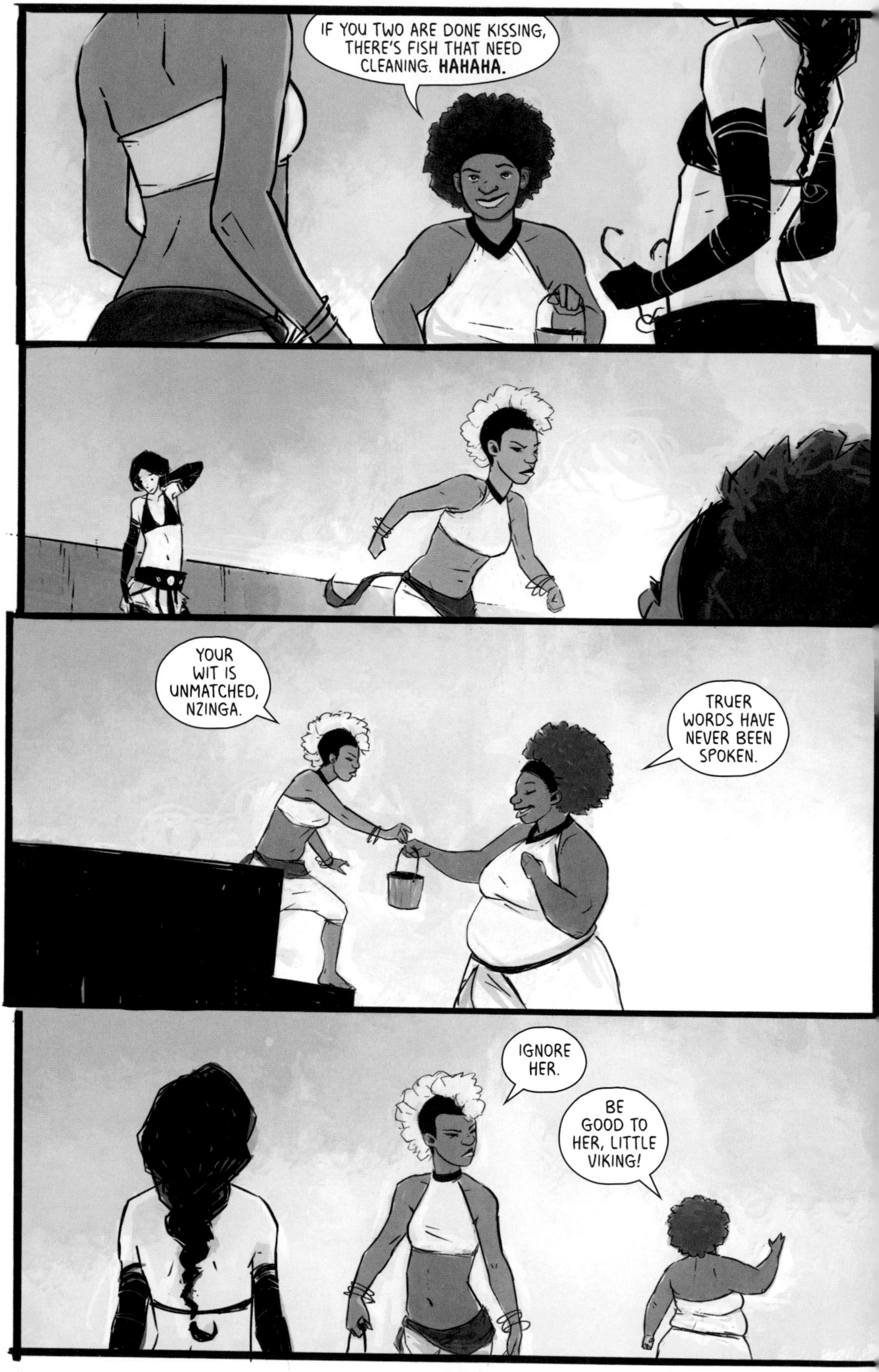
IF YOU TWO ARE DONE KISSING, THERE'S FISH THAT NEED CLEANING. **HAHAHA.**
YOUR WIT IS UNMATCHED, NZINGA.
TRUER WORDS HAVE NEVER BEEN SPOKEN.
IGNORE HER.
BE GOOD TO HER, LITTLE VIKING!

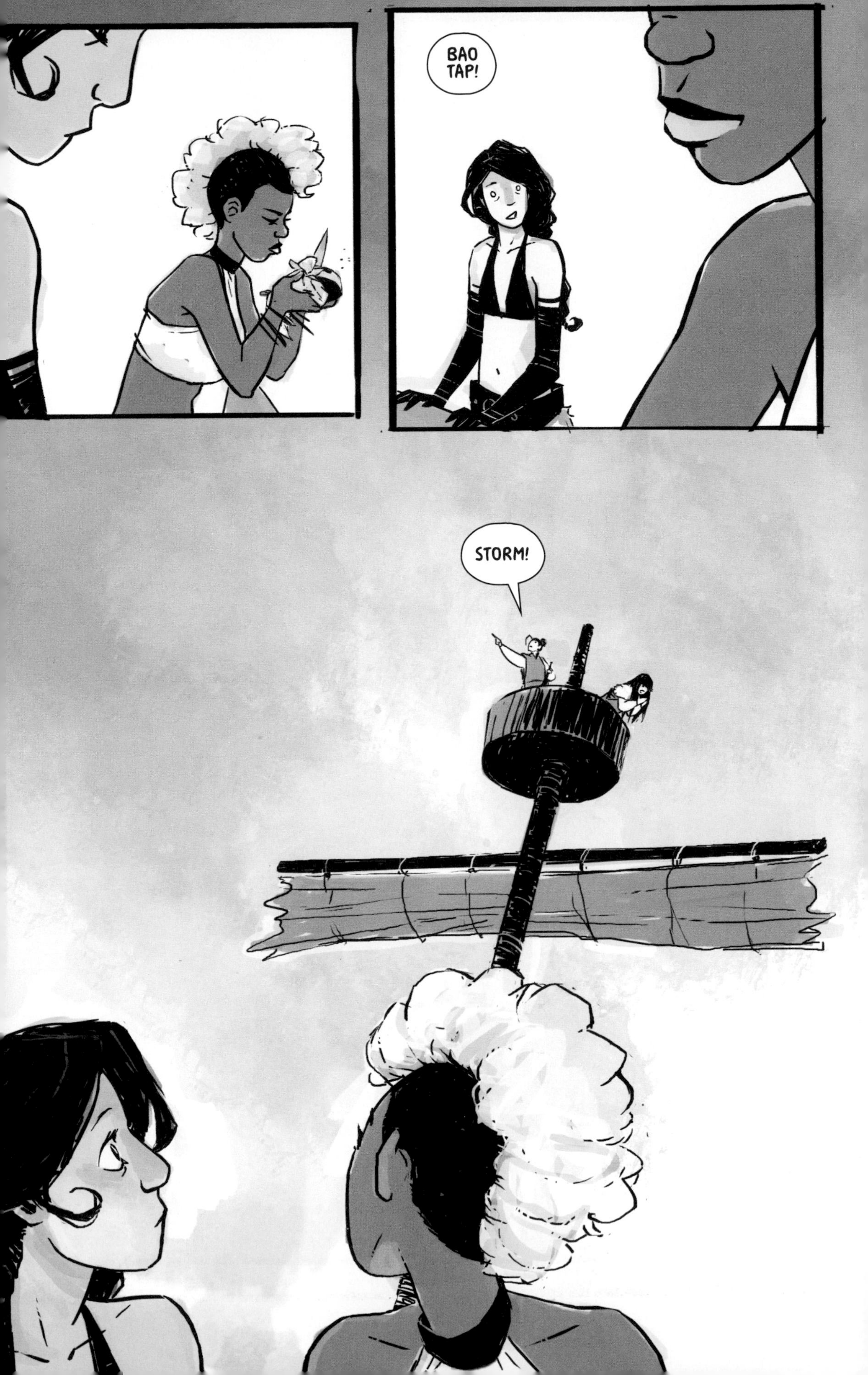
BAO TAP!
STORM!

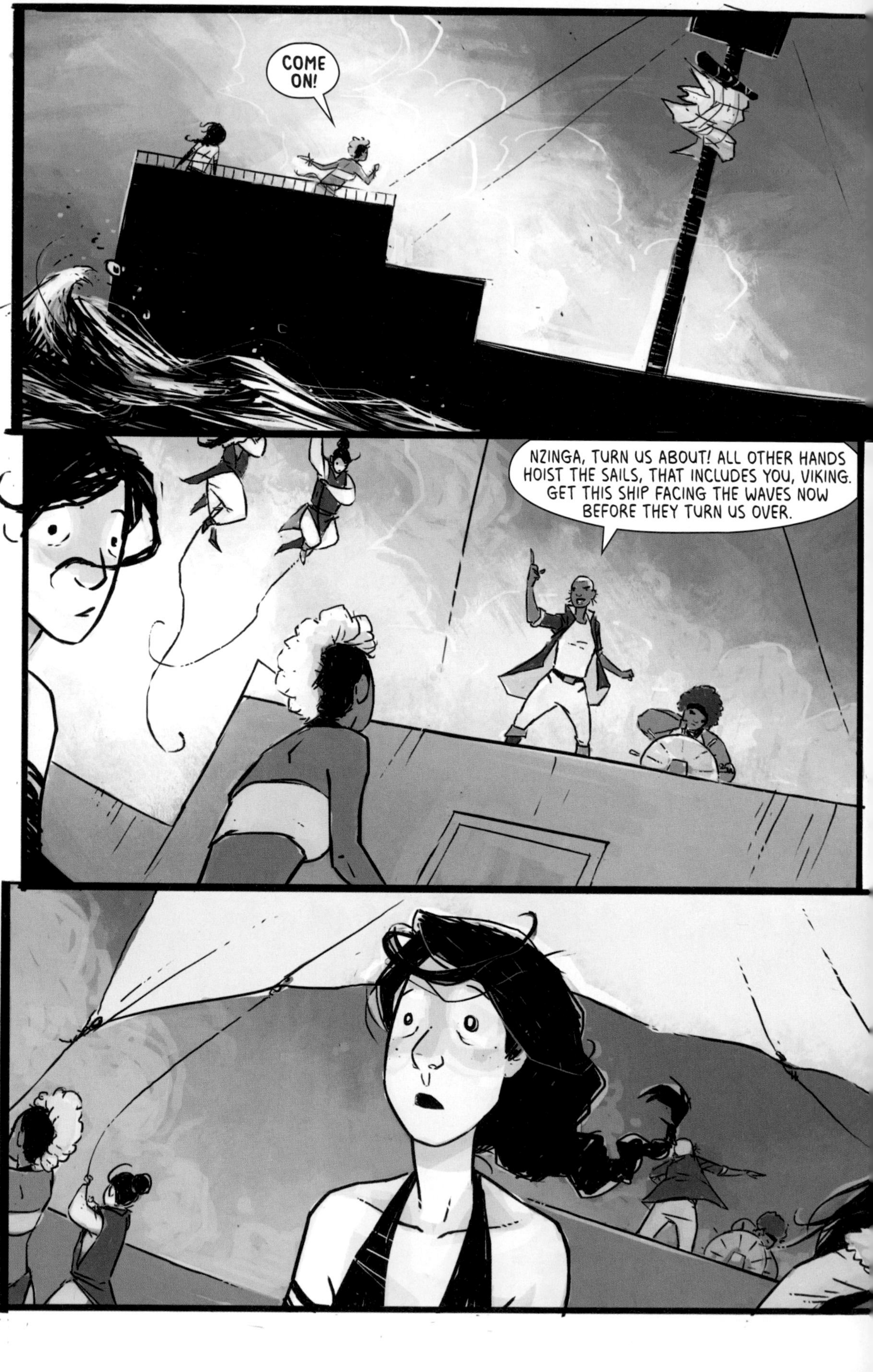
COME ON!
NZINGA, TURN US ABOUT! ALL OTHER HANDS HOIST THE SAILS, THAT INCLUDES YOU, VIKING. GET THIS SHIP FACING THE WAVES NOW BEFORE THEY TURN US OVER.

THERE HAS TO BE ROOM FOR COMPROMISE. OF COURSE HUMANS CAN BE EVIL, BUT I HAVE ALSO LEARNED THE DEPTH OF THEIR COMPASSION. THEY RESPOND SURPRISINGLY WELL TO MORE GENTLE METHODS OF PERSUASION. LOVE RATHER THAN FEAR. YOU'VE FORGOTTEN THAT.

NO, MY LOVE, YOU ARE THE ONE THAT'S FORGOTTEN.

YOU SEE THEM AS INNOCENTS, AS PETS YOU CAN DOTE ON. WERE IT NOT FOR YOUR IMMORTALITY, THOSE MEN YOU KEEP WOULD RAPE AND KILL YOU.

THEY ARE NOT ANIMALS, DEAR. LIVING IN THE SHADOW OF YOUR WRATH HAS TURNED THEM INTO FRIGHTENED BEASTS, LASHING OUT DEFENSIVELY AT IMAGINARY ENEMIES. THEY CAN BE TAUGHT A BETTER WAY.

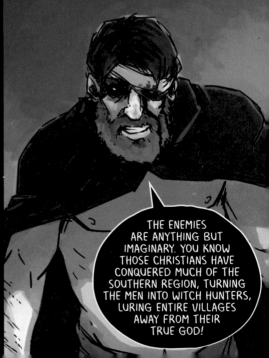

THE ENEMIES ARE ANYTHING BUT IMAGINARY. YOU KNOW THOSE CHRISTIANS HAVE CONQUERED MUCH OF THE SOUTHERN REGION, TURNING THE MEN INTO WITCH HUNTERS, LURING ENTIRE VILLAGES AWAY FROM THEIR TRUE GOD!

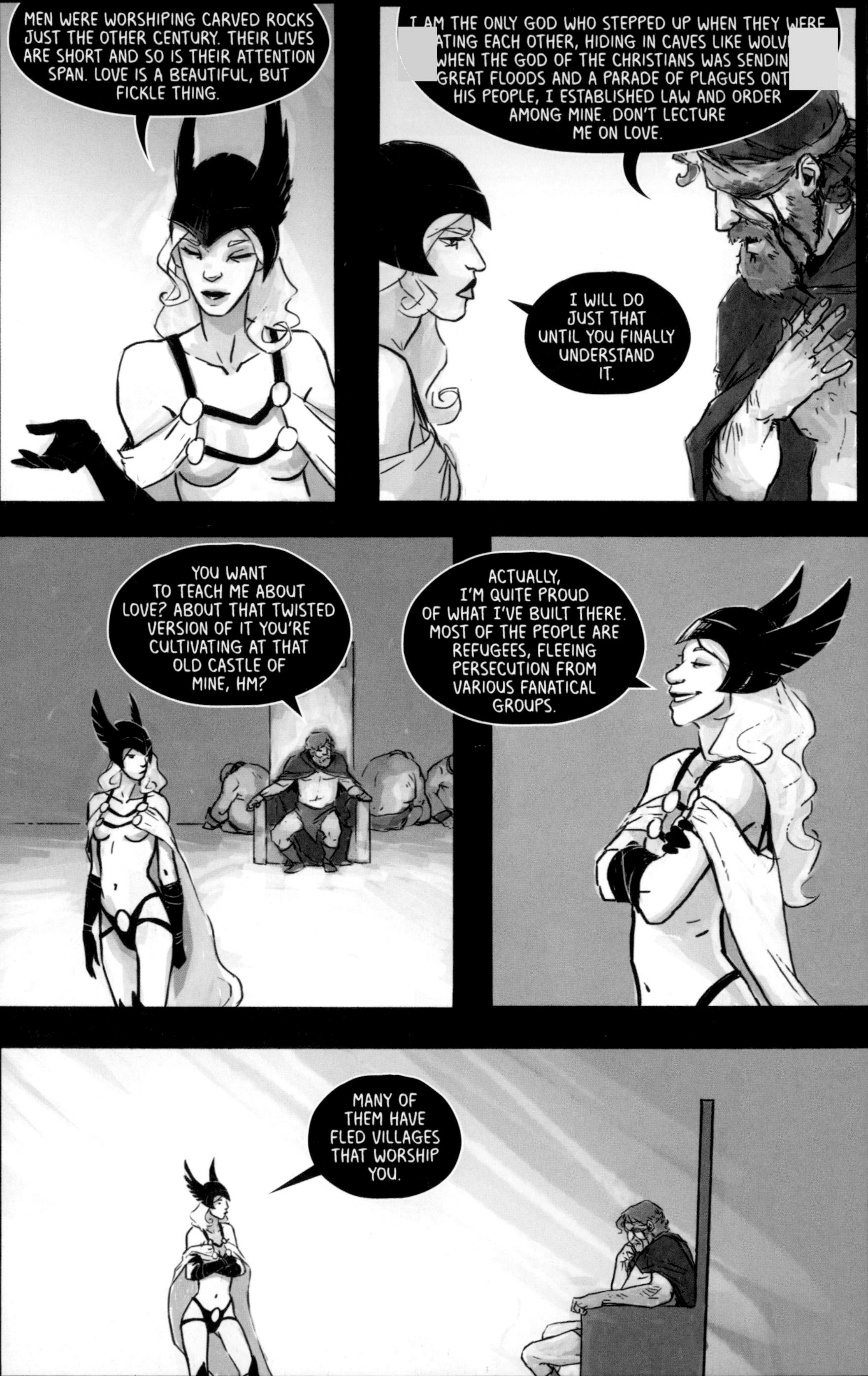
MEN WERE WORSHIPING CARVED ROCKS JUST THE OTHER CENTURY. THEIR LIVES ARE SHORT AND SO IS THEIR ATTENTION SPAN. LOVE IS A BEAUTIFUL, BUT FICKLE THING.
I AM THE ONLY GOD WHO STEPPED UP WHEN THEY WERE ATING EACH OTHER, HIDING IN CAVES LIKE WOLV WHEN THE GOD OF THE CHRISTIANS WAS SENDIN GREAT FLOODS AND A PARADE OF PLAGUES ONT HIS PEOPLE, I ESTABLISHED LAW AND ORDER AMONG MINE. DON'T LECTURE ME ON LOVE.
I WILL DO JUST THAT UNTIL YOU FINALLY UNDERSTAND IT.
YOU WANT TO TEACH ME ABOUT LOVE? ABOUT THAT TWISTED VERSION OF IT YOU'RE CULTIVATING AT THAT OLD CASTLE OF MINE, HM?
ACTUALLY, I'M QUITE PROUD OF WHAT I'VE BUILT THERE. MOST OF THE PEOPLE ARE REFUGEES, FLEEING PERSECUTION FROM VARIOUS FANATICAL GROUPS.
MANY OF THEM HAVE FLED VILLAGES THAT WORSHIP YOU.

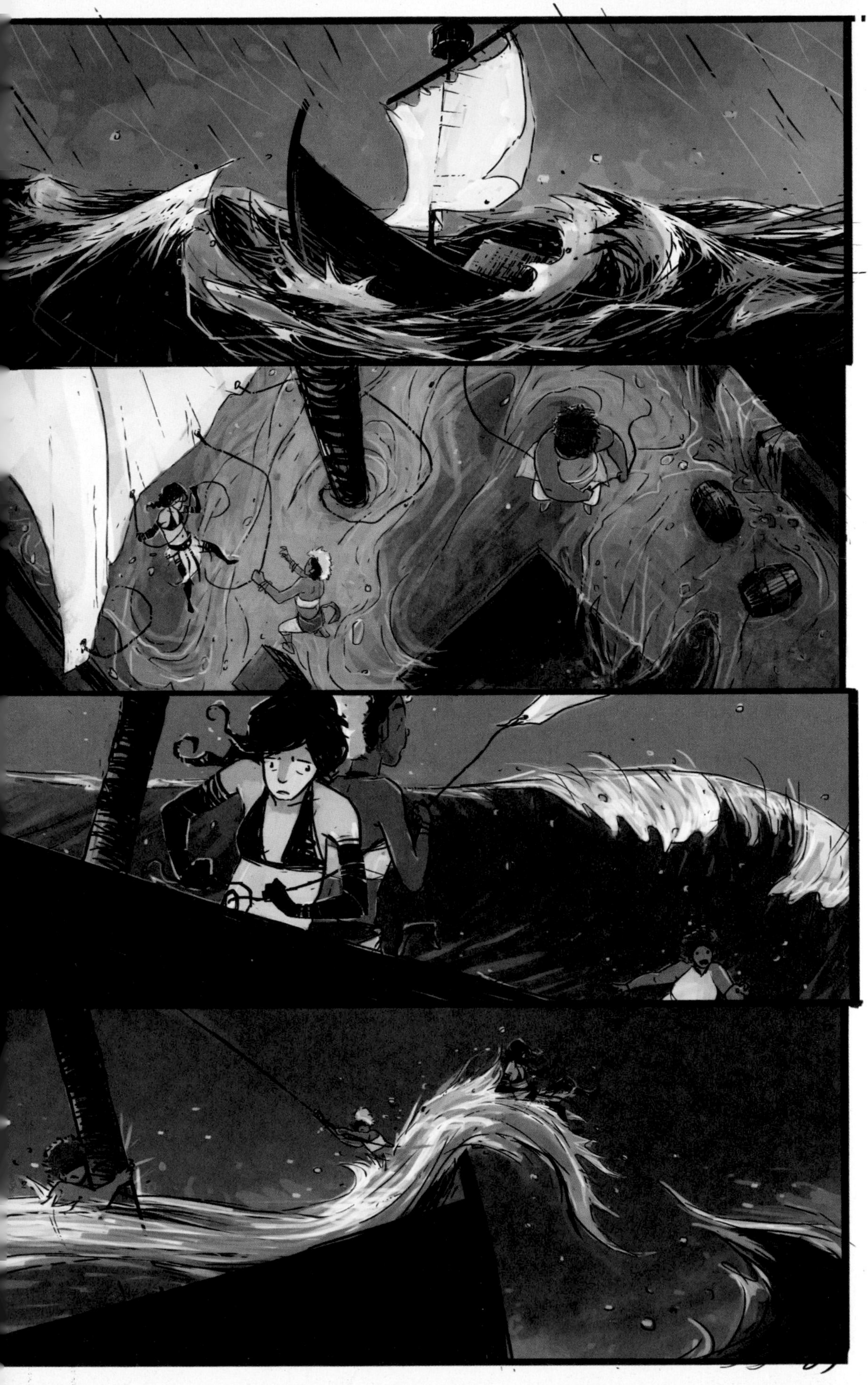

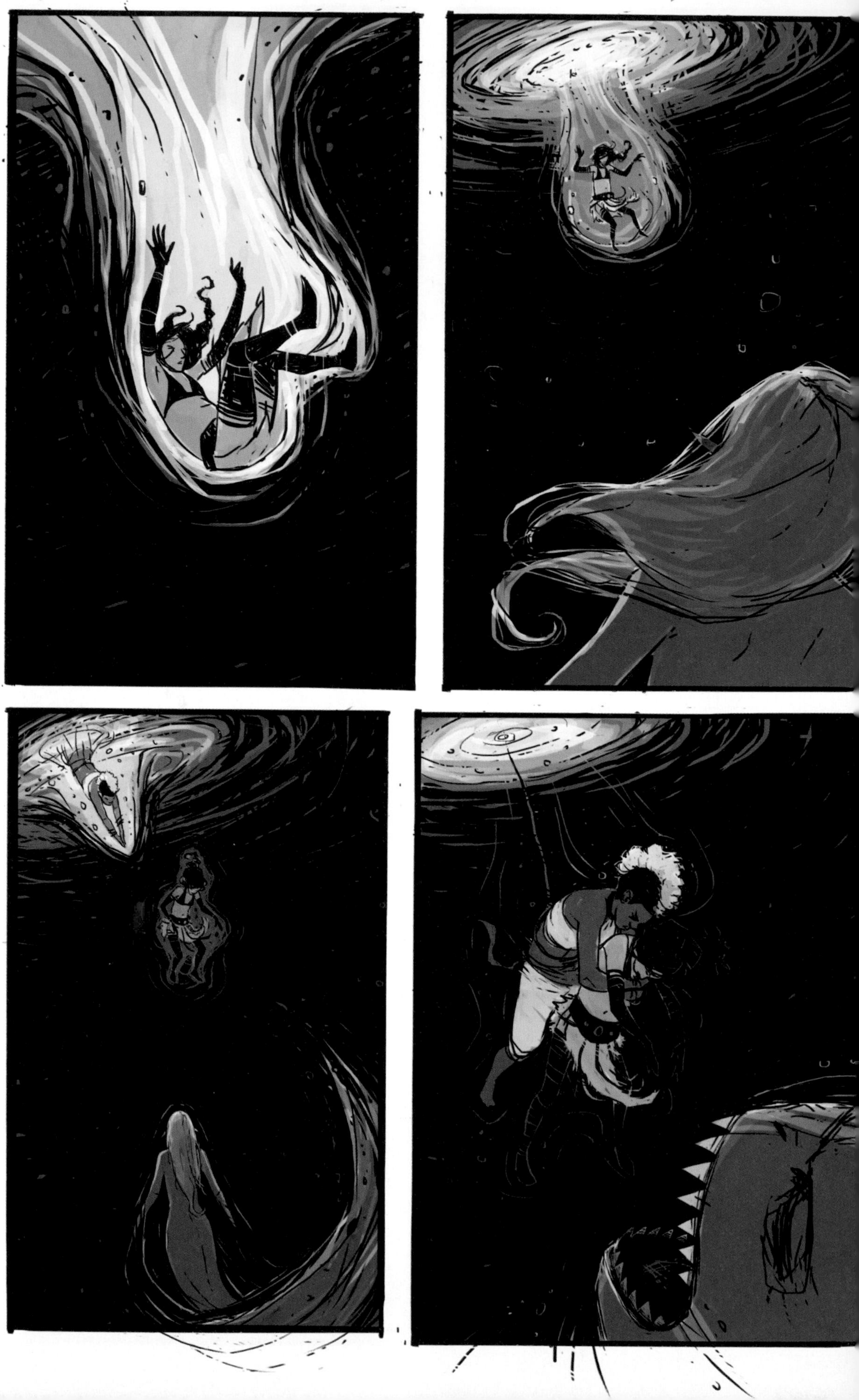

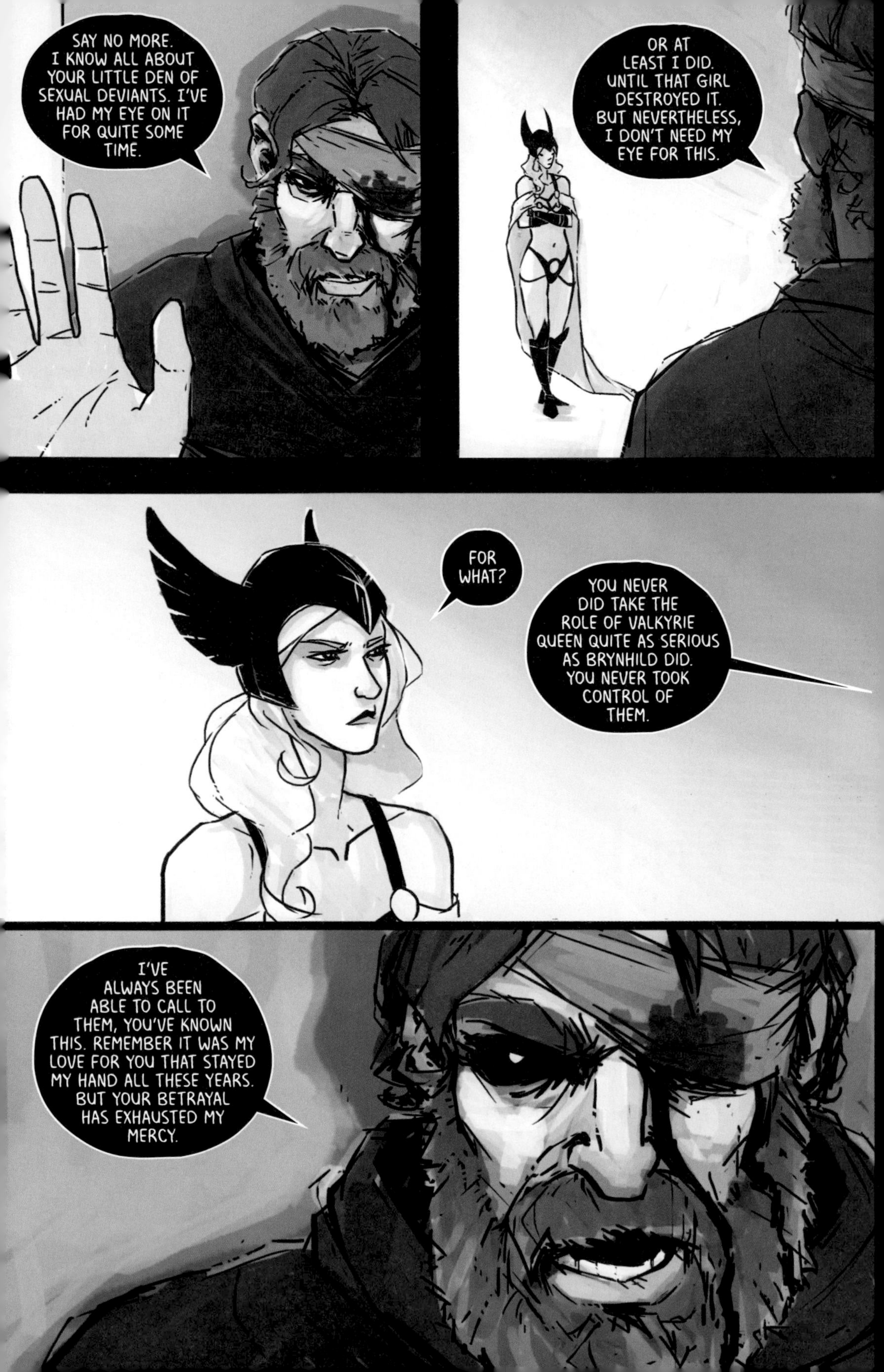
SAY NO MORE. I KNOW ALL ABOUT YOUR LITTLE DEN OF SEXUAL DEVIANTS. I'VE HAD MY EYE ON IT FOR QUITE SOME TIME.
OR AT LEAST I DID. UNTIL THAT GIRL DESTROYED IT. BUT NEVERTHELESS, I DON'T NEED MY EYE FOR THIS.
FOR WHAT?
YOU NEVER DID TAKE THE ROLE OF VALKYRIE QUEEN QUITE AS SERIOUS AS BRYNHILD DID. YOU NEVER TOOK CONTROL OF THEM.
I'VE ALWAYS BEEN ABLE TO CALL TO THEM, YOU'VE KNOWN THIS. REMEMBER IT WAS MY LOVE FOR YOU THAT STAYED MY HAND ALL THESE YEARS. BUT YOUR BETRAYAL HAS EXHAUSTED MY MERCY.

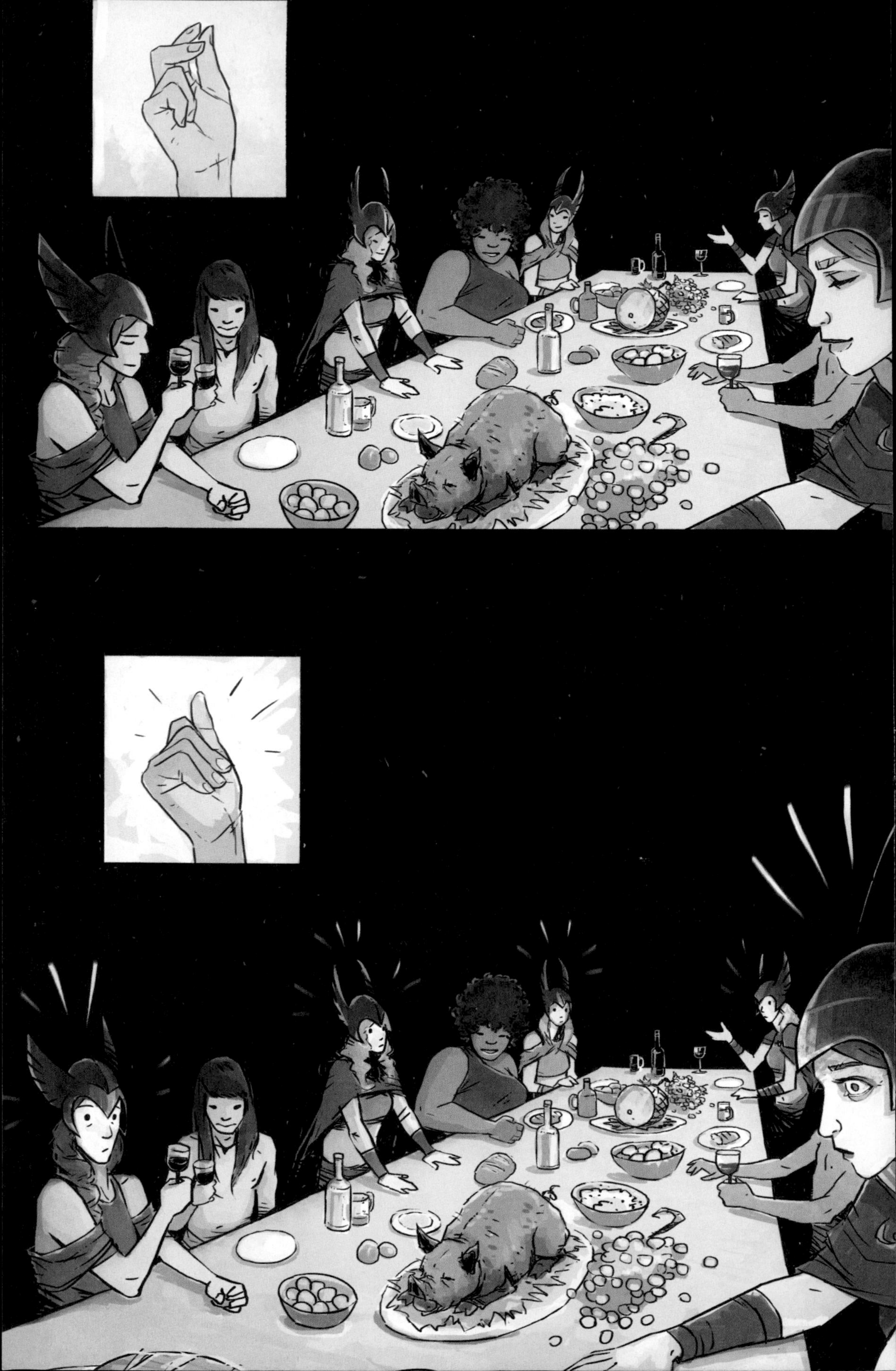

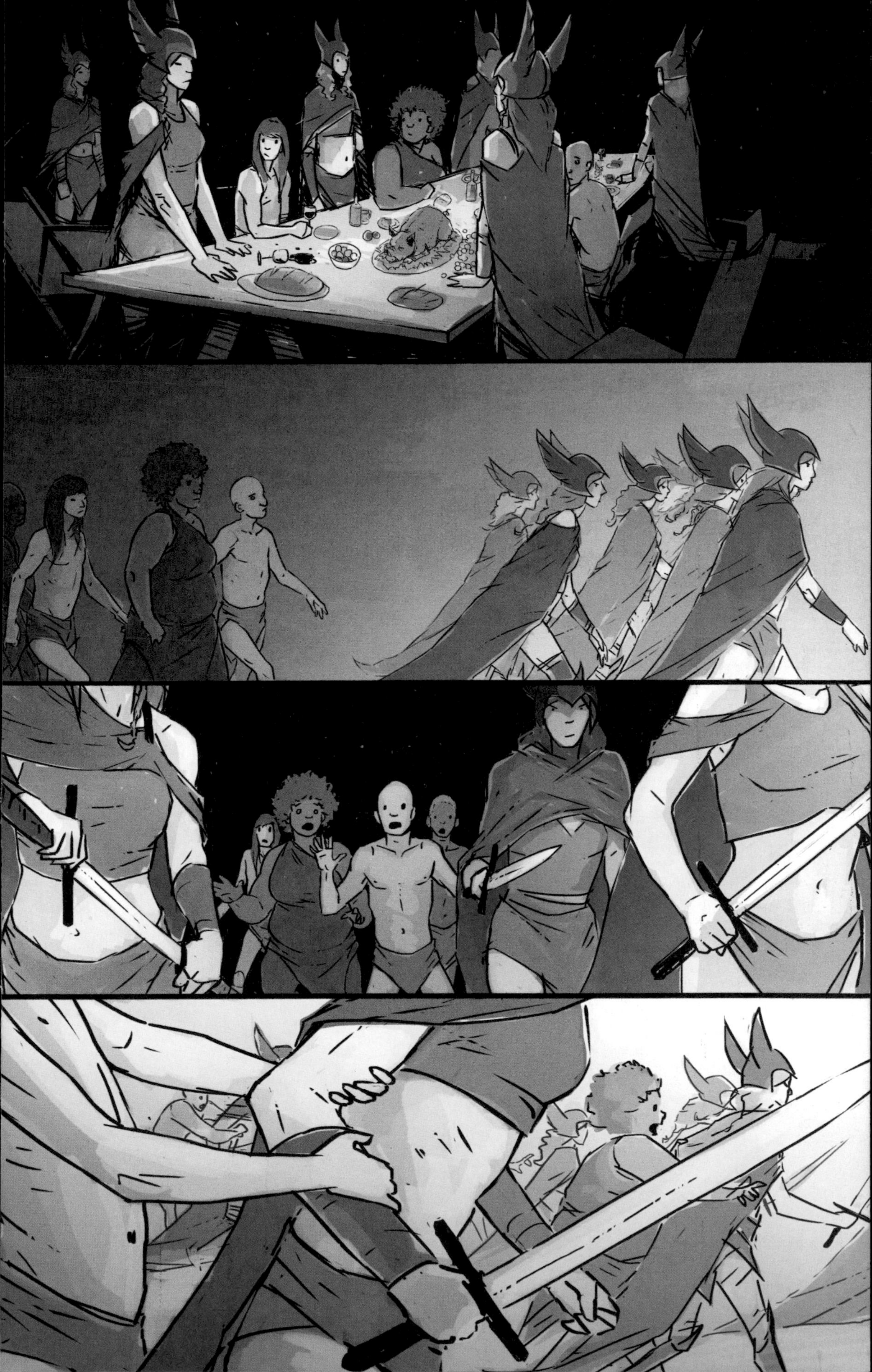

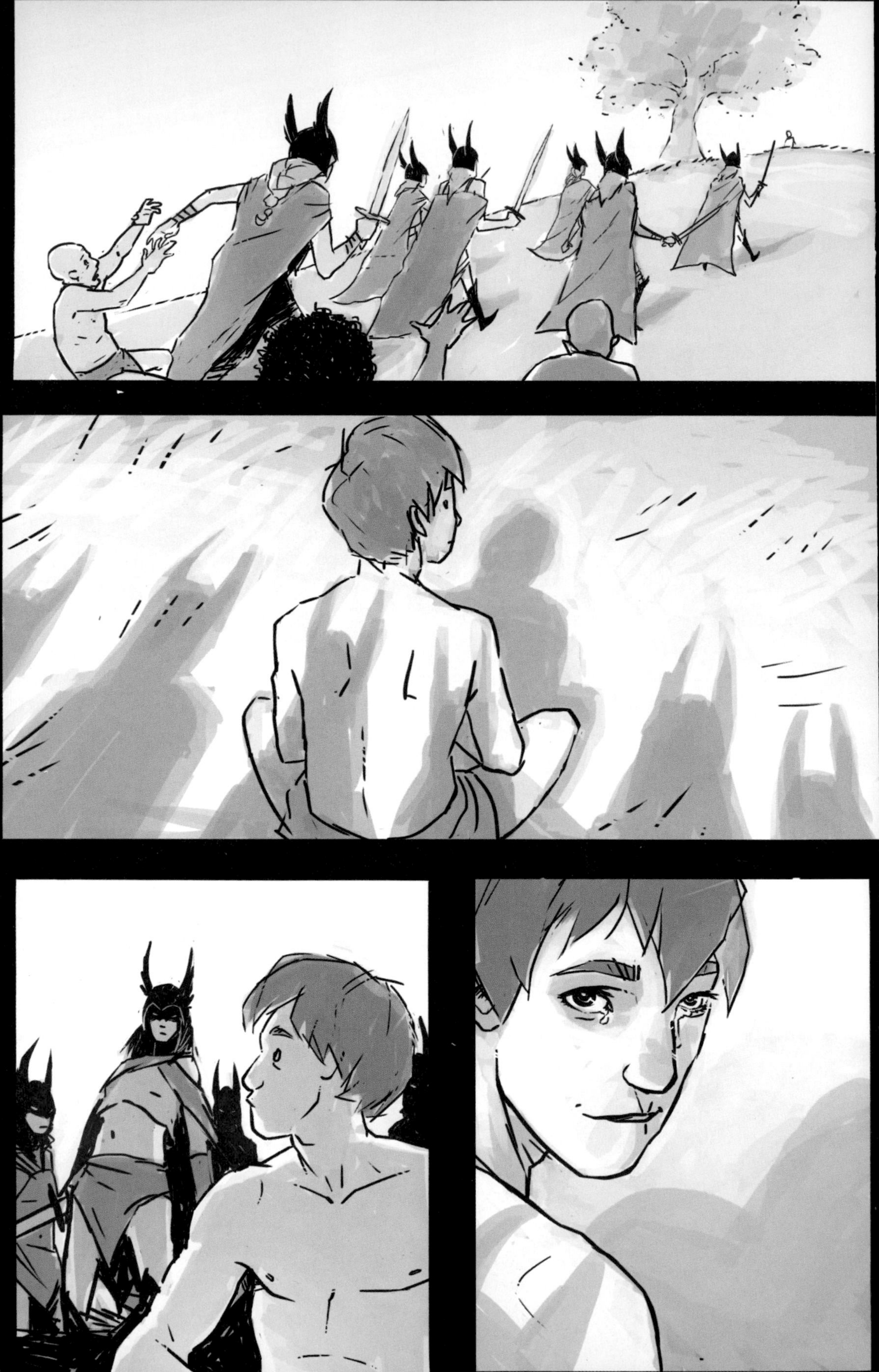

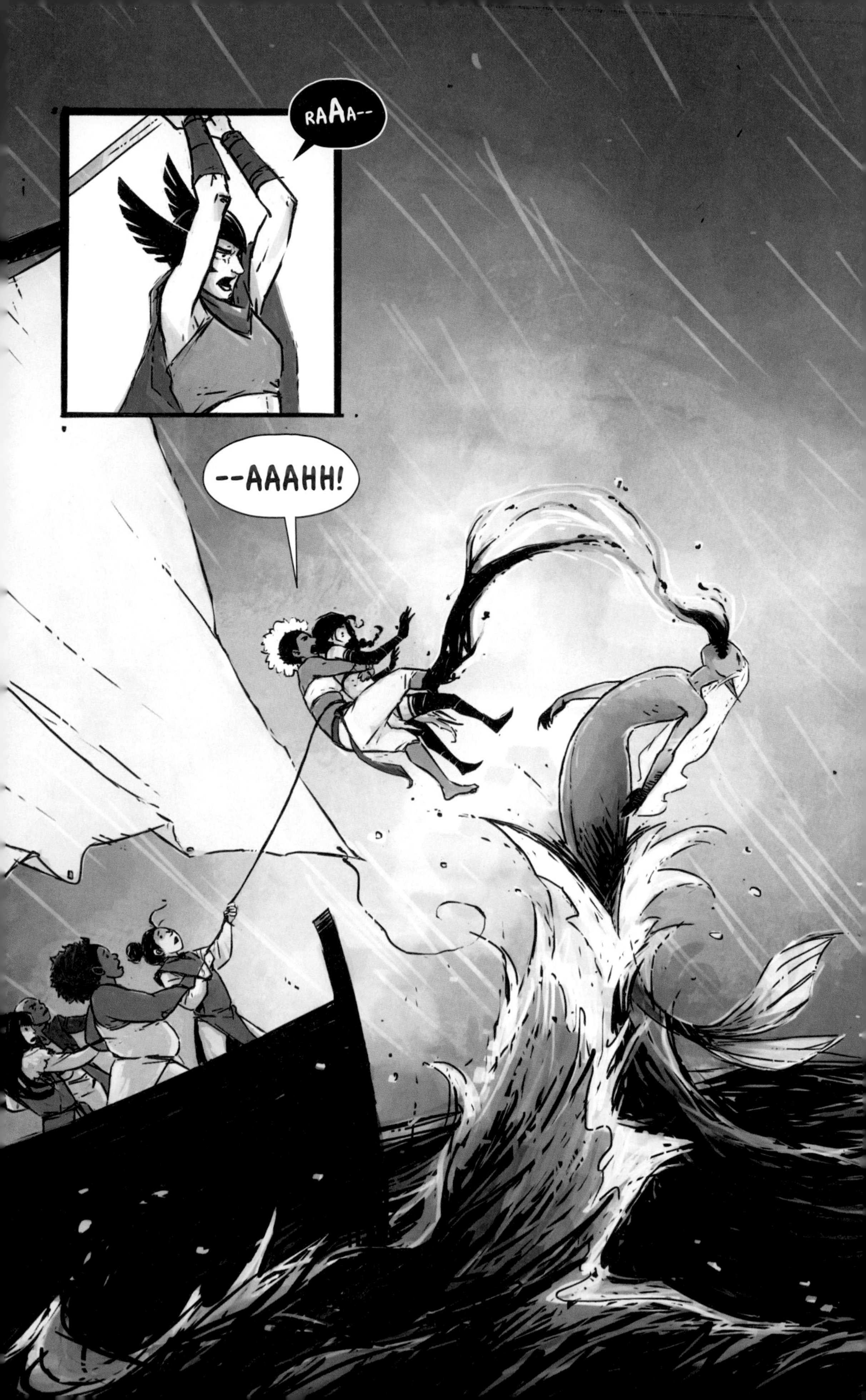
RAAA--
--AAAHH!

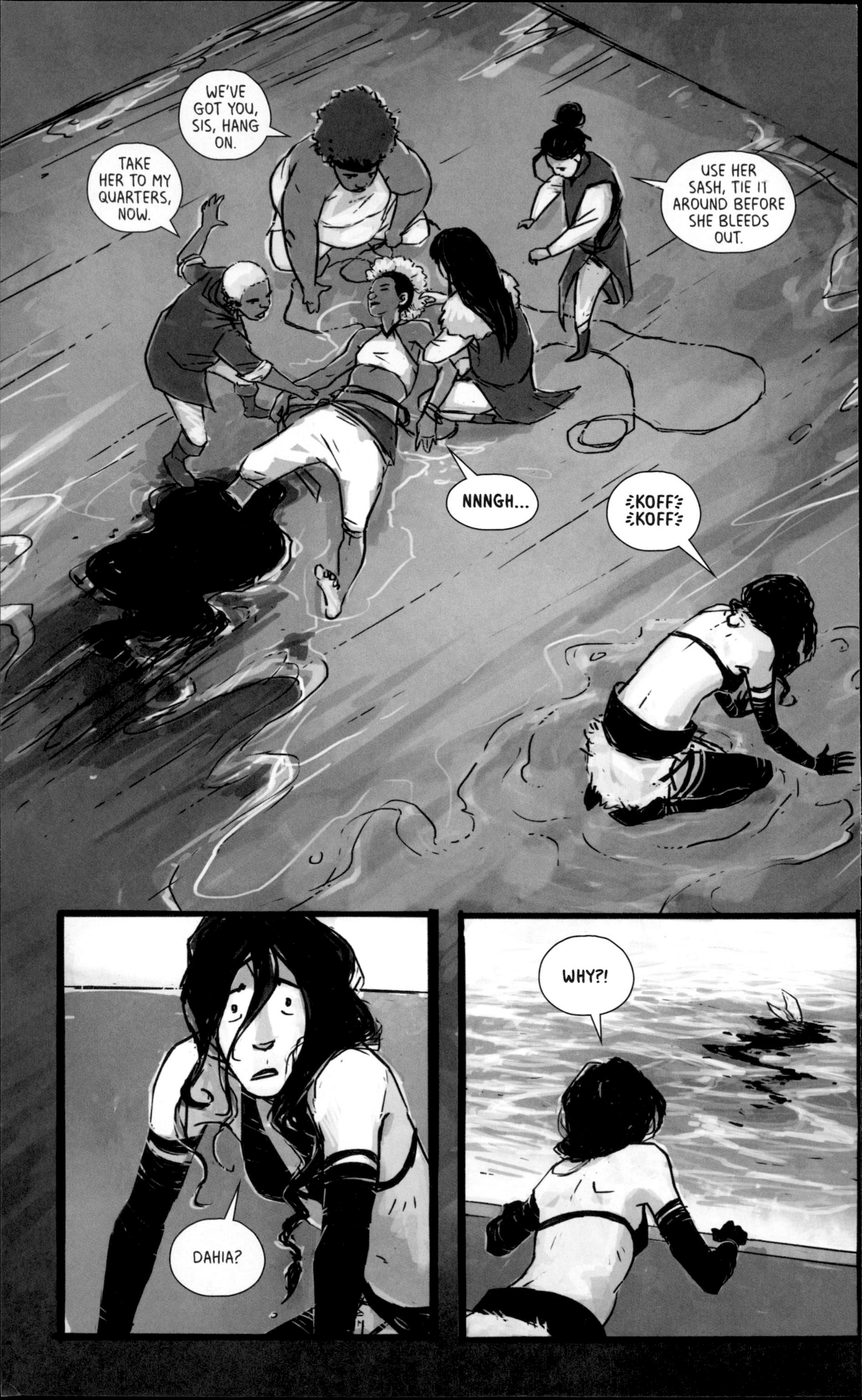
WE'VE GOT YOU, SIS, HANG ON.
TAKE HER TO MY QUARTERS, NOW.
USE HER SASH, TIE IT AROUND BEFORE SHE BLEEDS OUT.
NNNGH...
KOFF KOFF
DAHIA?
WHY?!

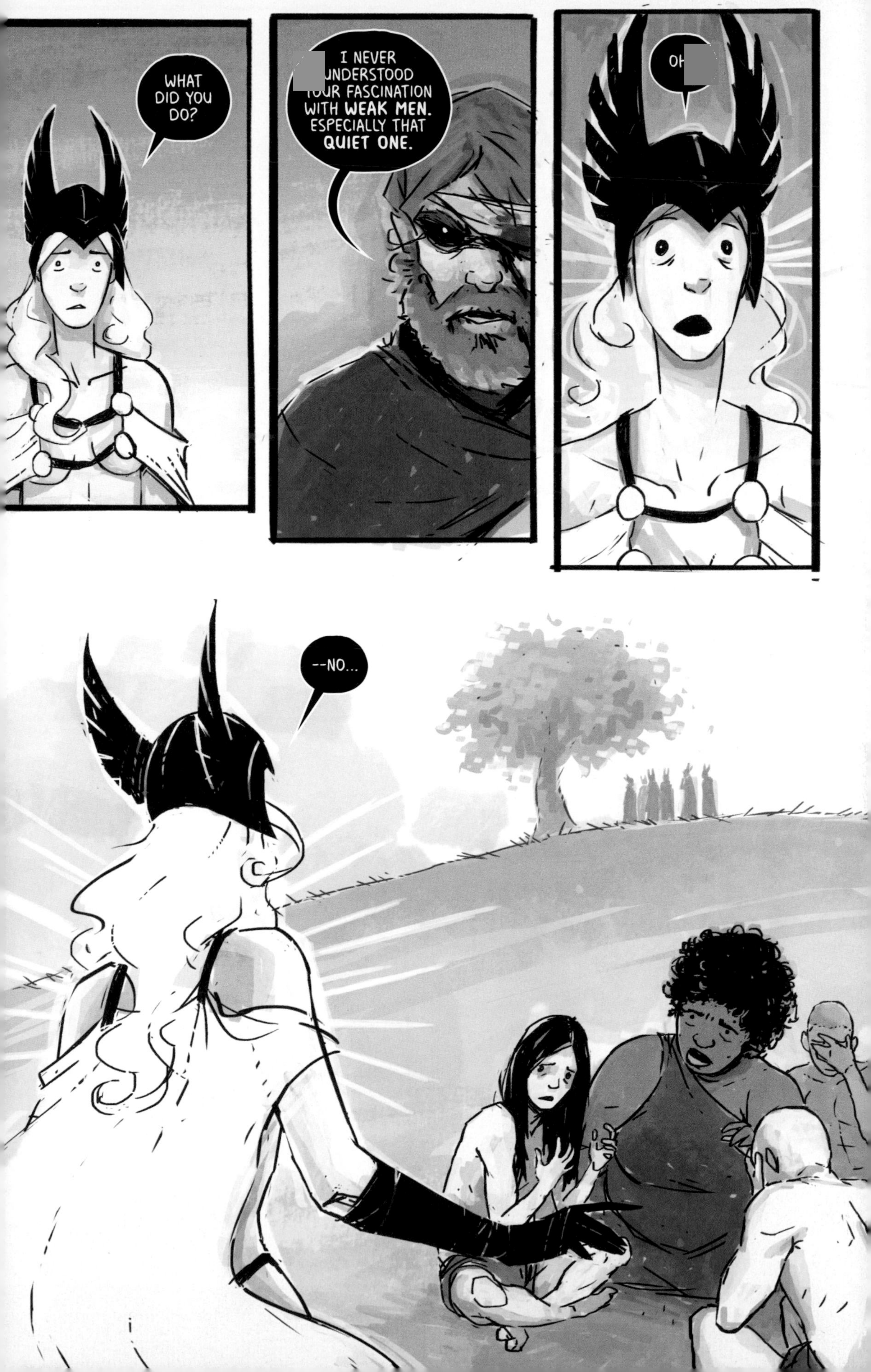
WHAT DID YOU DO?
[redacted] I NEVER UNDERSTOOD [redacted]OUR FASCINATION WITH WEAK MEN. ESPECIALLY THAT QUIET ONE.
OH[redacted]
--NO...

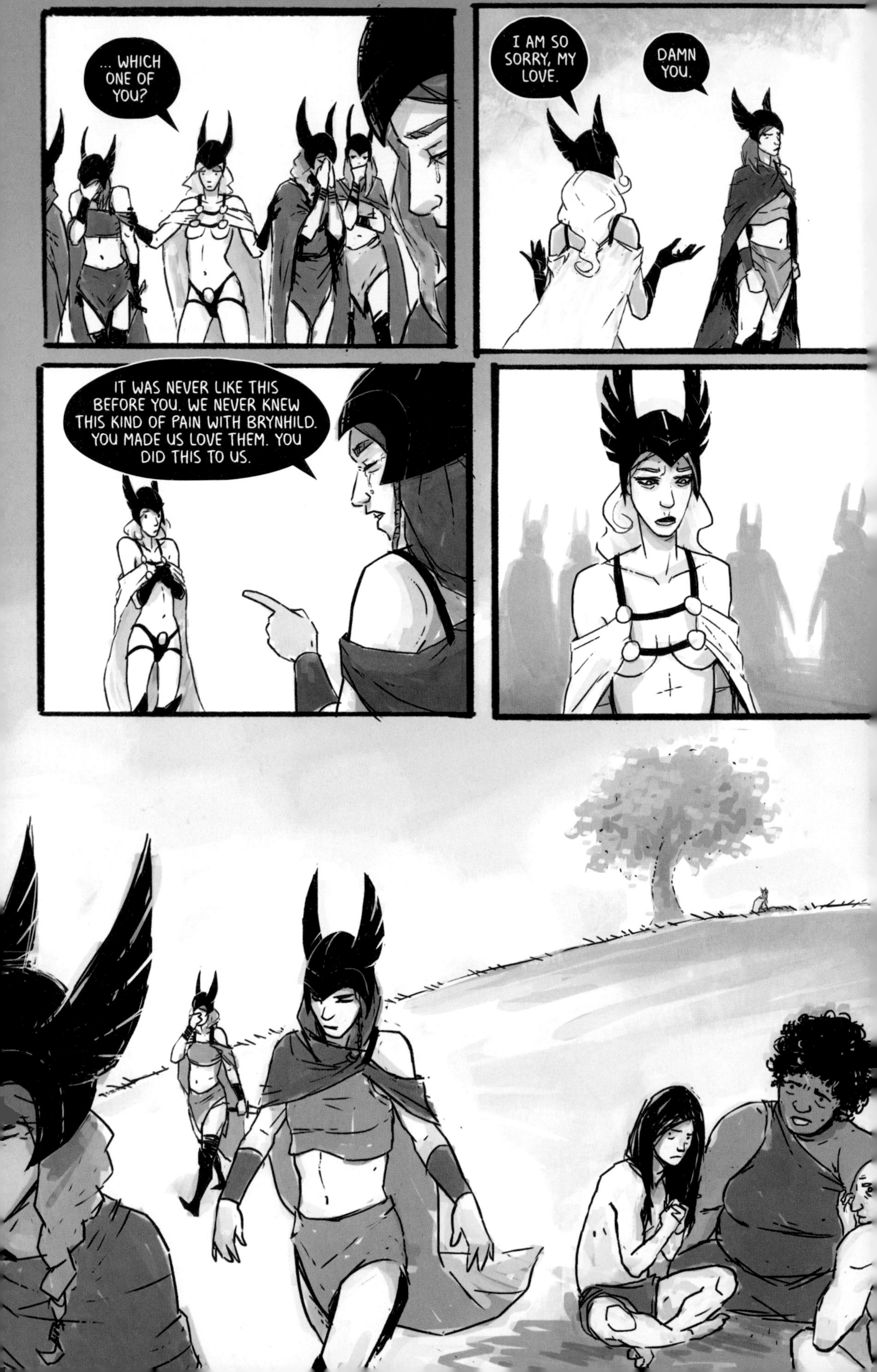
... WHICH ONE OF YOU?
I AM SO SORRY, MY LOVE.
DAMN YOU.
IT WAS NEVER LIKE THIS BEFORE YOU. WE NEVER KNEW THIS KIND OF PAIN WITH BRYNHILD. YOU MADE US LOVE THEM. YOU DID THIS TO US.

CHAPTER 8

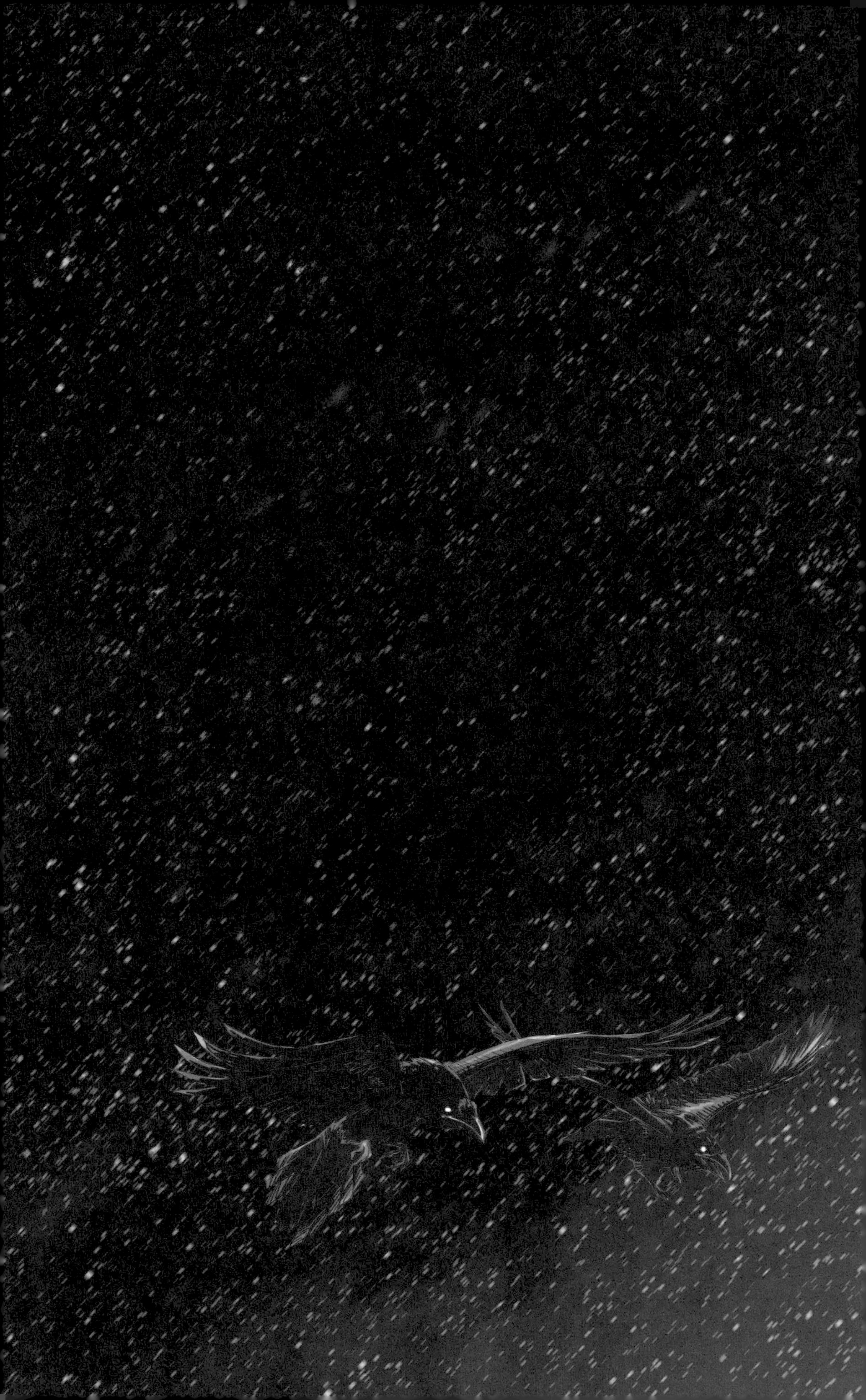

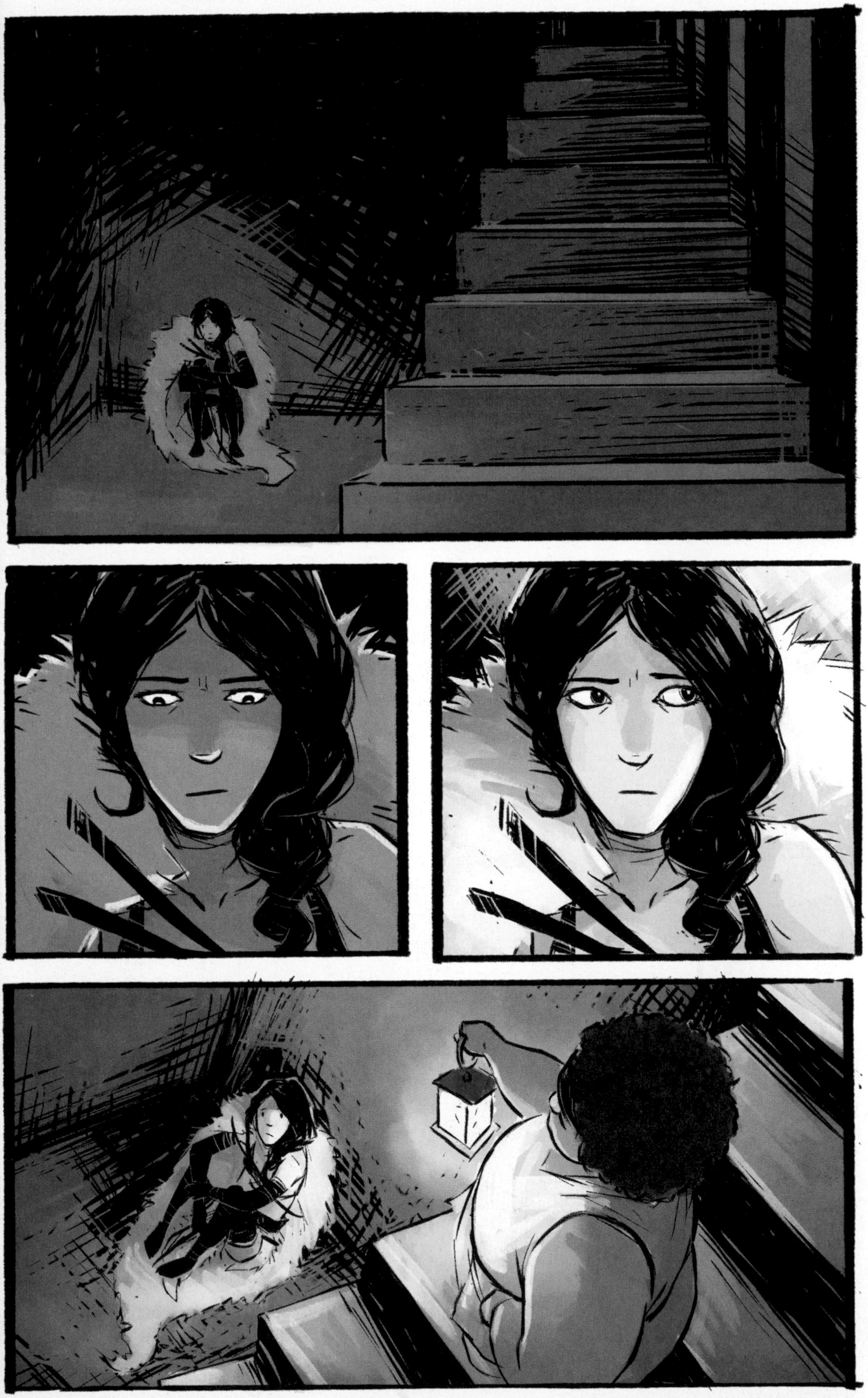

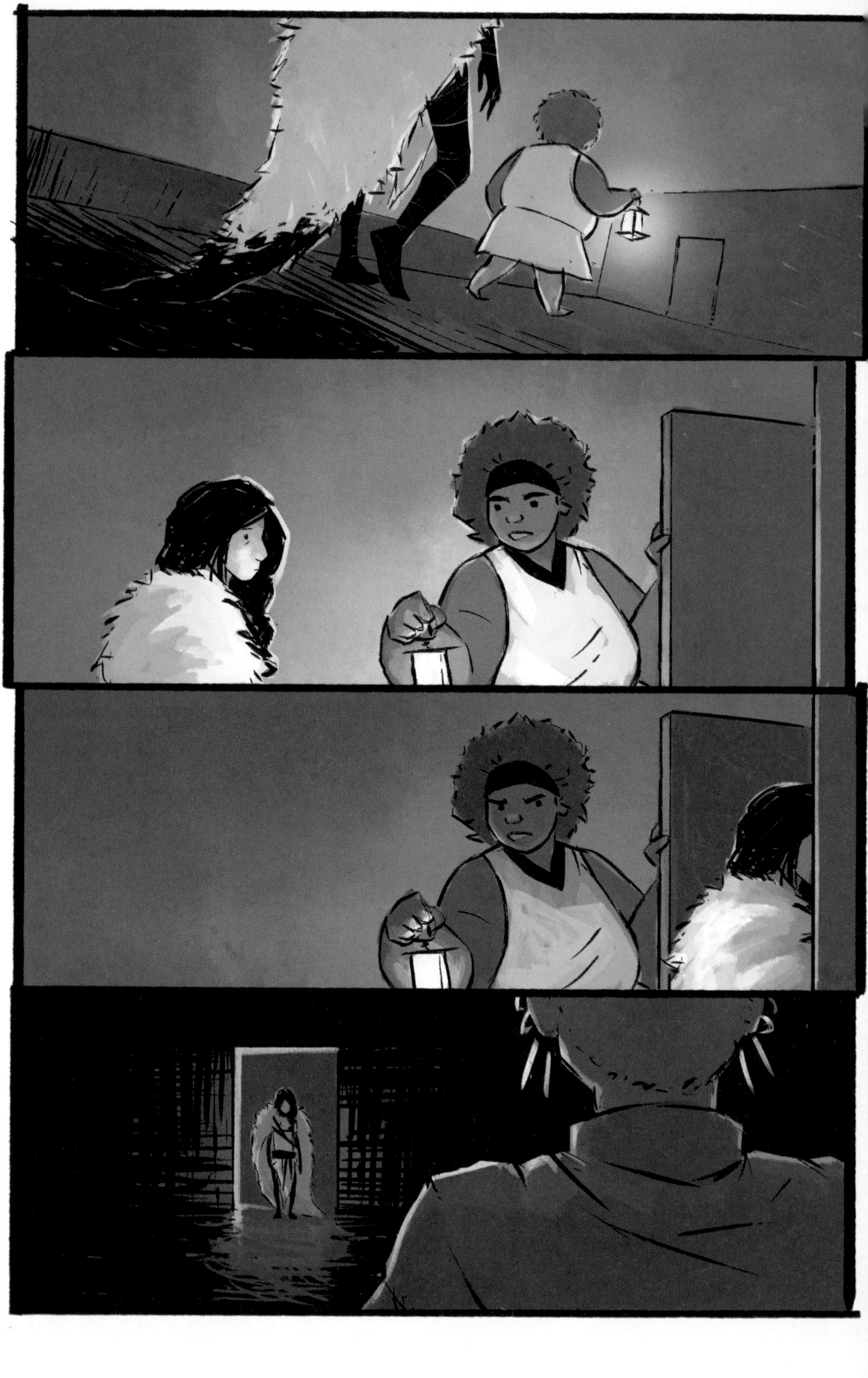

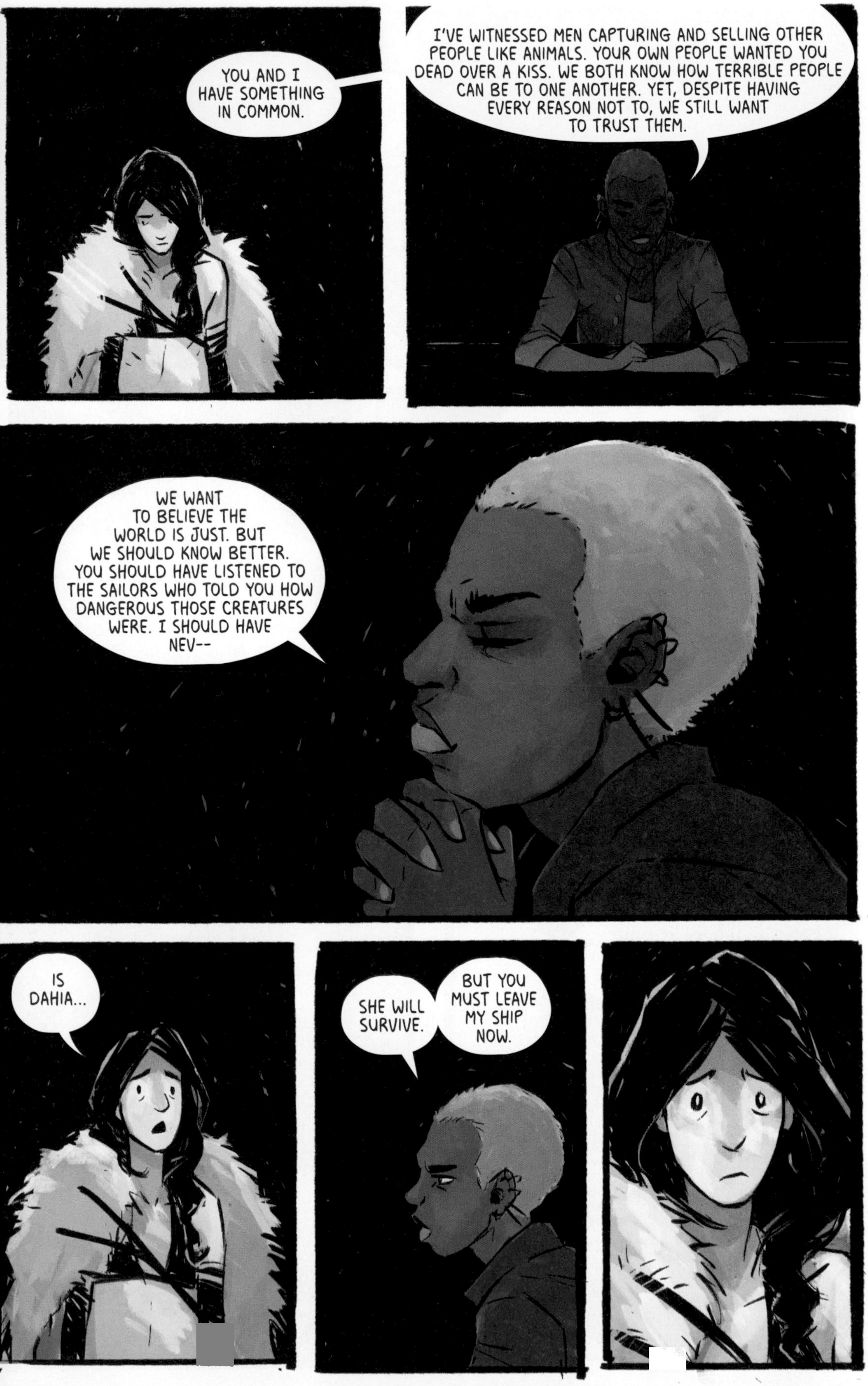
YOU AND I HAVE SOMETHING IN COMMON.
I'VE WITNESSED MEN CAPTURING AND SELLING OTHER PEOPLE LIKE ANIMALS. YOUR OWN PEOPLE WANTED YOU DEAD OVER A KISS. WE BOTH KNOW HOW TERRIBLE PEOPLE CAN BE TO ONE ANOTHER. YET, DESPITE HAVING EVERY REASON NOT TO, WE STILL WANT TO TRUST THEM.
WE WANT TO BELIEVE THE WORLD IS JUST. BUT WE SHOULD KNOW BETTER. YOU SHOULD HAVE LISTENED TO THE SAILORS WHO TOLD YOU HOW DANGEROUS THOSE CREATURES WERE. I SHOULD HAVE NEV--
IS DAHIA...
SHE WILL SURVIVE.
BUT YOU MUST LEAVE MY SHIP NOW.

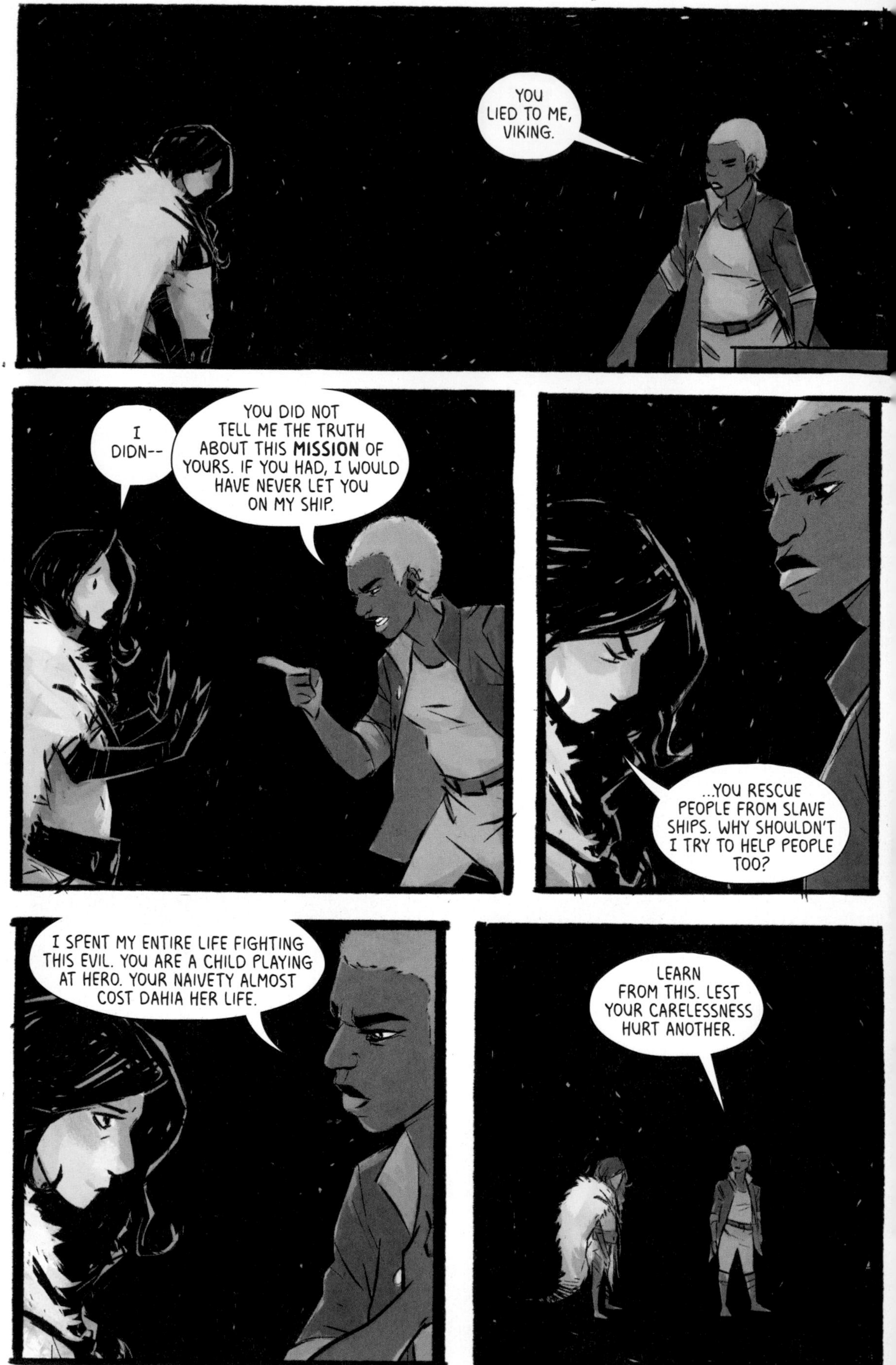

YOU LIED TO ME, VIKING.
I DIDN--
YOU DID NOT TELL ME THE TRUTH ABOUT THIS **MISSION** OF YOURS. IF YOU HAD, I WOULD HAVE NEVER LET YOU ON MY SHIP.
...YOU RESCUE PEOPLE FROM SLAVE SHIPS. WHY SHOULDN'T I TRY TO HELP PEOPLE TOO?
I SPENT MY ENTIRE LIFE FIGHTING THIS EVIL. YOU ARE A CHILD PLAYING AT HERO. YOUR NAIVETY ALMOST COST DAHIA HER LIFE.
LEARN FROM THIS. LEST YOUR CARELESSNESS HURT ANOTHER.

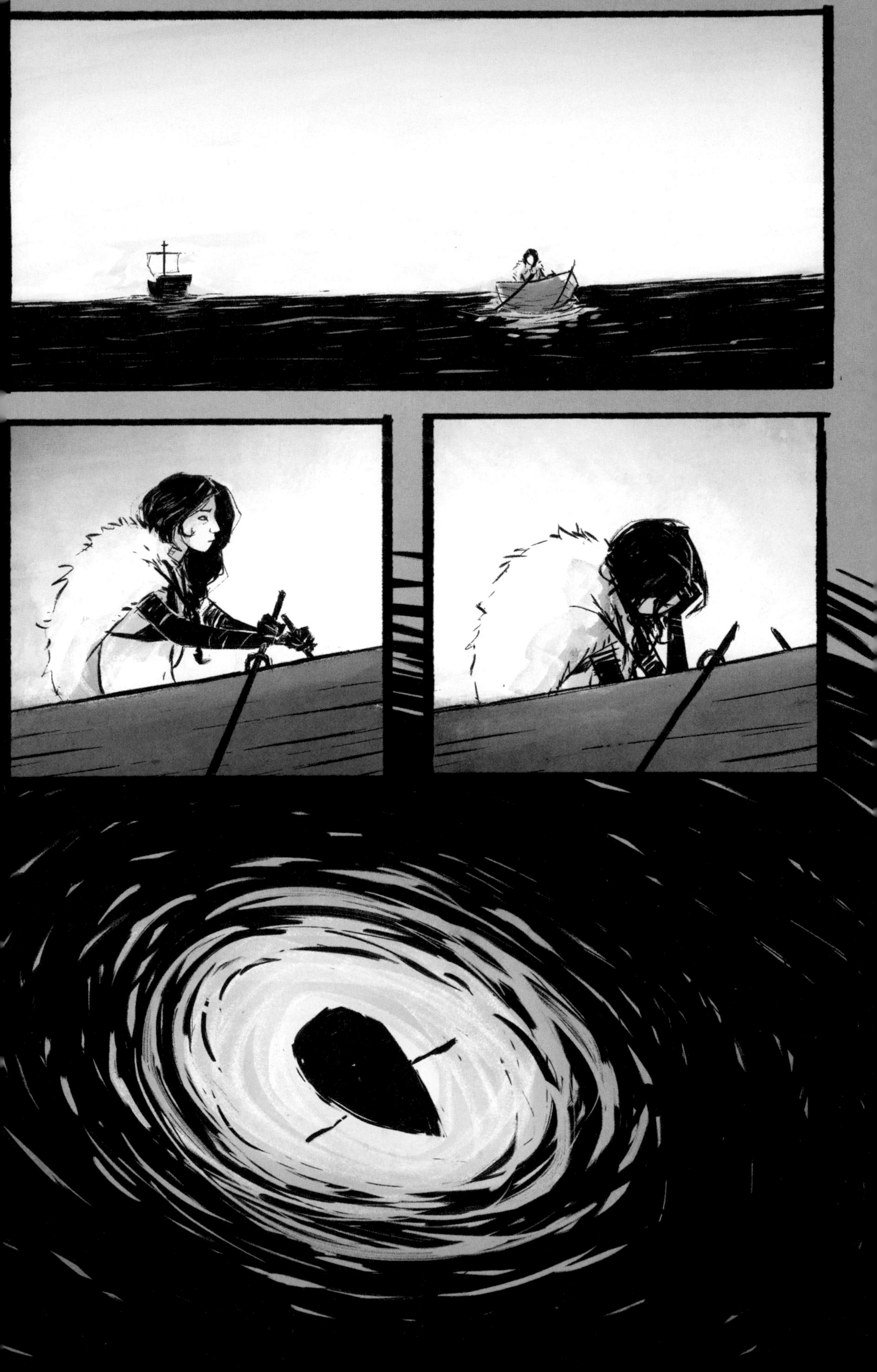

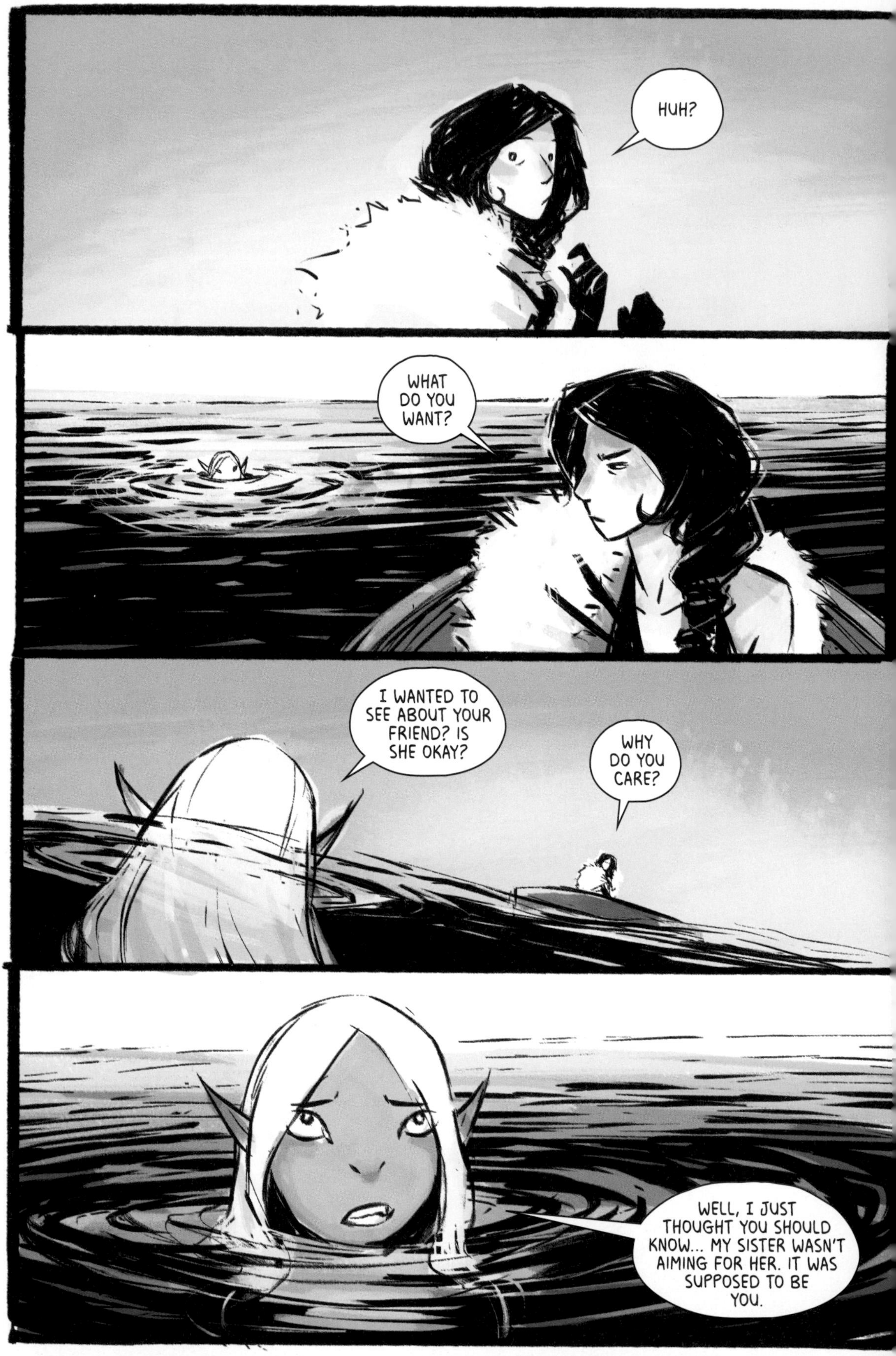
HUH?
WHAT DO YOU WANT?
I WANTED TO SEE ABOUT YOUR FRIEND? IS SHE OKAY?
WHY DO YOU CARE?
WELL, I JUST THOUGHT YOU SHOULD KNOW... MY SISTER WASN'T AIMING FOR HER. IT WAS SUPPOSED TO BE YOU.

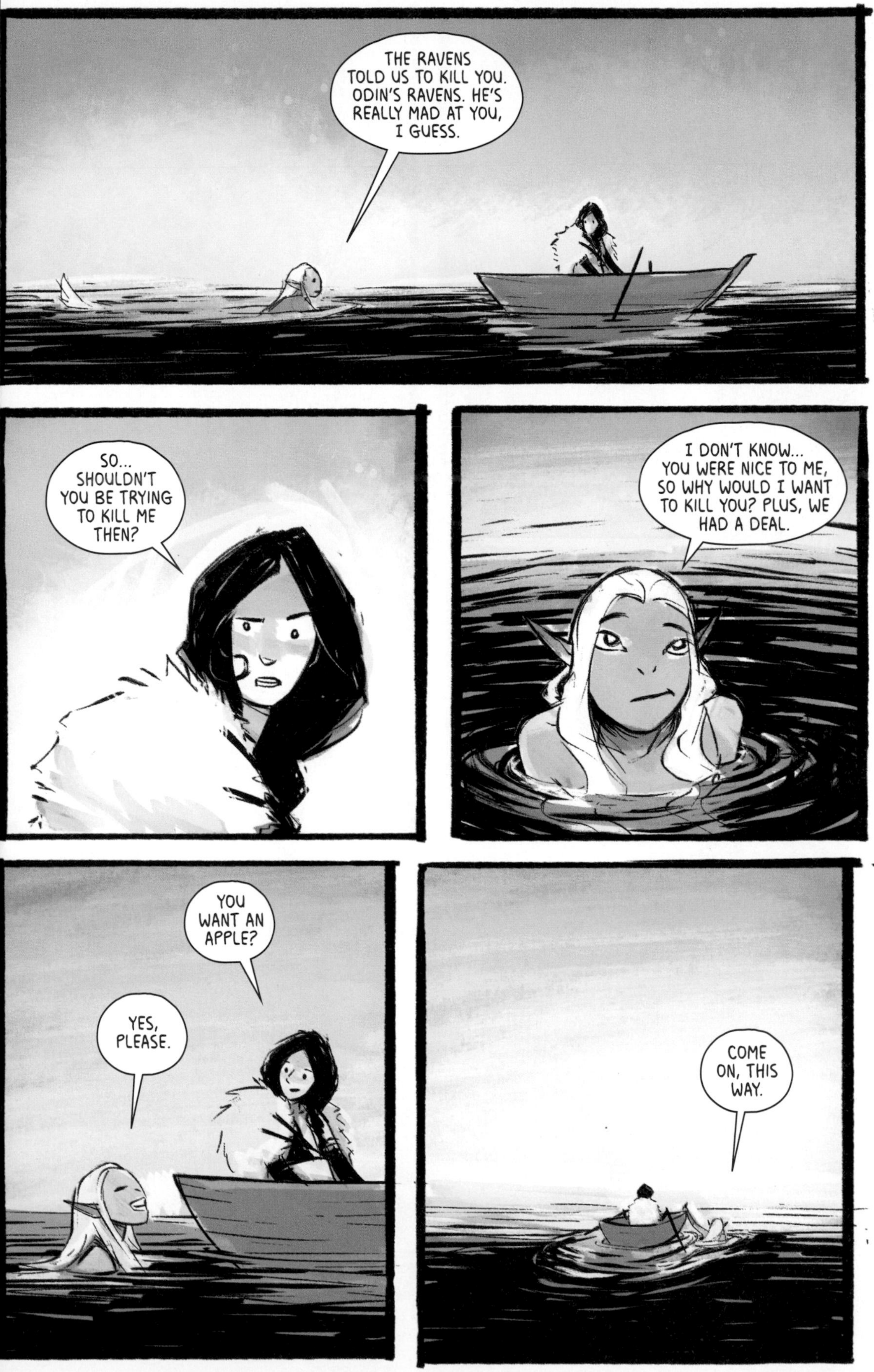
THE RAVENS TOLD US TO KILL YOU. ODIN'S RAVENS. HE'S REALLY MAD AT YOU, I GUESS.
SO... SHOULDN'T YOU BE TRYING TO KILL ME THEN?
I DON'T KNOW... YOU WERE NICE TO ME, SO WHY WOULD I WANT TO KILL YOU? PLUS, WE HAD A DEAL.
YOU WANT AN APPLE?
YES, PLEASE.
COME ON, THIS WAY.

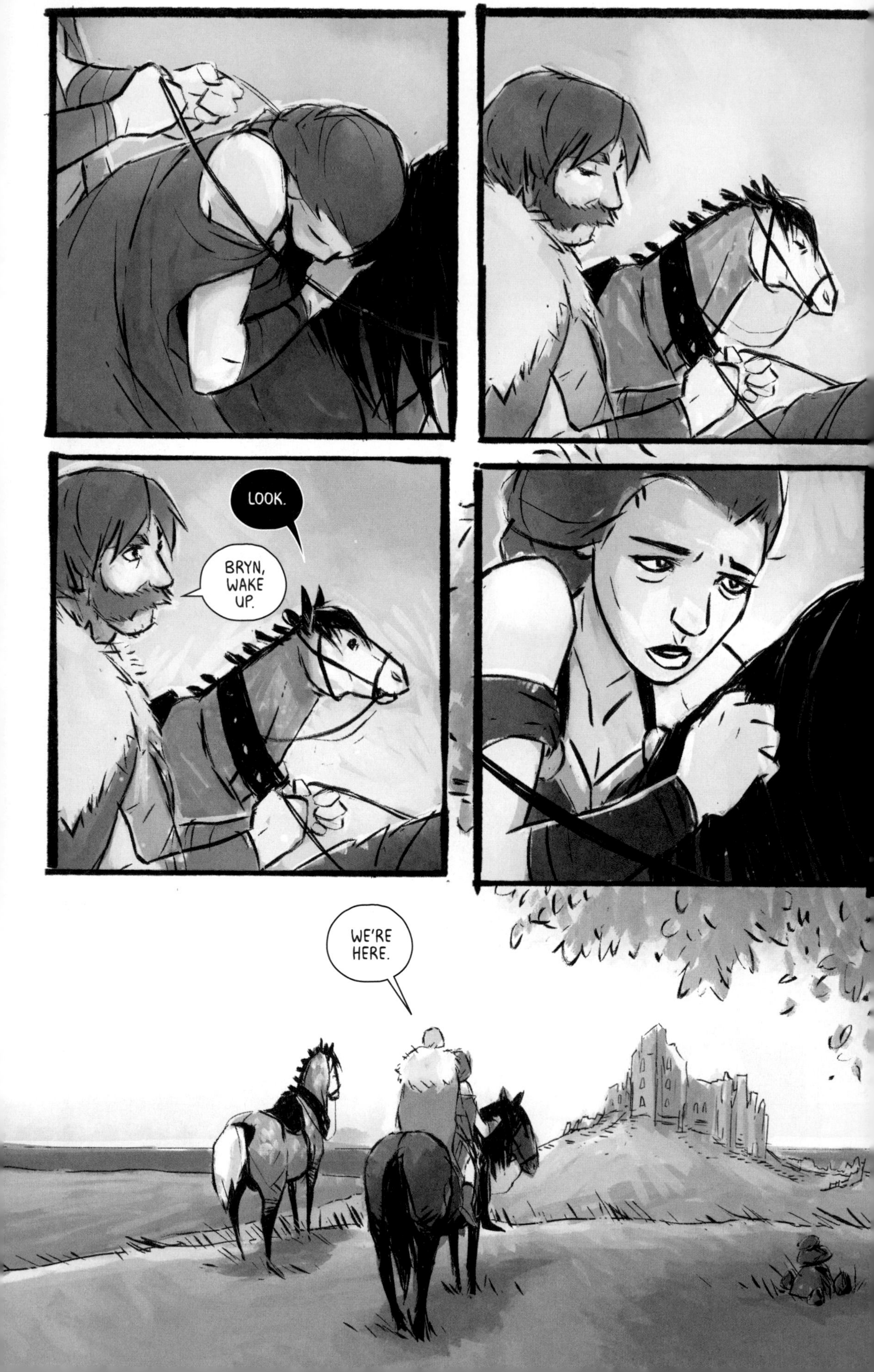
LOOK.
BRYN, WAKE UP.
WE'RE HERE.

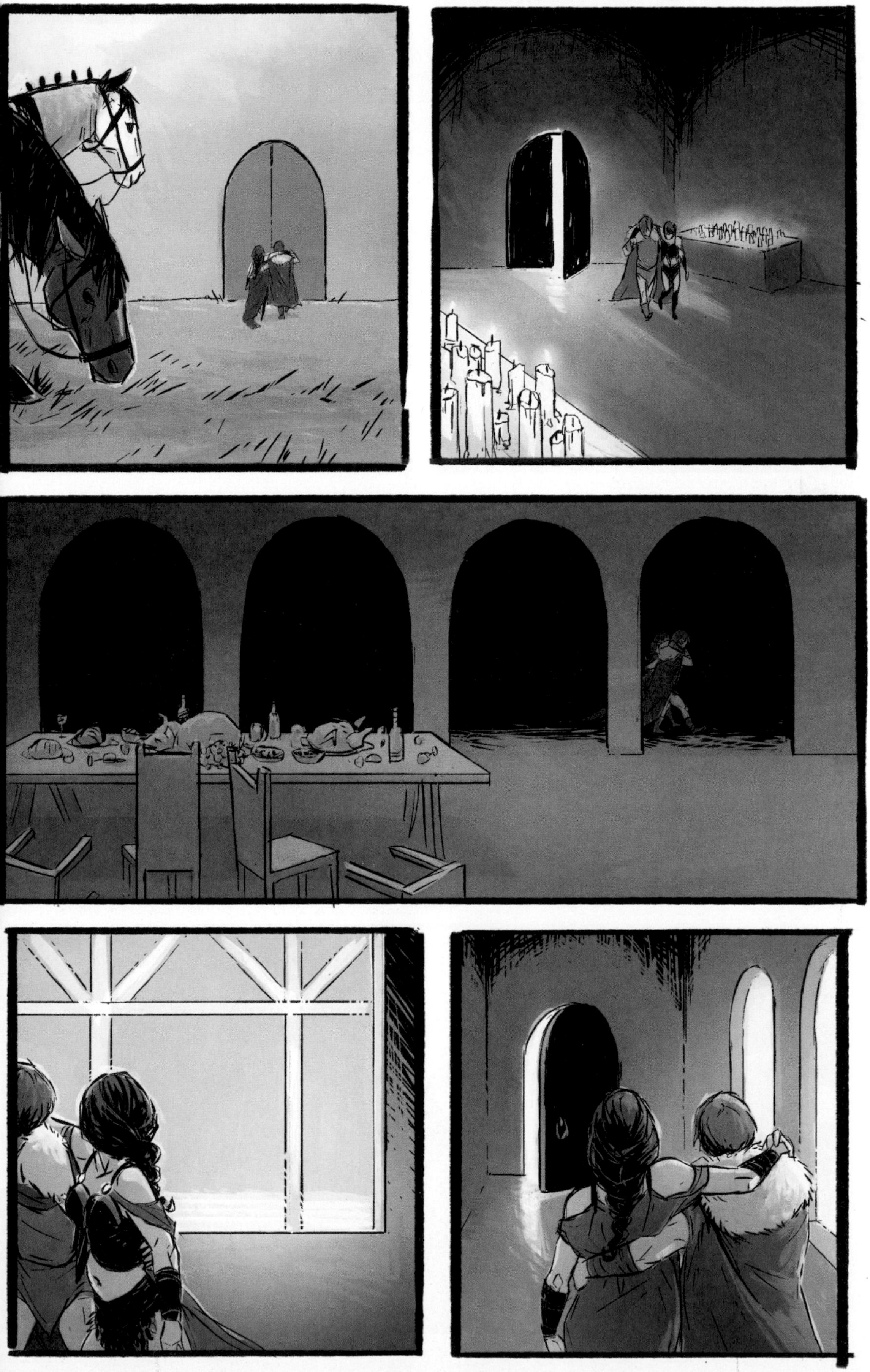

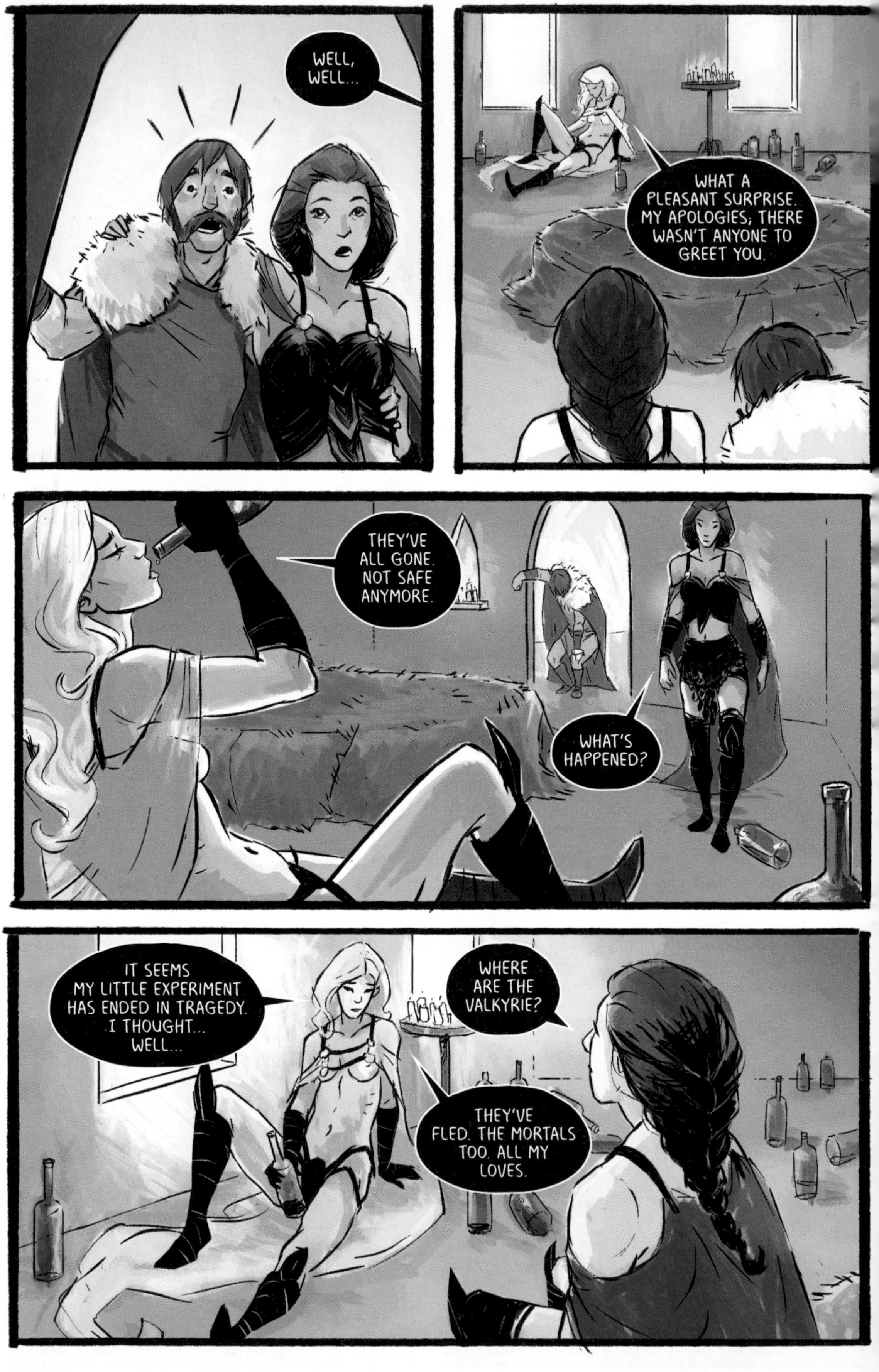
WELL, WELL...
WHAT A PLEASANT SURPRISE. MY APOLOGIES; THERE WASN'T ANYONE TO GREET YOU.
THEY'VE ALL GONE. NOT SAFE ANYMORE.
WHAT'S HAPPENED?
IT SEEMS MY LITTLE EXPERIMENT HAS ENDED IN TRAGEDY. I THOUGHT... WELL...
WHERE ARE THE VALKYRIE?
THEY'VE FLED. THE MORTALS TOO. ALL MY LOVES.

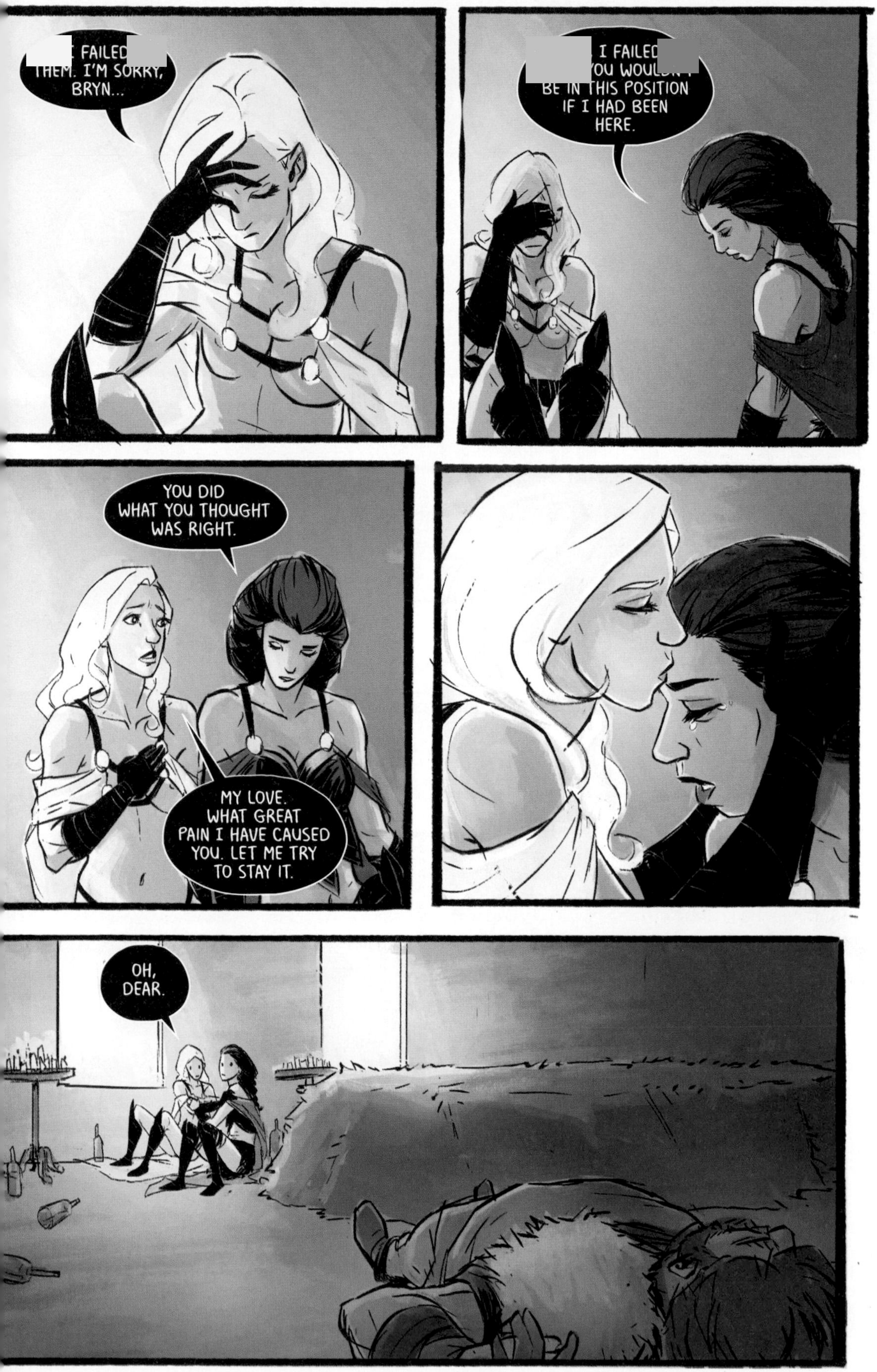

[redacted] I FAILED [redacted] THEM. I'M SORRY, BRYN...
[redacted] I FAILED [redacted] YOU WOUL[redacted] BE IN THIS POSITION IF I HAD BEEN HERE.
YOU DID WHAT YOU THOUGHT WAS RIGHT.
MY LOVE. WHAT GREAT PAIN I HAVE CAUSED YOU. LET ME TRY TO STAY IT.
OH, DEAR.

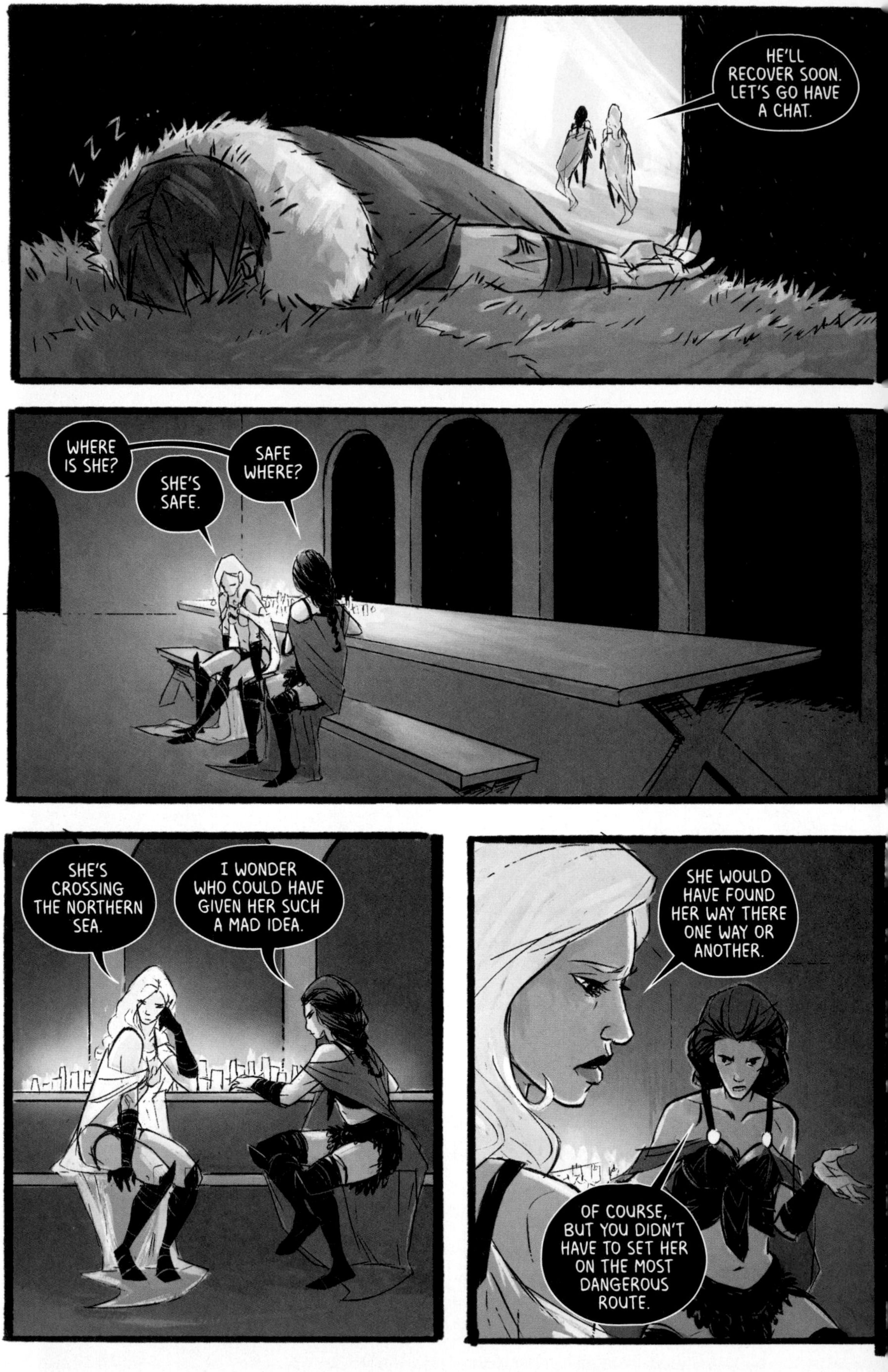
Z Z Z . . .
HE'LL RECOVER SOON. LET'S GO HAVE A CHAT.
WHERE IS SHE?
SHE'S SAFE.
SAFE WHERE?
SHE'S CROSSING THE NORTHERN SEA.
I WONDER WHO COULD HAVE GIVEN HER SUCH A MAD IDEA.
SHE WOULD HAVE FOUND HER WAY THERE ONE WAY OR ANOTHER.
OF COURSE, BUT YOU DIDN'T HAVE TO SET HER ON THE MOST DANGEROUS ROUTE.

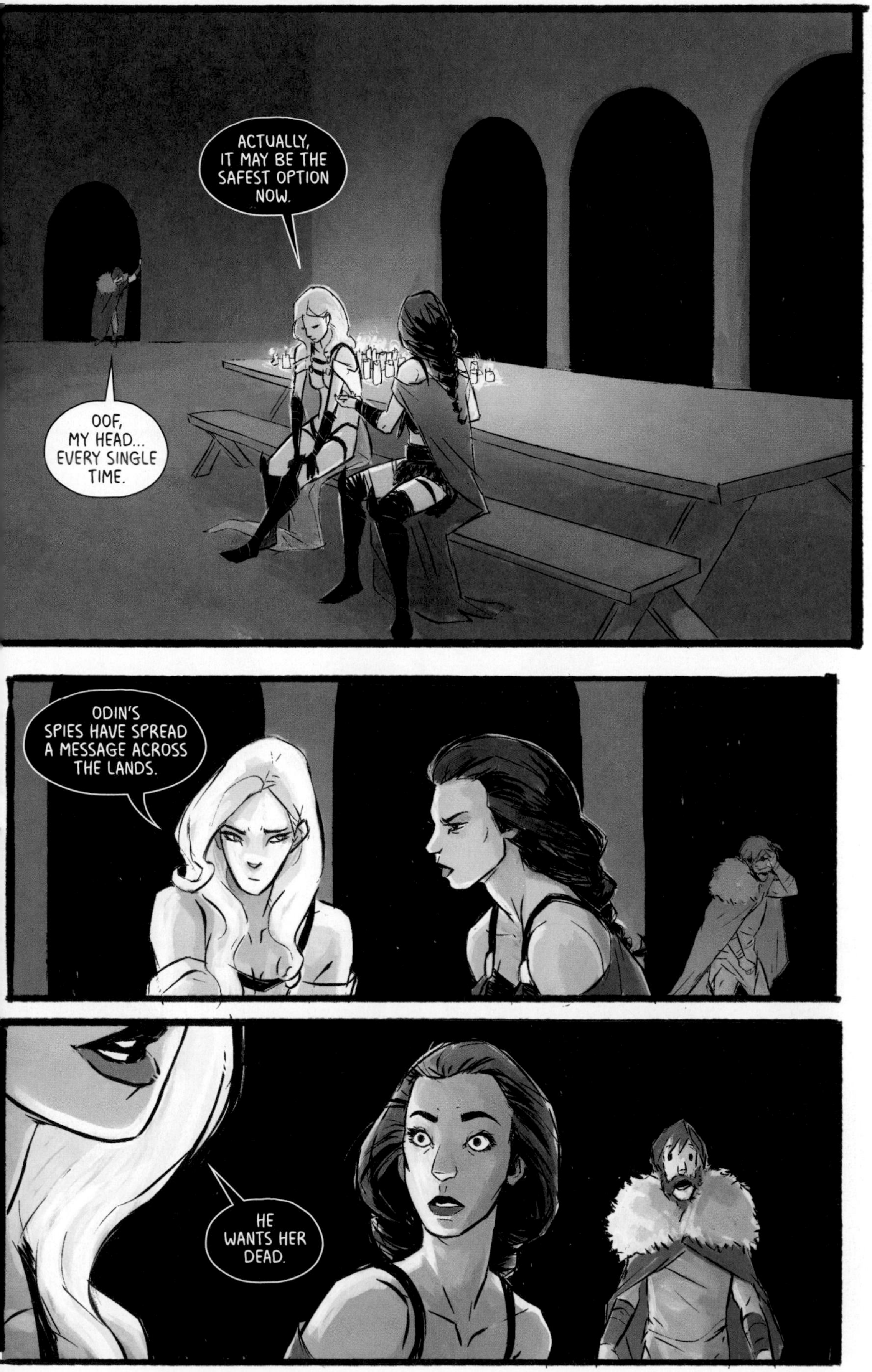
OOF, MY HEAD... EVERY SINGLE TIME.
ACTUALLY, IT MAY BE THE SAFEST OPTION NOW.
ODIN'S SPIES HAVE SPREAD A MESSAGE ACROSS THE LANDS.
HE WANTS HER DEAD.

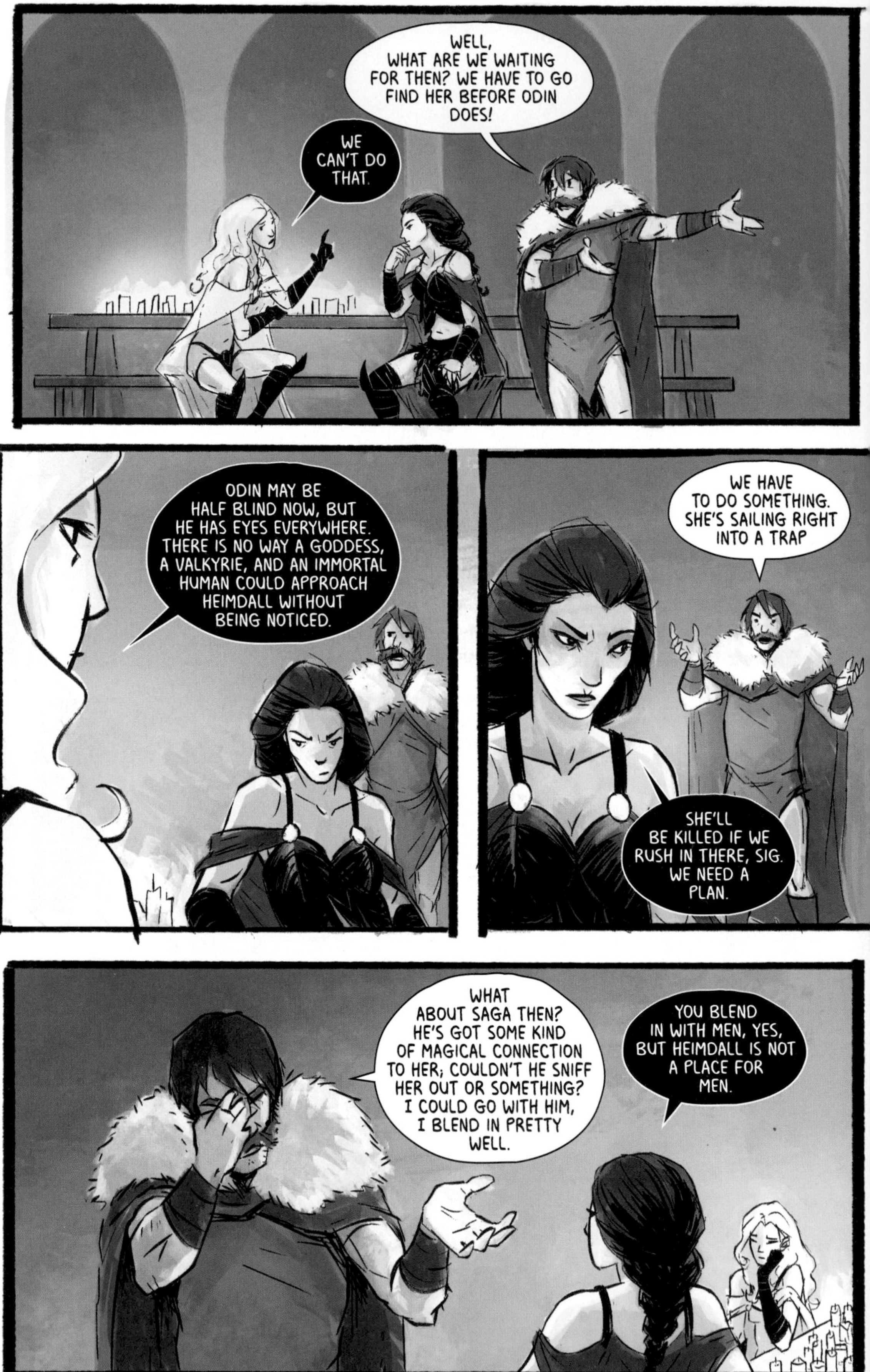
WELL, WHAT ARE WE WAITING FOR THEN? WE HAVE TO GO FIND HER BEFORE ODIN DOES!
WE CAN'T DO THAT.
ODIN MAY BE HALF BLIND NOW, BUT HE HAS EYES EVERYWHERE. THERE IS NO WAY A GODDESS, A VALKYRIE, AND AN IMMORTAL HUMAN COULD APPROACH HEIMDALL WITHOUT BEING NOTICED.
WE HAVE TO DO SOMETHING. SHE'S SAILING RIGHT INTO A TRAP
SHE'LL BE KILLED IF WE RUSH IN THERE, SIG. WE NEED A PLAN.
WHAT ABOUT SAGA THEN? HE'S GOT SOME KIND OF MAGICAL CONNECTION TO HER; COULDN'T HE SNIFF HER OUT OR SOMETHING? I COULD GO WITH HIM, I BLEND IN PRETTY WELL.
YOU BLEND IN WITH MEN, YES, BUT HEIMDALL IS NOT A PLACE FOR MEN.

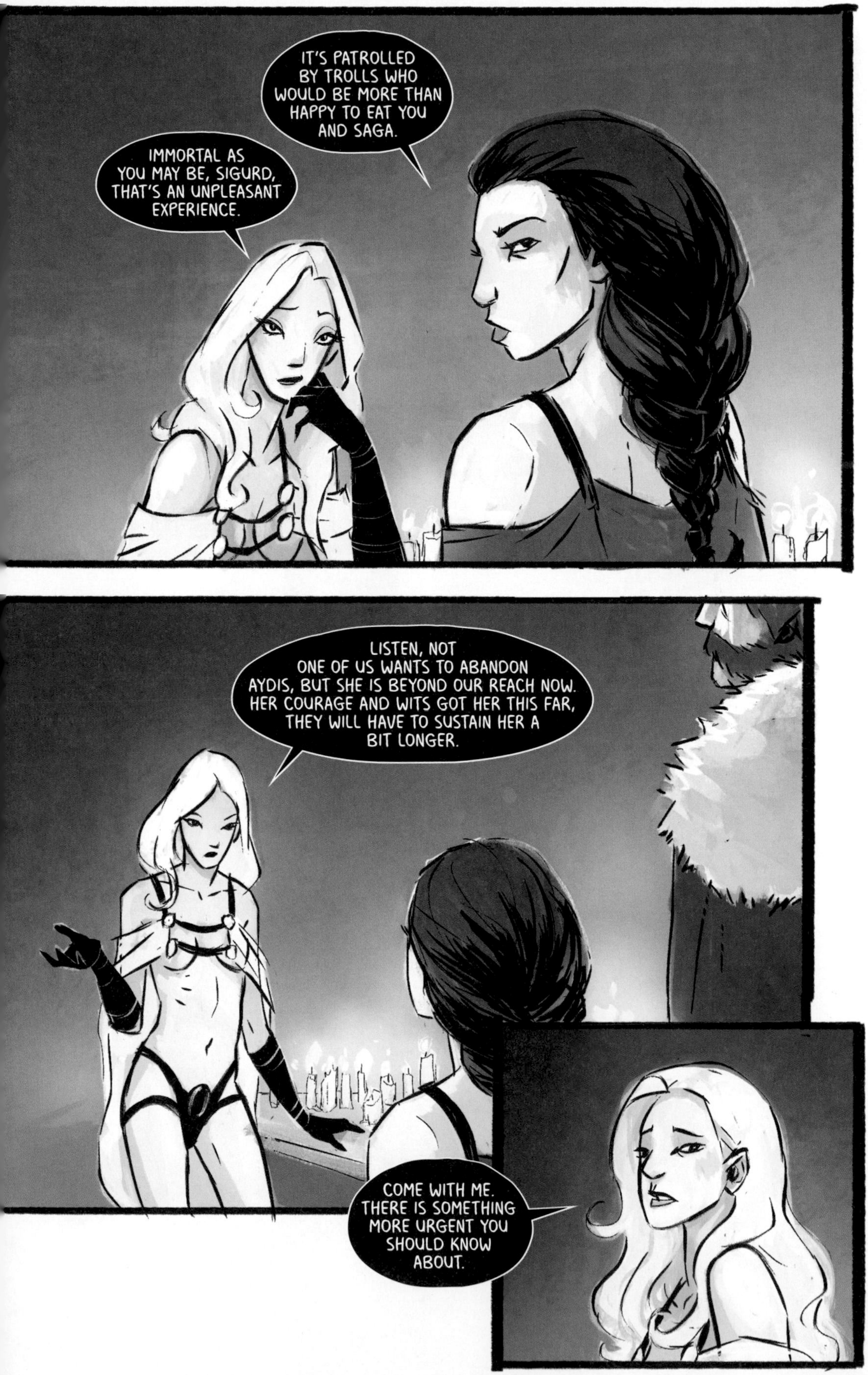
IMMORTAL AS YOU MAY BE, SIGURD, THAT'S AN UNPLEASANT EXPERIENCE.
IT'S PATROLLED BY TROLLS WHO WOULD BE MORE THAN HAPPY TO EAT YOU AND SAGA.
LISTEN, NOT ONE OF US WANTS TO ABANDON AYDIS, BUT SHE IS BEYOND OUR REACH NOW. HER COURAGE AND WITS GOT HER THIS FAR, THEY WILL HAVE TO SUSTAIN HER A BIT LONGER.
COME WITH ME. THERE IS SOMETHING MORE URGENT YOU SHOULD KNOW ABOUT.

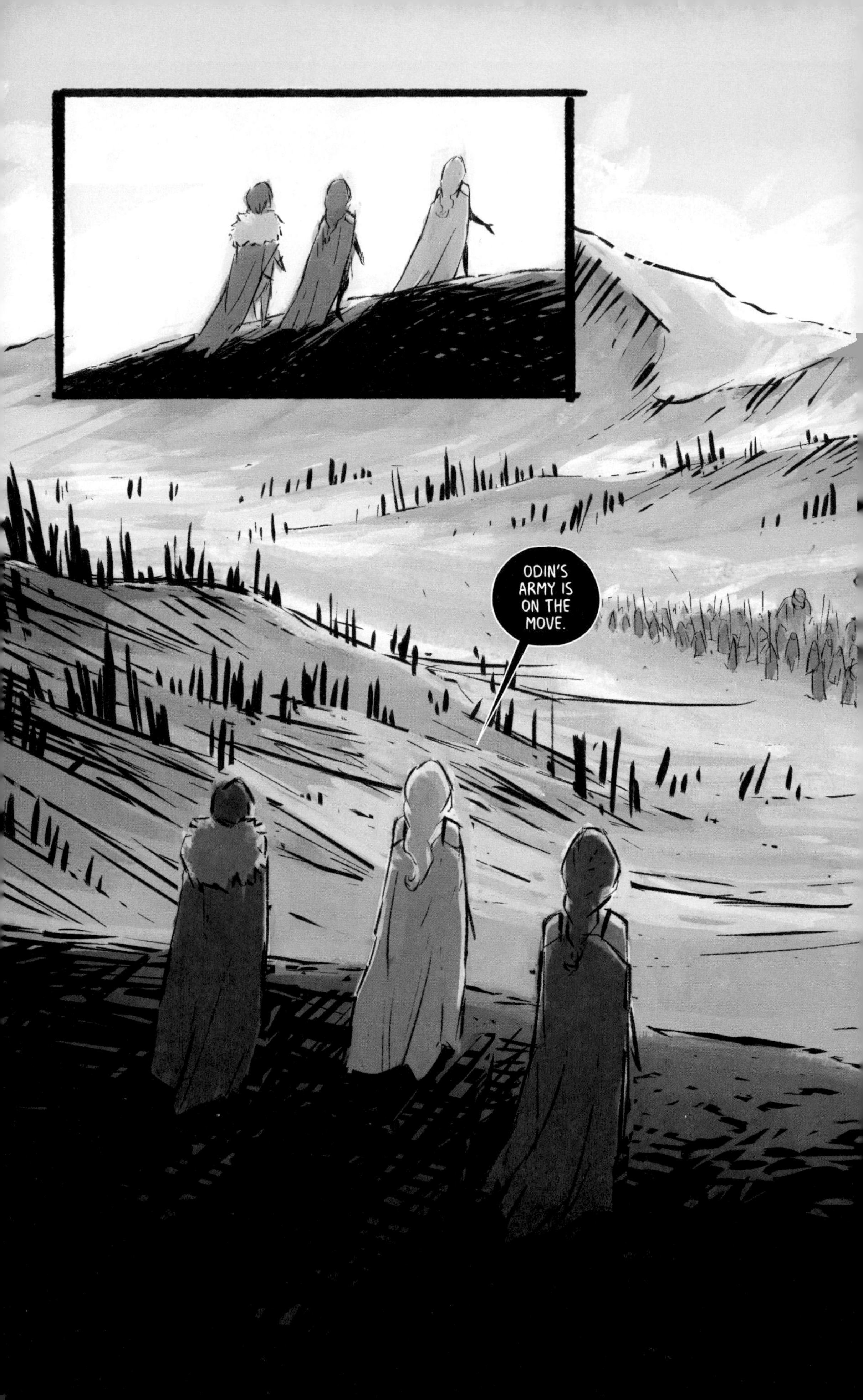
ODIN'S ARMY IS ON THE MOVE.

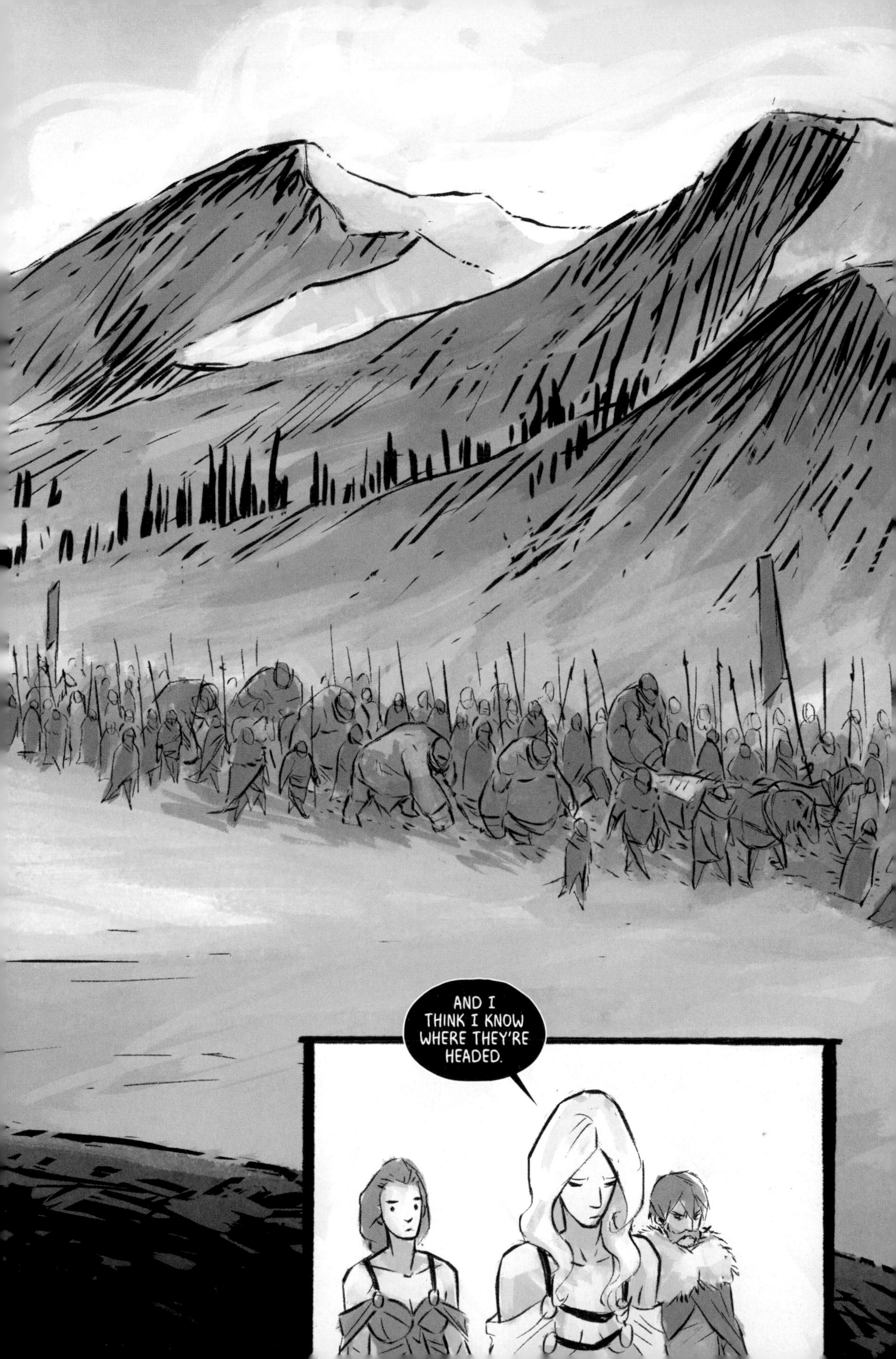
AND I THINK I KNOW WHERE THEY'RE HEADED.

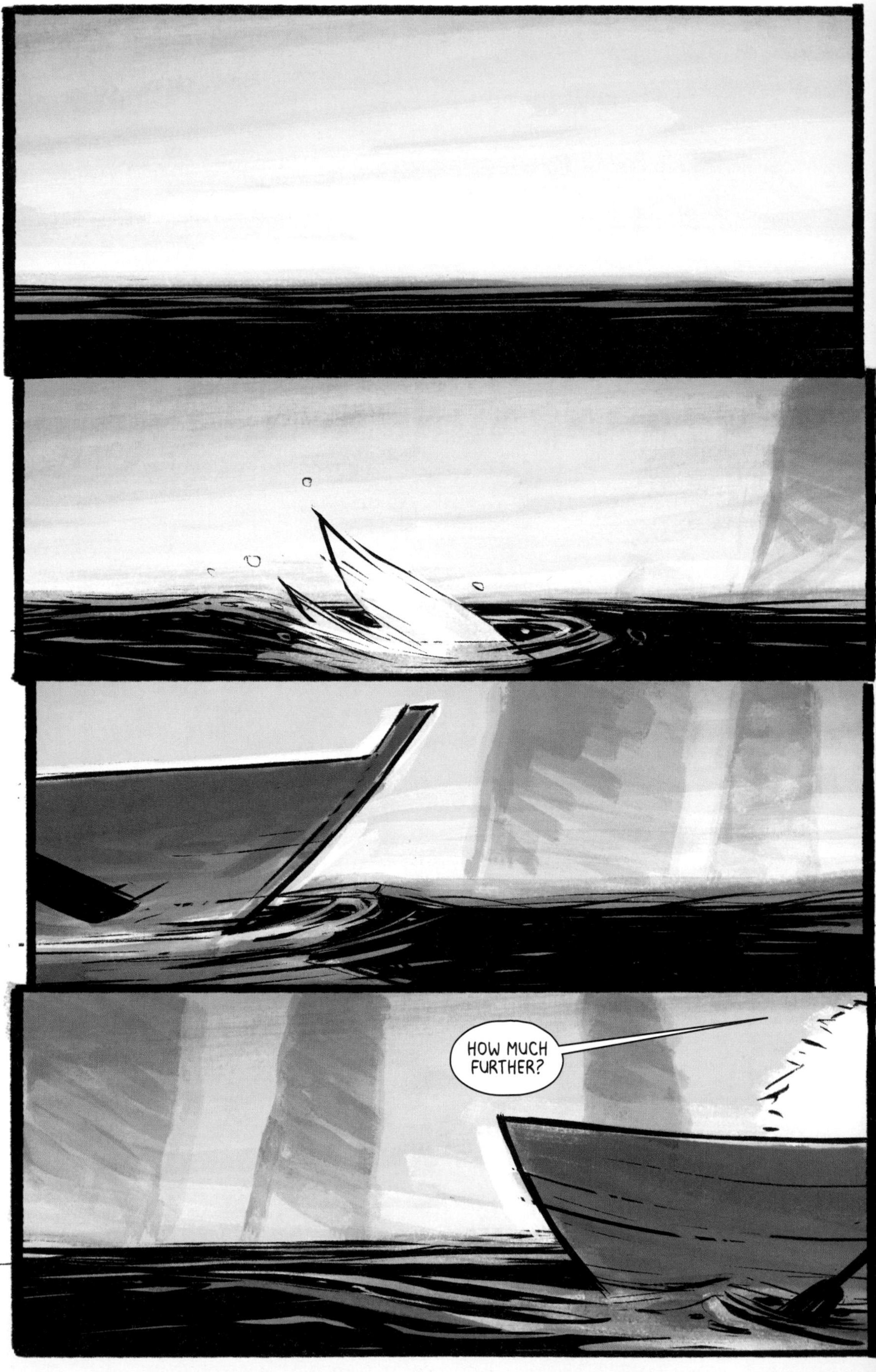
HOW MUCH FURTHER?

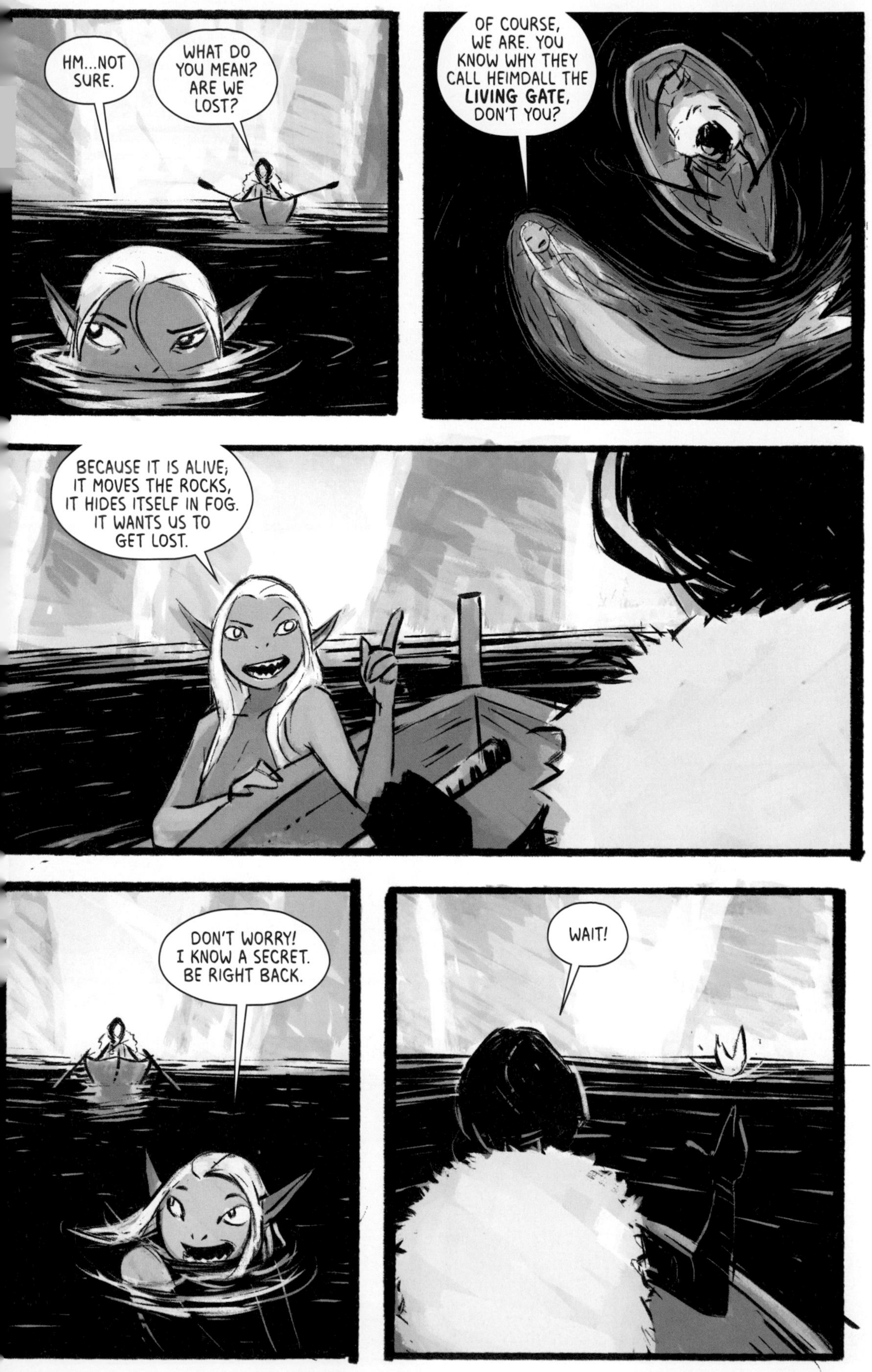
HM...NOT SURE.
WHAT DO YOU MEAN? ARE WE LOST?
OF COURSE, WE ARE. YOU KNOW WHY THEY CALL HEIMDALL THE **LIVING GATE**, DON'T YOU?
BECAUSE IT IS ALIVE; IT MOVES THE ROCKS, IT HIDES ITSELF IN FOG. IT WANTS US TO GET LOST.
DON'T WORRY! I KNOW A SECRET. BE RIGHT BACK.
WAIT!

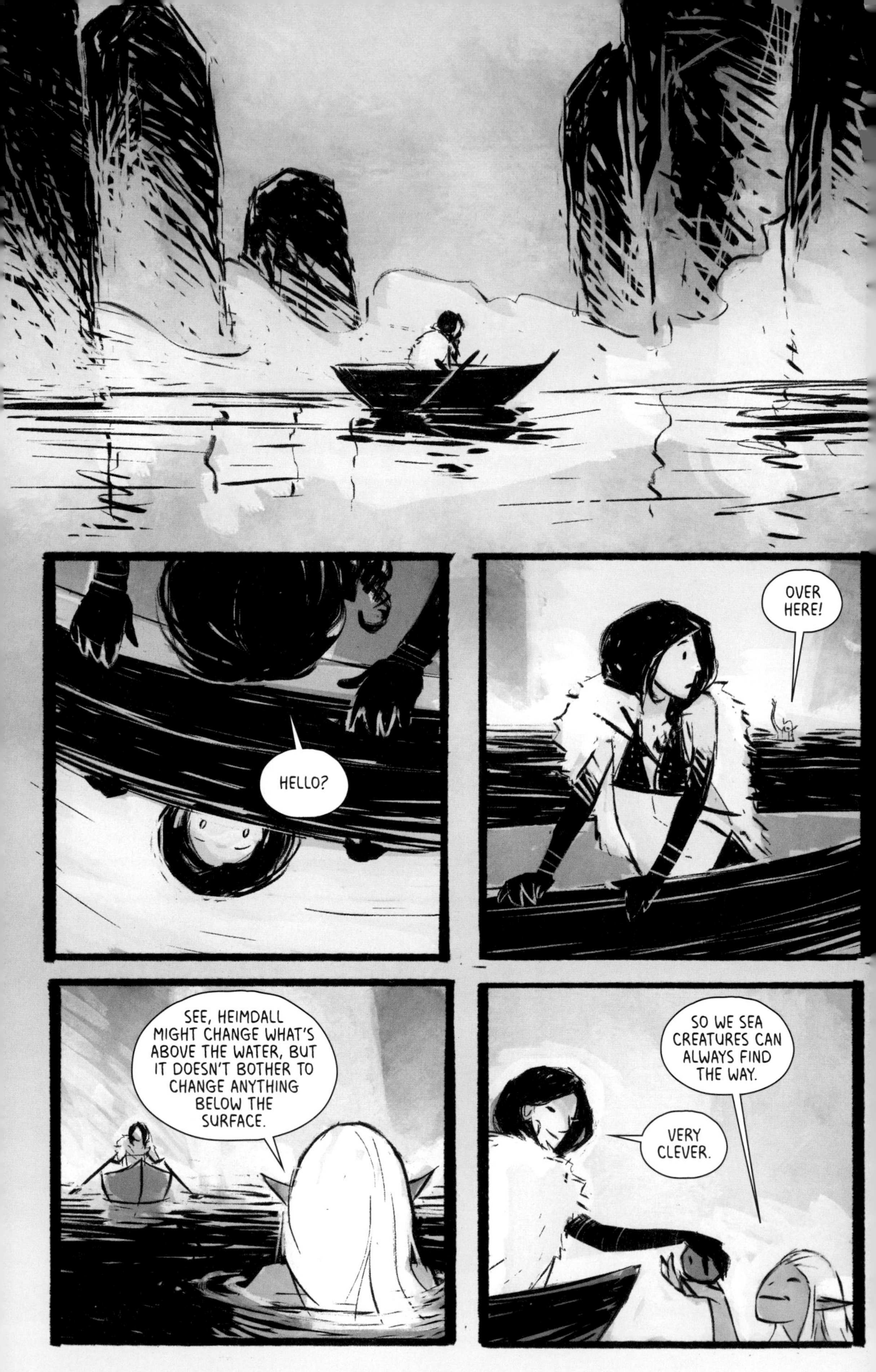
HELLO?
OVER HERE!
SEE, HEIMDALL MIGHT CHANGE WHAT'S ABOVE THE WATER, BUT IT DOESN'T BOTHER TO CHANGE ANYTHING BELOW THE SURFACE.
SO WE SEA CREATURES CAN ALWAYS FIND THE WAY.
VERY CLEVER.

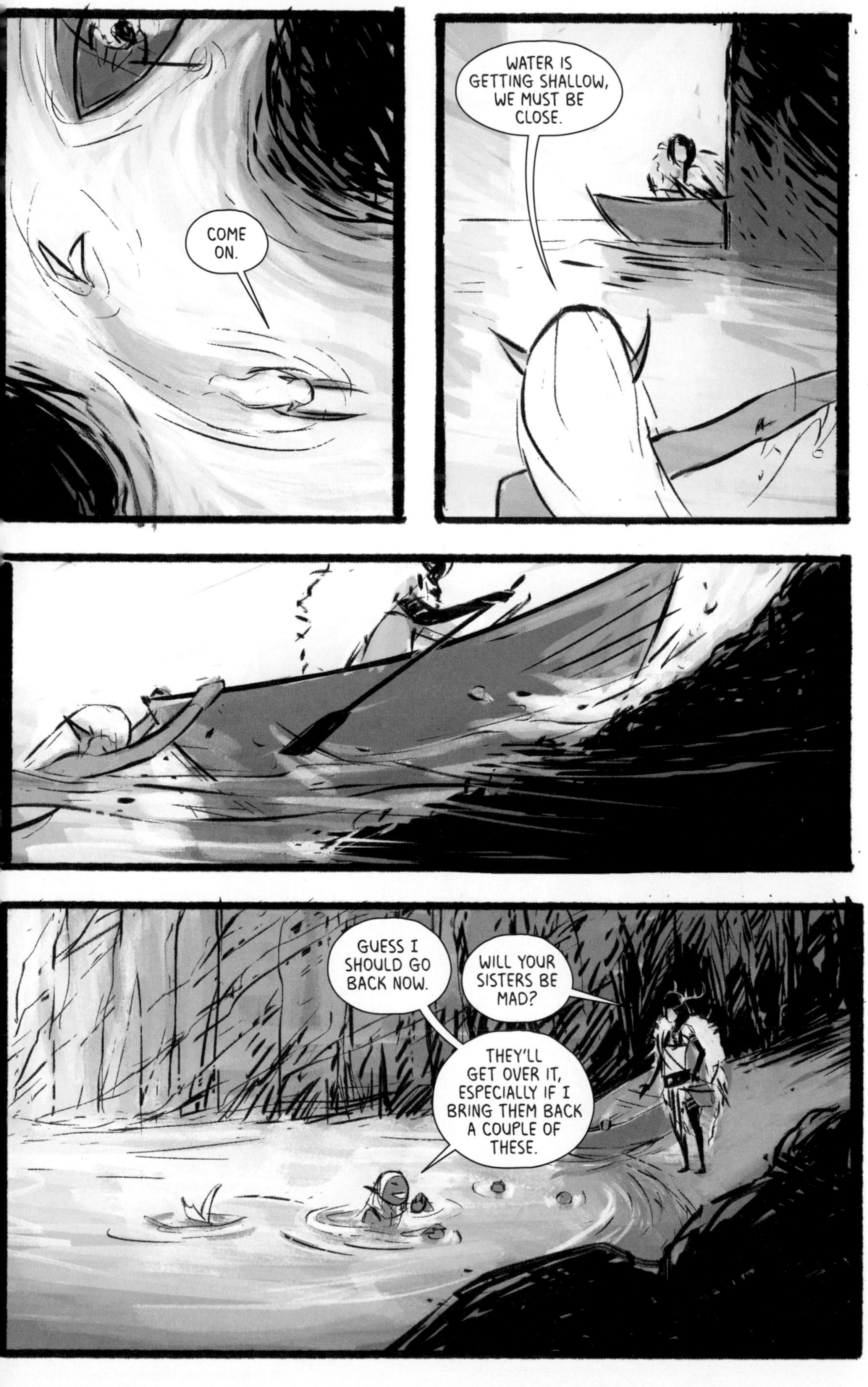
COME ON.
WATER IS GETTING SHALLOW, WE MUST BE CLOSE.
GUESS I SHOULD GO BACK NOW.
WILL YOUR SISTERS BE MAD?
THEY'LL GET OVER IT, ESPECIALLY IF I BRING THEM BACK A COUPLE OF THESE.

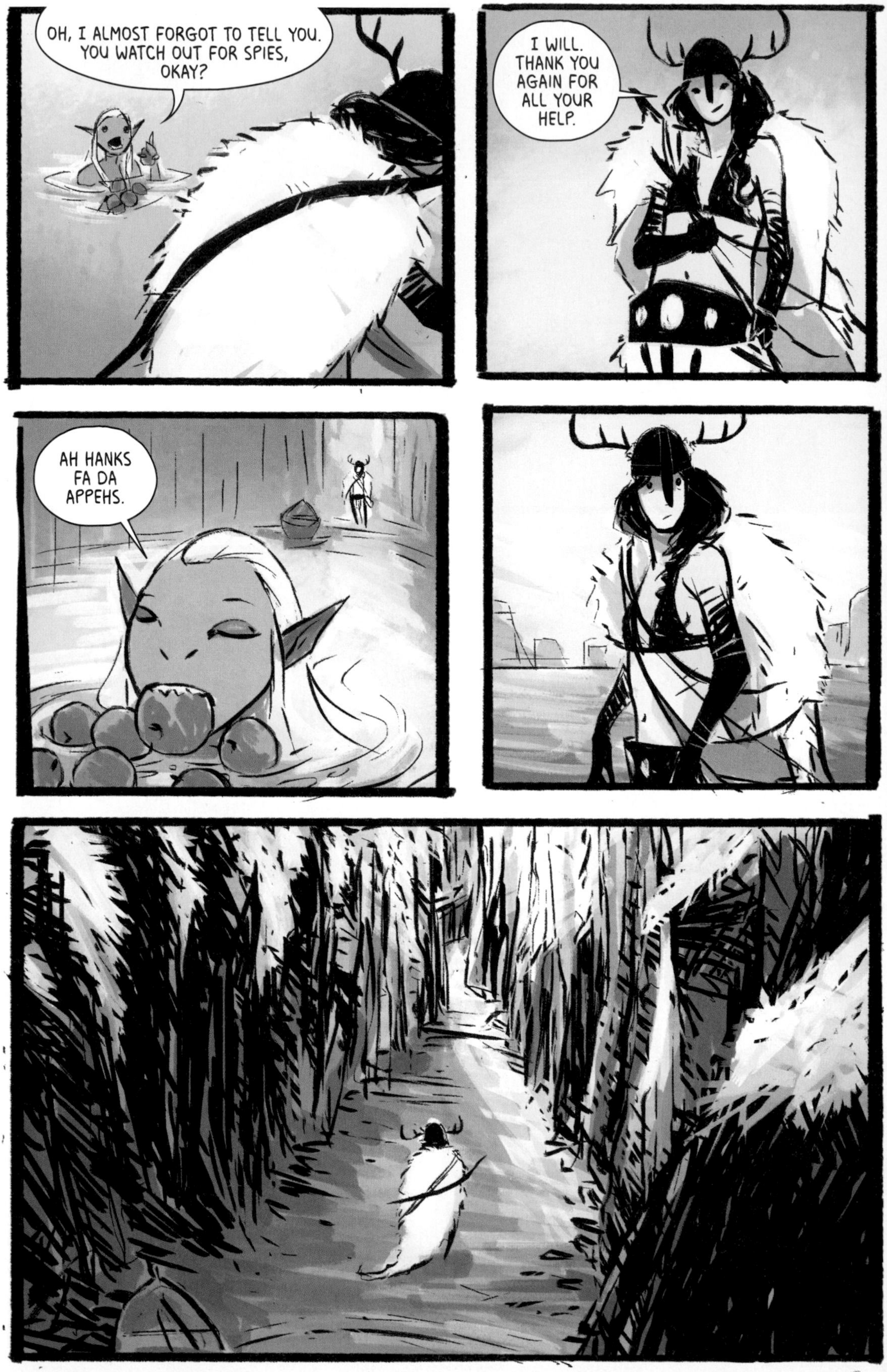
OH, I ALMOST FORGOT TO TELL YOU. YOU WATCH OUT FOR SPIES, OKAY?
I WILL. THANK YOU AGAIN FOR ALL YOUR HELP.
AH HANKS FA DA APPEHS.

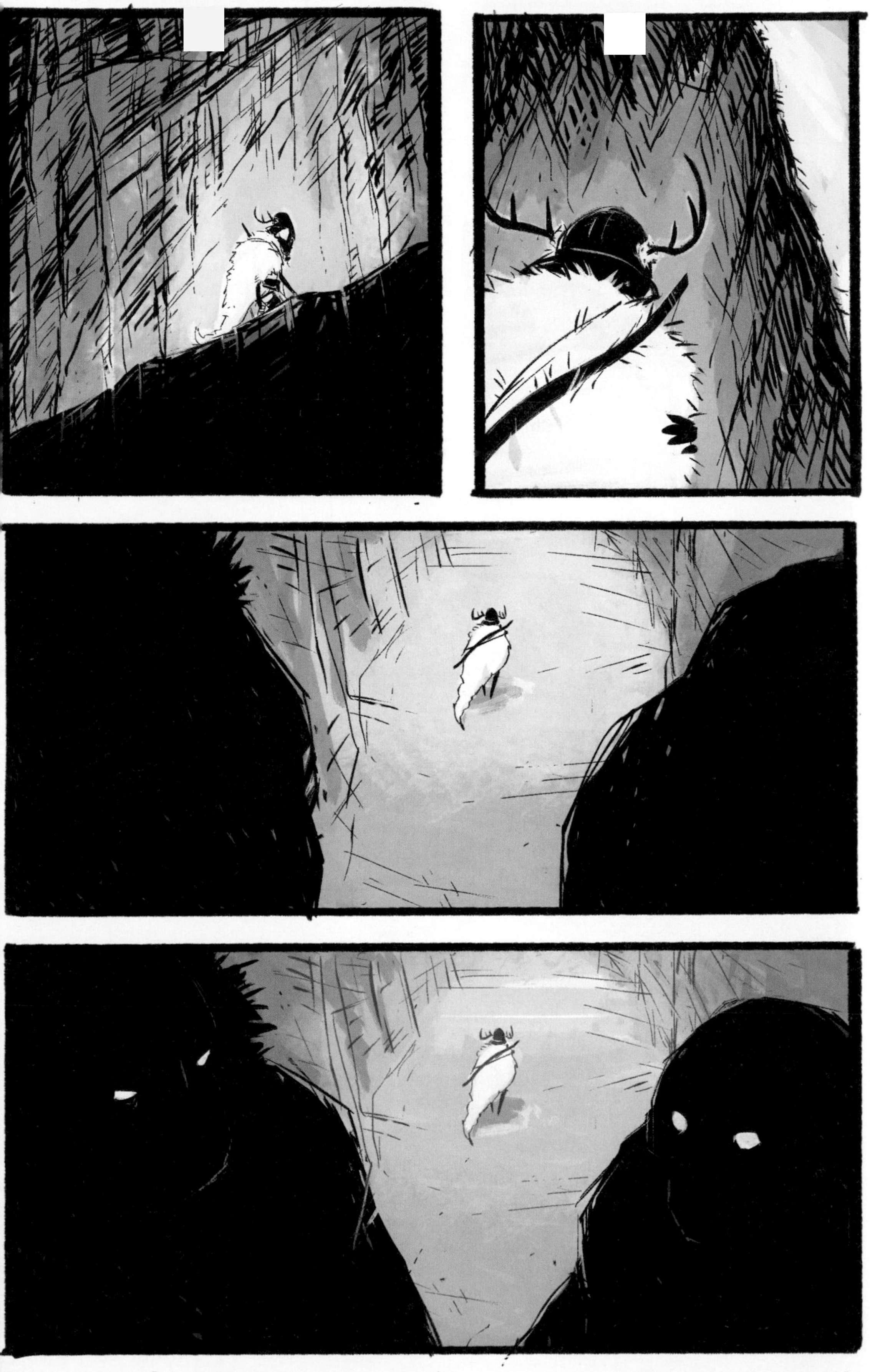

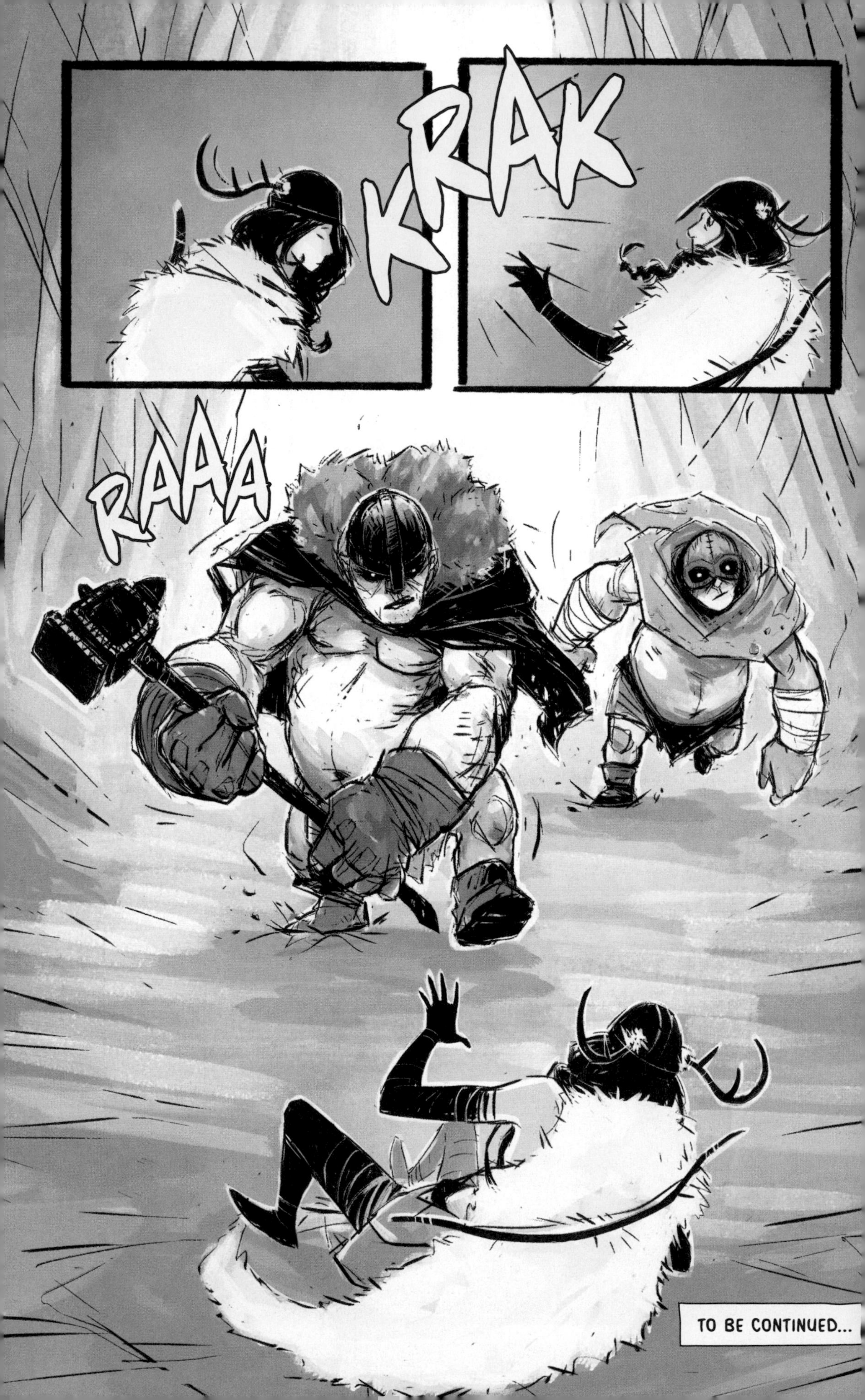
KRAK
RAAA
TO BE CONTINUED...

THE ART OF HEATHEN
COVER GALLERY

FEATURING

NATASHA ALTERICI

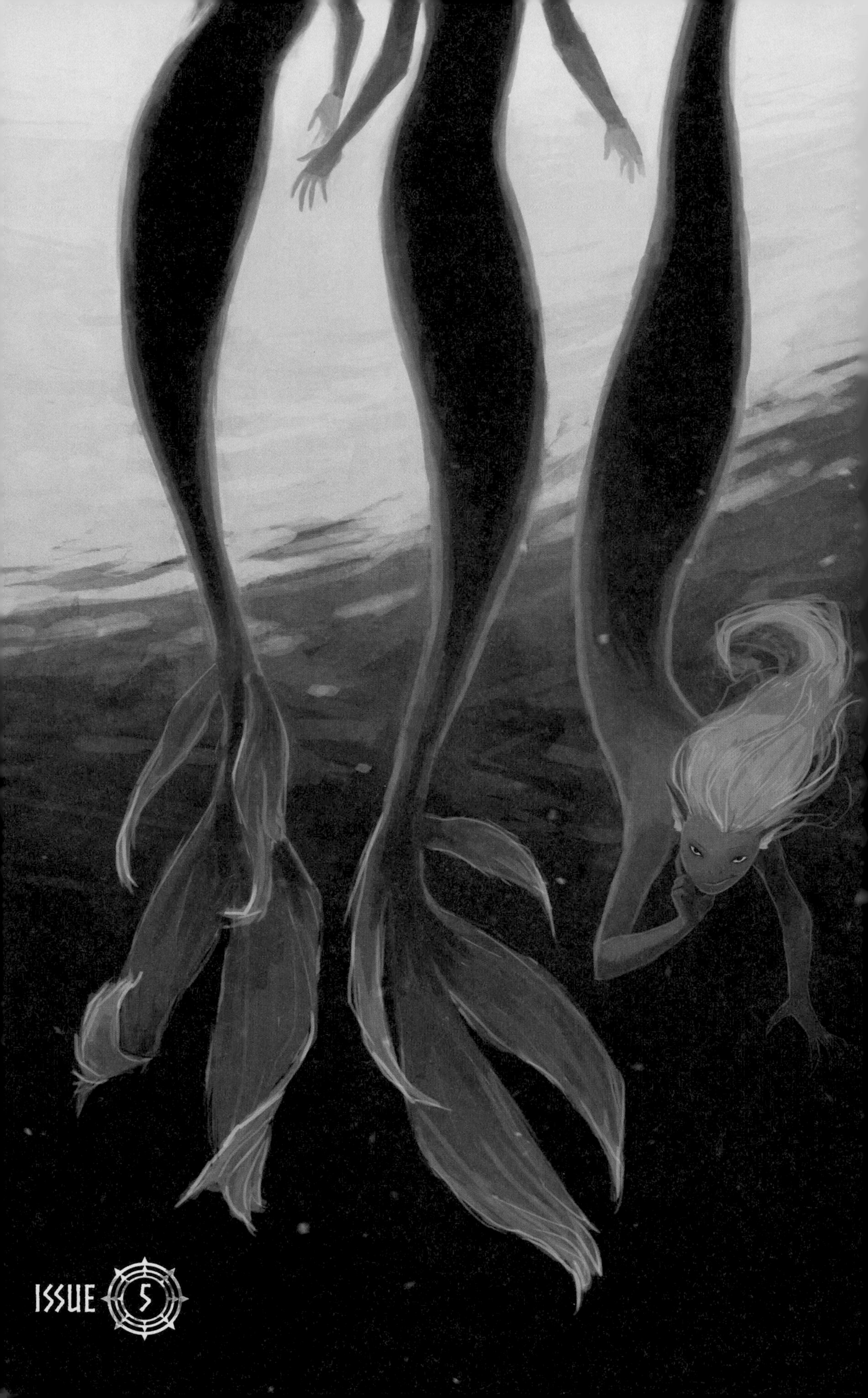
ISSUE 5

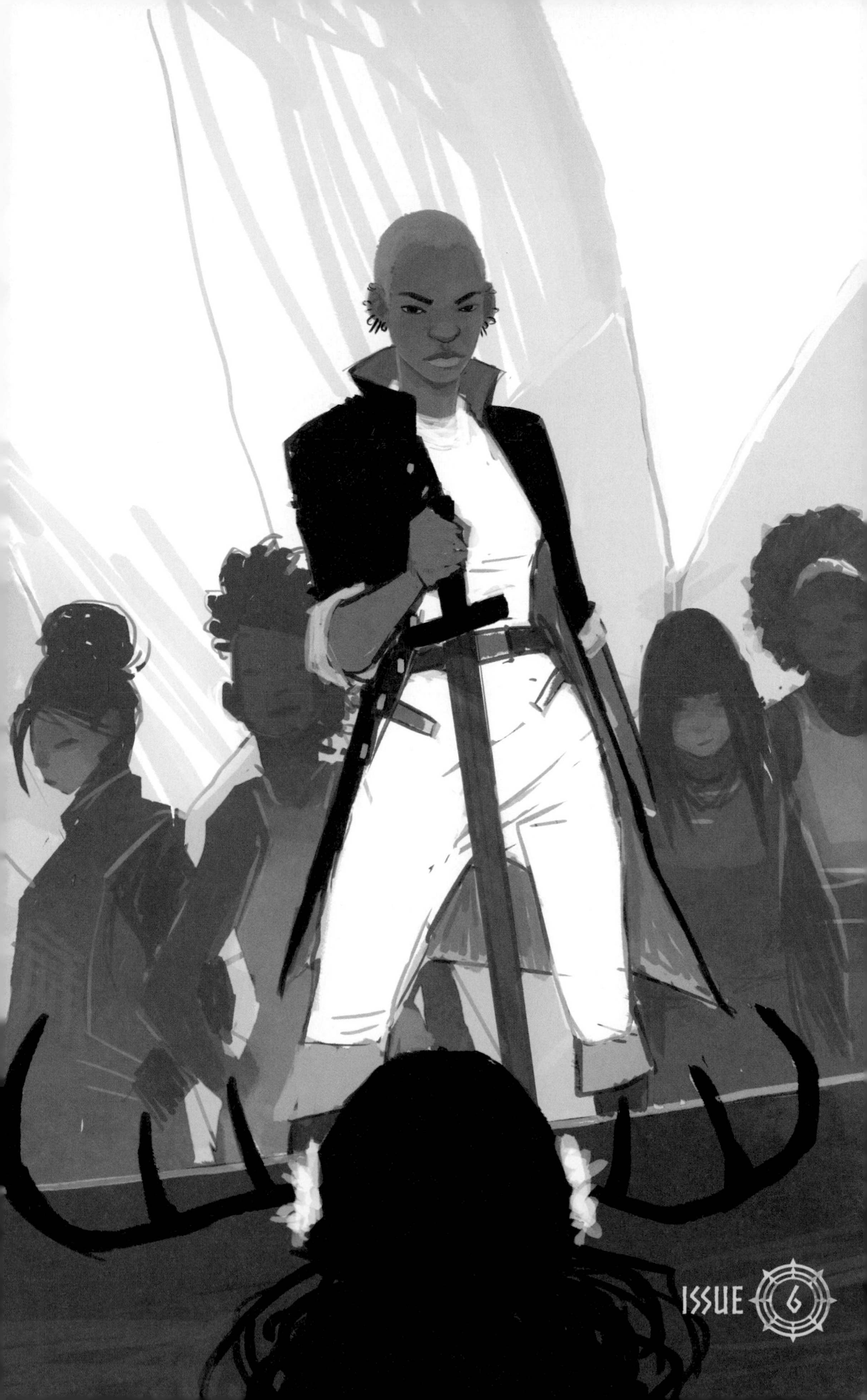
ISSUE 6

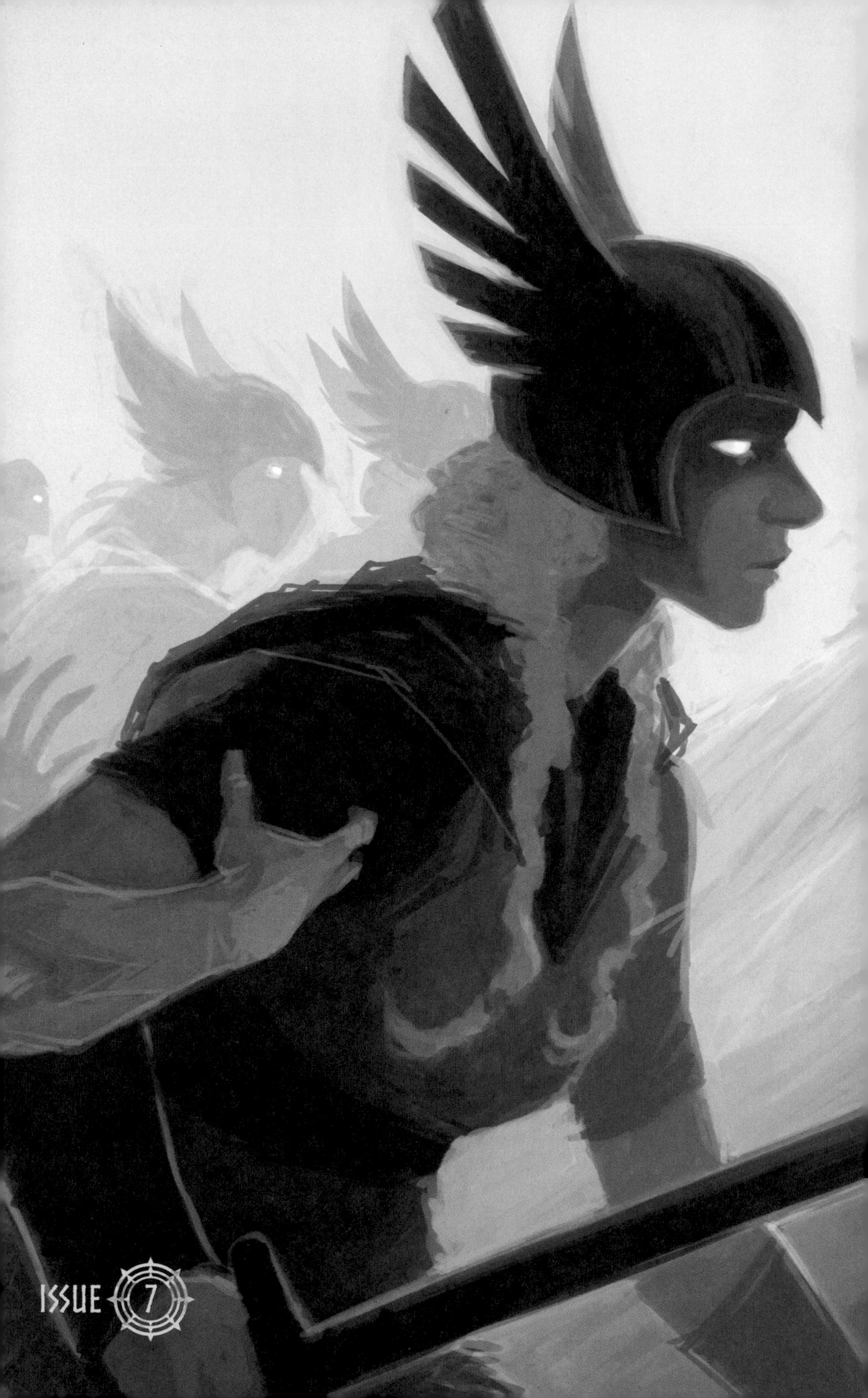
ISSUE 7

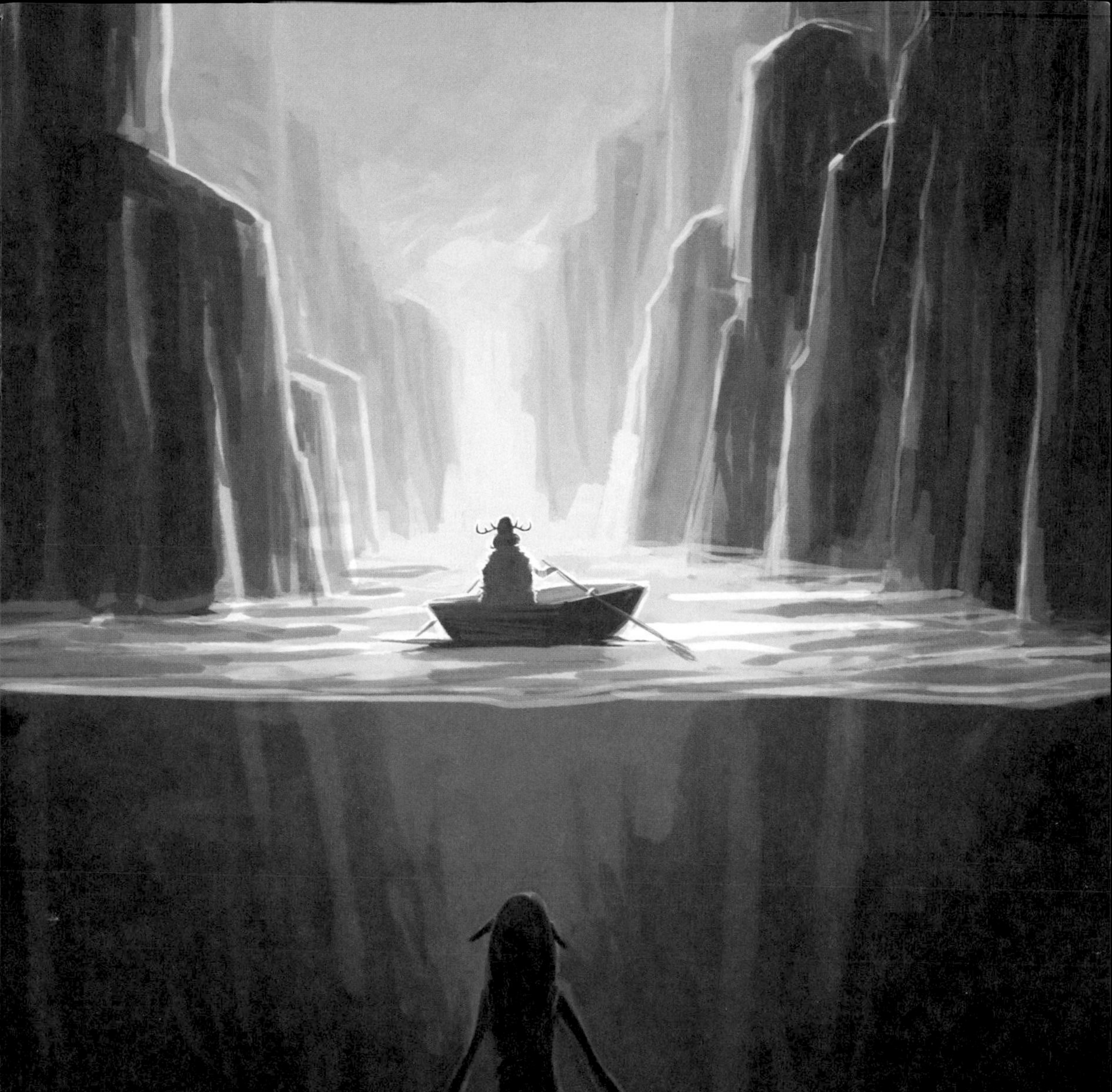

VIKING. WARRIOR. WOMAN. OUTCAST.

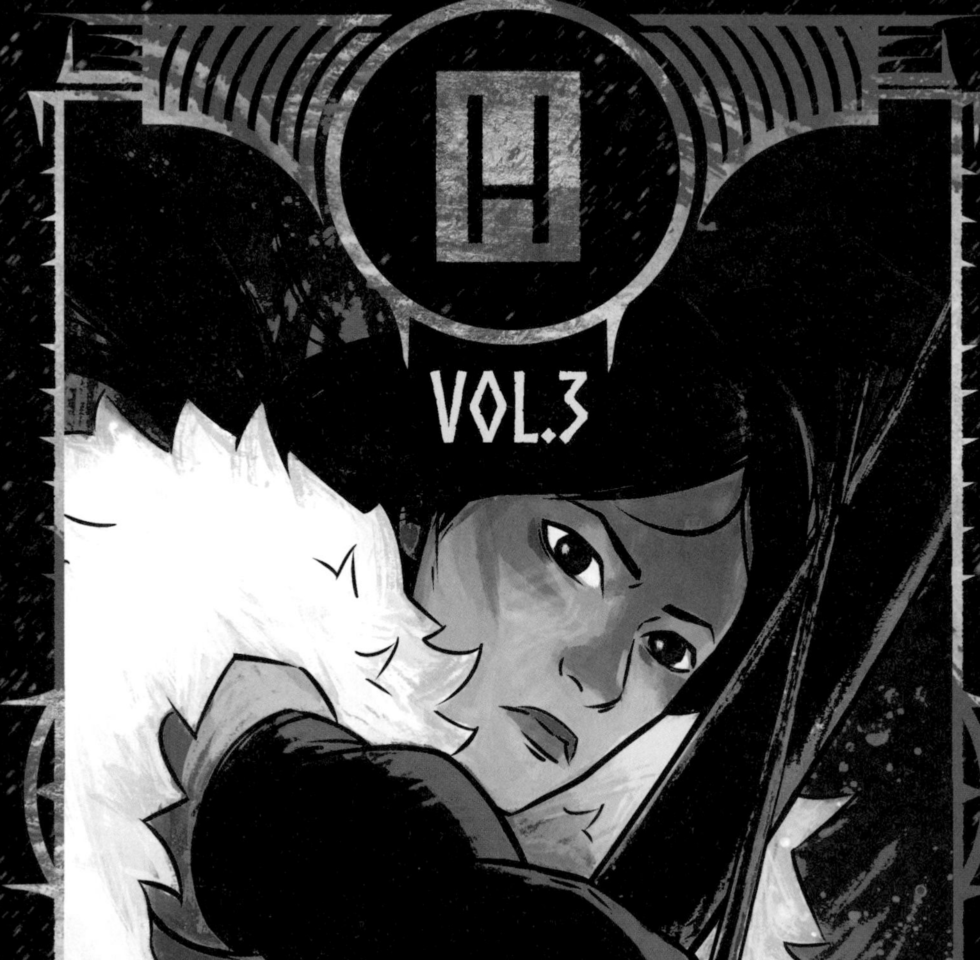
VOL.3

AIMING TO END THE GOD-KING ODIN'S OPPRESSIVE REIGN.

ALTERICI - WOODS - DEERING

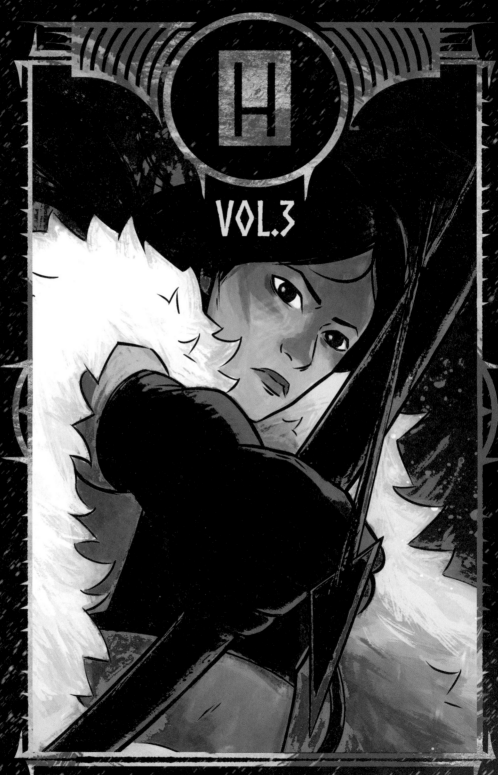